MOCKINGBIRD

MOCKINGBIRD

Mockingbird

SEAN STEWART

ACE BOOKS, NEW YORK

MOCKINGBIRD

An Ace Book
Published by The Berkley Publishing Group,
a member of Penguin Putnam Inc.,
200 Madison Avenue, New York, NY 10016
The Penguin Putnam Inc. World Wide Web site address is
http://www.penguinputnam.com

Copyright © 1998 by Sean Stewart

Book design by Oksana Kushnir

ISBN 0-441-00547-0

Printed in the United States of America

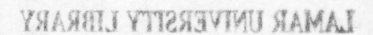

MOCKINGBIRD

ONE

When you get down to the bottom of the bottle, as Momma used to say, this is the story of how I became a mother. I want that clear from the start. Now, it's true that mine was not a typical pregnancy. There was some magic mixed up in there, and a few million dollars in oil-field speculation, and some people who died, and some others who wouldn't stay quite dead. It would be lying to pretend there wasn't prophecy involved, and an exorcism, and a hurricane, and I scorn to lie. But if every story is a journey, then this is about the longest trip I ever took, from being a daughter to having one.

It starts the day we buried Momma.

It is embarrassing to admit that your mother can see the future, read minds, perform miracles, and raise the dead. It was something I held against her for a long time. I hated the agonizing moment when a kid on my baseball team or a high-school classmate would ask me if the stories were really true, and I would have to say yes. It would have been easier—and safer—to say no, to say that Momma was a bit eccentric but had no special powers. But I was always a willfully, rudely honest little girl. If someone asked me point-blank, I had to admit that my mother was a witch, and the little gods who ruled her were real.

When I told folks what Momma could do they figured I was fibbing, or that my sister and I suffered from delusions brought on by too much drinking, blows to the head, or the repressed memories of incest or devil worship. Now, it is true my mother was a liar. It is true she drank too much and she slapped me more than once when I was growing up. But I promise you, worshipping the Riders was the farthest thing from her mind. They were Life's collection agents. When Momma drew too much on her gifts, the Riders would take their due. Unless you worship the IRS, drop the whole idea that Momma loved her gods.

Momma's magic was real. When she predicted IBM stock would go up, it went up, and the money her investors made was real too. Once I even saw Momma raise the dead, although that went so badly that we all agreed, even her, never to do it again.

It wasn't exactly a person that Momma resurrected. It was Geronimo the frog.

I had better explain that.

The chief feature of my parents' house in Houston, Texas, was the glorious garden in our backyard. The whole wall of the house facing it was French doors, which Momma left open all the time, so it was hard to tell where the garden ended and our kitchen began. My little sister, Candy, and I spent a lot of time in the garden, hiding from Momma and catching frogs. Now, the early seventies in

Texas were a doll-crazy time for little girls. Besides a le-
gion of Barbies, I had a bunch of Kiddles, little weensy
dolls whose clothes would fit a good-sized frog just right.
I still have Polaroids of Geronimo in a pink doll tutu that
is to die for. At first Geronimo didn't like being caught
and dressed up, but he seemed to get used to it. After we
had been acquainted a while, he would come squat on our
hands and let us dress him up, so long as we bribed him
with mealworms and doodlebugs.

Just after my eleventh birthday I found Geronimo dead,
floating in the little concrete pond under the banana tree.
Candy and I were inconsolable. At first Momma was sym-
pathetic, but our whining and snivelling soon commenced
to aggravate her. I was a sulky girl at the best of times,
and made life miserable for everyone with my moping.
Finally Momma took the frog over to the cabinet where
she kept her gods and stuffed him in the Preacher's cubby
and lit a candle and told us to get out of the room. Then
she did something she had seen in New Orleans when she
was younger. I never knew the details, but the next morning we found Geronimo in the garden again, shouldering
his way heavily through the monkey grass.

But he wasn't really alive. He never ate, he never sang.
He just staggered after us as if hungry for our warmth. He
was worse than dead: he was a Zombie Frog, a horrible
pathetic remnant of himself. Candy, who was only seven,
started screaming whenever he came near. Finally I
squashed Geronimo flat with a shovel from the garden
shed. Then I stood on the blade, pinning him to the flag-
stone path, while Candy ran and got an empty milk carton. I could feel the shovel jerking and trembling under
my foot as Geronimo tried to get away. When Candy got
back I opened the spout end of the carton and shoved

Geronimo inside. Then I held it closed with my foot while Candy got the big stapler off Daddy's desk. Together we stapled the end of the milk carton shut and then we crept out of the yard and ran to the storm drain at the end of the block and stuffed the milk carton into its big dark mouth, with poor Geronimo still bumping and hopping inside.

It was an awful episode. I mention it as an example of how real Momma's magic was, though it wasn't always that ghastly. I have to admit that as they lowered Momma's coffin into her grave, I wasn't crying and grieving like Candy was. I was listening for the sound of Momma bumping and knocking against the lid, trying to get out.

My name is Antoinette Beauchamp, pronounced BEECH-um, and I am my mother's daughter only in DNA. I have a degree in mathematics from Rice University and am a Fellow of the Society of Actuaries. I hate lying. Leave the prayers and possessions and the Riders in the wardrobe, the stories of Sugar and the Widow and the Little Lost Girl—leave all that buried with Momma, along with the tears and the scenes and the Bloody Marys. Buried with her where they belong.

Even in death my mother was a schemer. Somehow she got herself planted in Glenwood, Houston's most exclusive cemetery. I do not doubt it gave her great satisfaction to be buried beyond her means.

Momma should have been stashed at Cherryhurst, or stuck under a few feet of sod at the old Confederate cemetery on Memorial Drive. Or she could have been cremated, that would have been like her; her ashes sprinkled into the sea at Galveston, or worked into a clay sculpture and stuck in the garden, or mixed up with lime juice and tequila and consumed at a wake where shadow-eyed zydeco gypsies with cat familiars would play on sweat-stained accordions with cracked ivory keys. Or she could have disappeared, no body left to find: vanished into the jungle in Costa Rica, or fallen off a shrimp boat in the Gulf of Mexico, or plucked up by a tornado; one pointy-toed witch's boot, size 7, left standing in the field below.

Any of those endings would have made sense.

But for her to die of cancer and be buried in Glenwood: that was a travesty. Glenwood is the cemetery of Houston's Establishment, chock full of Hoffheinzes, Holcombes, Cullens, and Friedrichs; a little Greek Revival village of white marble cenotaphs chiseled with the same names you see in the lobbies of the city's museums and theatres and hospitals. Howard Hughes is buried in Glenwood. Cardinal Richelieu probably should be, along with Lorenzo de' Medici and Vasco de Gama. But my mother has no business being there.

The first few days of being dead are very rushed. Usually I am careful and scrupulous and I pay attention to things. But in the week after Momma died, my focus seemed to slip away. Funeral plans and insurance forms and calls to relatives fluttered over and around me, half-noticed, like birds passing through a garden. I wasn't sad, not for a minute. Candy was. Candy cried and cried. But I felt no grief. Just that lack of focus, and a tightness in my chest almost like anger.

When old Mr. Friesen offered to take care of things, I made the mistake of letting him. I had been dreading what funeral arrangements Candy would suggest: hair fetishes, voodoo, St. Anthony's candles at the reception, midnight

Masses—God knew what kind of spookery. At the time, it seemed easier to let Bill Friesen handle it.

My mistake. Never, never, never be beholden to anyone.

By the time I realized Mr. Friesen meant to plant Momma in Houston's most exclusive neighborhood—you can't depart more dearly than at Glenwood—it was too late to make other arrangements. So Glenwood it was, on a glorious November afternoon. The gulf coast breeze blew softly through the ash and the towering white-barked sycamores, the massive live oaks and the tremendous lanky pines whose limbs branched upward like green ball-lightning. The grave was a long black gash of turned earth amid the sweet grass. Leaf-shadow trembled over it from a live oak so old its limbs were furred with moss and ferns that had rooted in its ancient bark.

William Friesen stood before us, reminiscing at the graveside. He was mostly bald, and his bare head with its collection of freckles and liver spots was the color of mashed potatoes with a few of the peels still in. He spoke at length. Like a lot of rich men, Bill Friesen never seemed to be troubled by the possibility his stories might be boring. "In 1958 I saw a pretty girl at the counter of the House of Pies," he said. "I didn't think much about women at the time, I was working long hours at the office, but suddenly there she was, and there I was, with my nice suit and my pretty smile. I reckoned I had a chance. So I walked over to her stool and asked if I could buy her a piece of pie."

We had all heard this story many times. It seemed to be stirring up some grief for Candy, judging by a new couple of tears trickling from her pretty eyes, but I was mostly wishing I could scratch my calf where my stockings itched.

The Grand Old Man of Friesen Investments grinned, remembering. "She turned to me and said, 'I'm not the woman you will marry, so don't get your hopes up. But if you still care to buy me that slice of pie, I b'lieve I'll try the pecan.' " Bill laughed. "Well, she had me there, didn't she? I couldn't back out after that. I ordered the pie and tried to keep up my end. 'Why be so sure we won't be married, little lady? This could be the start of a beautiful friendship.'

" 'Oh yes, we'll be friends,' this gal said. 'But your wife will be a blonde, five foot four, with small hands and a pretty face.' Well, my jaw dropped at that, and dropped again one week later when I met the woman she had described." Bill Friesen looked fondly at his wife, Penny, who stood beside him at the grave head.

(I am fifteen. I have just applied for a summer temp job at Friesen Investments and Bill Sr. has told this story to me during my job interview. Momma is driving me home. "Expurgated old turd," she laughs. "What I really said was, 'Your wife will have small hands, cold feet, little breasts that turn up at the nipples, and lots and lots of money.' Lord but he blushed. Though I daresay he doesn't remember it that way now. He's very good at forgetting things, Bill is. Too bad for poor Penny.")

But in the end it was poor Penny standing beside the grave, while Momma lay at the bottom of it.

"Well," Bill Sr. went on, "Elena Beauchamp was right about my wife, and over the years she was right about a lot of other things. She had a rare talent, a God-given gift. I learned to listen carefully to what she had to say. My family has always been the better for it." This was certainly true. It was Momma's advice that made the Friesens rich. Unfortunately, Momma was even better at spending money than she was at making it, and we never did prosper so well as Bill Sr. had. There's probably a parable in there somewhere. Momma could have found it. She had a story for everything.

At the front of Momma's plot, beyond the newly turned earth, stood her headstone, black marble with steel letters inset:

ELENA BEAUCHAMP
1933 – 1995
There are some gifts
Which cannot be refused.

Two weeks earlier the hospital had sent her home to die with a day nurse and a supply of morphine. The weather had been beautiful beyond hope. We moved a chaise lounge from the first floor into the garden and Momma lay on it all day amid the monkey grass and hibiscus, watching the lizards scoot across the stone paths and listening to the mockingbirds.

After an hour or so she asked me to bring her a glass of iced tea with a wedge of lime in it and a shot of vodka. She also asked for a notebook and a pen, but she was too weak to use them. I held her glass and let her take the tea in little sips, lips working, head shaking, bald from the radiation therapy. Then she made me write down that epitaph and read it back to her, twice, and promise to call the stonecutter so the headstone would be ready for her funeral. The epitaph was a message meant for me, I knew that, but Momma wouldn't come out and say so, and I wouldn't ask.

She died the afternoon they called to say the stone was ready. Houston is a refinery town, covered in a hazy blanket of industrial hydrocarbons of the sort that make a sky beautiful, and that day the sunset was magnificent; long halls and galleries of cloud turning peach in the tall sky, then bright breathing gold, then smoldering down and going out in a sky darkly blue and luminous, like the sea.

My mother could see the future. My mother said "give me some sugar" when she wanted our kisses, which she required like a Roman empress, and like tribute we surrendered them. My mother made Bloody Marys and drank them in the afternoons, walking around our tile floors in her stocking feet with her hips sashaying. There was a hole in my mother's life that she never talked about, stretching from the time she quit high school to the day she met Bill Friesen. My mother knew a hundred ways to cry. My mother once broke every mirror in our house, smashing them with the heel of one white pump. She must have slapped me a hundred times and twice she cut my cheek with the diamond wedding ring my father bought her in New Orleans. I still remember every color of her nail polish: pearl, pink, carmine, true red, scarlet, and gold too and silver, like the black girls wear. My mother took an hour to put her makeup on and I will remember the smell of her hairspray always. My mother wanted to go to Paris, she had boxes of oil pastels and watercolors and she painted me the most beautiful birthday cards in the world, great blooming hydrangeas or sand-colored starfish or fine watercolor horses, bay, chestnut, dapple, and palomino. My mother lied and lied and lied, to me and everybody.

There are some gifts which cannot be refused.

I refuse.

• • •

After the burial Daddy and Candy and I went back to the house to wait for our condolence visits. I meant to mop the tile floors and order in some food, at least muffins and coffee, but instead I wandered through the kitchen, where pots of thyme and sage and sweet basil rested along the window ledge, along with two bushy mints Momma kept to flavor her iced tea. Overhead, wire baskets full of onions and garlic hung next to ropes of dried peppers: red and yellow chilis, green Anaheim peppers, and the darker, rounder, hotter poblano peppers that make the best chili rellenos; and also jalapeños and firecracker peppers and explosive habaneros that looked like cherry bombs and blew up in your mouth.

Leaving the kitchen, I wandered by the long farmhouse table and the French doors that open into the garden. Finally I turned to face the tall cabinet where Momma kept her Riders.

All her life, my mother was afflicted by possessions. Days might go by, or weeks, or even months in which she was only herself; but sooner or later she would pull out that cursed magic Gold Card and ring up a purchase against her talent. She would ask the Riders for help, which they would give—at a price. In exchange for their services, they would come into her head, banishing her God knows where, and for an hour or two these small gods could walk the earth.

After a Rider left and Momma came back, she would be confused, shocky and shaking with exhaustion. She never had any memory of what the Rider had done or said while in her head. It was terrible, as a child, to see my mother torn up and thrown away by these little gods who mounted her, and then to watch her struggle to put herself back together like Humpty-Dumpty from the fragments left behind. When you saw her go through that hideous ordeal time after time, you could never doubt her strength. "Takes more than birdshot to bring me down," she used to say, and she was right.

There were six Riders, plus the Little Lost Girl. Each of them wanted different things. Daddy had built the cabinet, which Momma called a chifforobe, at Momma's request. Behind its polished cherry-wood doors were three tiers of two cubbyholes each. In each cubby Momma had put a doll representing one Rider, along with a few gifts or knickknacks. Offerings, you might call them.

The top cubby on the left belonged to the Mockingbird, represented by a hand puppet, a long leather glove with the skins of two mockingbirds sewn to it. Momma's index finger made the beak; when she opened and closed her hand, the wings flapped.

A mockingbird isn't much to look at. She's bigger than a wren and smaller than a crow, with flashing, white-barred wings. Of all God's creatures she has the loveliest songs. She will sing the calls of other birds more beautifully than they can do it themselves. When she tires of that, she can make a song out of a creaking gate or a door slamming or wash flapping in the wind.

When the Mockingbird was riding Momma, she became many people, changing her song every few minutes. She might be Daddy first, telling road stories he had collected on his last swing through Louisiana or Oklahoma as a traveling rep for American Express. The next minute she might be old Mr. Friesen, talking to one of his brokers over the intercom. Then Momma would be back, laughing and making herself a Bloody Mary and lighting a cigarette. Then it would be her friend Mary Jo, or Greg, the boy who lived across the street, or Mr. MacReady, our neighbor next door who had opened a convenience store in his garage. There were dozens of other voices too, many we girls didn't recognize.

The Mockingbird was a terrible copycat, and Candy used to strike up conversations with her just for the fun of seeing herself reflected, as if in a living mirror. Even I had done it a few times. The Mockingbird was never dangerous, and it was rather delicious to hear my opinions coming out of Momma's mouth. Daddy thought this was disrespectful, though, so we never did it if he was around.

The right-hand cubby on the top shelf was for the Preacher. His doll was a cross made from two lengths of sawn broom handle lashed together, a white dog's skull on top, a child's black Sunday coat hanging from the crossbrace like a scarecrow's jacket. On top of the skull sat an old collection plate like they pass around at the Baptist church, turned upside down and worn like a hat. The Preacher was a fearsome Rider, very hard. He smelled like old books. He was a scourge on the vanities of this world, a grim man who spoke only bitter truths. Candy learned to hide her makeups after the day the Preacher came into our bedroom when she was twelve and without a word snapped all her eyebrow pencils, washed her nail polish down the sink, crushed her lipsticks under his foot and then threw the crumpled tubes away.

Momma never put anything in the bottom of the Preacher's cubby but a black leather Bible.

(By the time I was five I understood that Momma and the Riders were quite different beings, with no overlap between them. When a Rider was in Momma's head, she was completely gone. Even though the Preacher was in a woman's body, he was still the Preacher, and a man, cold and hard.)

Beneath the Mockingbird, on the middle shelf, sat Sugar. Sugar loved to be flattered, and would always flirt with the loveliest person in the room (man or woman; she wasn't fussy). She was my favorite, even though she ignored me whenever pretty Candy was around. She didn't look scary, and also, when Momma told the Rider stories, Sugar was the kindest to the Little Lost Girl. Sugar's fetish was like a regular doll, only she had pointed cat's ears and eyes made from green marbles. She wore a short dress made of black lace and red patent leather shoes, and she smelled of peaches.

Each time after Sugar mounted her, Momma went out and bought one new piece of clothing for the goddess to try on next time she came. I used to think this was just Momma's way of spending money on filmy underwear, but she was very scrupulous about never messing with the stuff in any of the cubbies herself, nor were we allowed to. Sugar's cubby was a clutter of lipticks and perfumes, which even the Preacher wouldn't touch, though the sight of them always made him sour. Candy tried to stash some of her makeups there once to keep them safe from the Preacher. Momma saw that directly and blacked her eye for it. Neither of us touched anything in the chifforobe after that.

Beneath the Preacher sat Pierrot. He was the only store-bought doll; Momma had found him in the French Quarter in New Orleans. He had white clown cheeks with red circles on them, a sharp pointed nose and sharp pointed chin, and a long pointed cap that leaned down in front of his eyes. He was very funny and very alone. Some days he would leave you breathless with laughter, but he could be cruel, too, like the time Candy's period left a stain on her pants and he made jokes about it to the boys in the mall we were in. He could juggle and breathe fire and he smelled of lighter fluid.

On the bottom row, beneath Sugar, was the Widow, whose body was a long stoppered test tube filled with dried-up spiders. Her head was a red pincushion, her eyes were glossy black buttons, and her hair was made of needles and pins. The Widow smelled of scorched cloth and silver polish; a dry, burnt, dizzy smell. Of all the Riders, we saw her the least, maybe only three or four times that I could remember, but I hated her the most. She took a particular and immediate interest in our family. She gave orders and we followed them, but I never once felt she loved us. If our family was a farm, she was the farmer, and would mow, seed, or slaughter us as she saw fit. She did not care about me as a person, or Candy, or even Momma. She was the one that twisted money out of Daddy like water from a rag to send me to Rice for my degree, when I could have gone to UT in Austin for far less, and gotten away from home in the bargain.

Last, beside the Widow, came Mr. Copper. Momma had carved him from hickory wood and polished him until he gleamed. His body was narrow and tremendously thin, like a primitive African statue. Around his shoulders hung a cloak made from squares of snakeskin she had sewn together. In his hand he held a long bone spear, its head made from a rattlesnake's rattle. Mr. Copper came with a smell of dust and gasoline and he was very good with money. He loved calculation, and would demand to play bridge or dominos with anyone good enough to give him a game, although he never lost. Mr. Copper was a user, a creature of pure power. As the old saying goes, he knew the price of everything and the value of nothing. In his cubby Momma always kept a pack of cards, a pair of bone dice, and a set of ivory dominos in a snakeskin case.

There never was a doll for the Little Lost Girl, nor did she have a cubbyhole of her own, though Momma said that if you listened very closely you could hear her walking through our house in the middle of the night.

The day they buried Momma I stood in front of the staring Riders for a long time. Then, fearfully, I reached out for the tall chifforobe doors, and swung them shut. The moment Momma's gods could no longer see me, a wonderful lightness came into my heart and head, making me giddy. Like a schoolgirl cutting class, I abandoned my chores and snuck out to the garden instead.

As I came through the patio doors the sound of birds assaulted me. Every November I could remember, Houston's skies had filled with birds, more of them every year. Many settled in for the winter; many more were just passing through, all on the wing from where *you* live, the dark countries, the cold places where winter comes. The day we buried Momma, the live oaks that lined our street were boiling with birds: bluejays, cardinals, redbirds and mockingbirds, and grackles and grackles and yet more grackles; the females olive-chested and poised, the men raucous, each the shiny blue-black of polished coal: eight of them perched along the neck of each street lamp, leering down like drunken magistrates in their black coats.

Most houses have yards, but Candy and I grew up in a garden, with a cranky white stucco house thrown in as an afterthought. The house had once belonged to Clark Gable's rich first wife back in the 1920s. It was laid out in the old Spanish style, one room per floor. Candy and I were stuck on the top, to broil in the summer heat.

Momma and Daddy slept underneath us. Both upper floors had long balconies with rust-spotted wrought-iron railings that squeaked and swayed when me and Candy swung on them.

The garden had crowded the house into the very corner of the lot, and was constantly attempting the spill into the ground floor. Momma loved to keep all the French doors open, so inside melted into outside, tile floor giving way to the stone-flagged patio and paths set in the foliage. This put the whole family on an intimate footing with ants, tree roaches, green anoles and mosquitoes, but Momma believed it was worth it.

The afternoon we buried Momma it was 76 degrees out, according to the thermometer hanging from the patio roof. My sister, Candy, was waiting for me at the wrought-iron table under the banana tree. "How's Daddy?" she asked.

"Watching basketball in their room. Not so good, I guess."

In her plain black funeral dress Candy looked like a young Mexican widow, with her dark eyes and pale skin and her hair pinned up señora style. She pointed to two shot glasses on the patio table, each with three fingers of some Dr. Pepper-colored liquid, a deep red-brown so dark as to be nearly black. Between the glasses stood one of Momma's recycled liquor bottles; the paper label on the front had *Mockingbird Cordial* written in her florid hand. The cap was off. "Momma told me to break this out when she was safely underground." Candy's eyes were red and the makeup on her cheeks was smudged with tear tracks.

I picked up the shot glass on my side of the table. The drink had the strangest fragrance, half-floral, half-industrial, like flowers and hot steel. "No thanks."

"I didn't make it, honest. I don't even know what's in it."

"There's a recommendation."

"For Christ's sake, Toni."

"No. Uh-uh. I did my deathbed scene with Momma. She may not reach out from beyond the grave and make me do another one."

"Why do you have to hate her so much?"

"I do not hate her."

"Yes you do! You've been stomping around in a fury since the moment she died. For Christ's sake, Toni! She's gone, our momma is gone, God bless her." Candy wiped another tear off her cheek with the back of her thumb. "Why can't you leave her alone?"

I said, "You get what you pay for."

"God, you're a vindictive bitch."

"You swear too much."

"Fuck off." Candy's fabulous breasts rose as she took a deep breath. "Please, Toni. I don't dare cross her. She can't get to you like she can get to me."

This was true enough. Candy is the one who inherited Momma's touch of magic. In Candy the gift was more direct, but less flexible. None of the Riders had ever mounted her. She could see the future sometimes, in dreams and visions, but with one curious qualifier: all she ever saw were happy things.

I picked up my glass and tipped a little of the Mockingbird Cordial into my mouth. It bit like a copperhead snake: rum, vanilla flowers; the feeling you get on the tip of your tongue when you touch it to a battery. The taste of pennies in your mouth when you were a child. I swallowed and Candy followed suit. "Thanks," she said.

"How long ago did you know she was going to die?"

"Maybe a year. I just . . . stopped dreaming about her anymore."

"How many happy dreams of her did you ever have?" I swirled another few drops of the cordial around my mouth and swallowed. "This stuff surely burns. Candy, are you all right? About Momma, I mean."

"No—Are you?"

"I'm all right."

Momma always liked Candy. Right from a baby, Candy was smiley and huggable. A great relief, as I had been colicky and a crosspatch from day one. "When I was having you, you were that set to come out sideways," Momma told me. "The doctor had to get in there and haul you out with forceps as big as a pair of steel salad forks. And cold! Like to have killed me," she would say, and laugh. I was horrified.

When she was in a good mood Momma called me ornery but durable. She liked that word: durable. To endure, which she pronounced with no y sound: en-doo-er. When she cried, which was often, I was a "poor baby," for having to be so tough so little, but it was good I was tough because in this life that's what you had to be. When she was angry, I was mean, or hateful, or sometimes the hatefulest child that ever was.

"I'm all right," I said. "You two were always closer ."

Candy choked and laughed. "The funny part is that you actually believe that."

"It's true!"

"Uh-huh."

I raised my glass. "To Momma. May I never be like her." Birds hopped and flittered among the branches overhead. The liquor ran down into my center and bloomed there, like flowers opening.

Candy stretched her legs out and crossed them at the ankles. "That bastard Carlos should have come to the funeral."

Carlos was Candy's current boyfriend, a Tex-Mex car detailer who lived at some strange intersection between Mexican folk magic and low rider gang membership. Carlos himself was small and lean and soft-spoken, a wonderful mechanic and something of a sorcerer who had lost part of one ear in a gang fight years before. Despite his angular face and tattoos and small black goatee no one had ever heard him cross his mother. I once saw him drink a shot glass full of 10W-40 motor oil to win a bet.

Candy had dated a lot of weird guys.

Actually, I thought they made a good couple: Carlos was pretty serious-minded, which she needed, and she was able to take the fact that he would occasionally visit with the spirits of the dead fairly much in stride. The most noticeable thing about Carlos was his car, a reconditioned hearse that he had turned into a rolling shrine. "Can you imagine Carlos bringing the Muertomobile into Glenwood? The security guards would have gunned him down in the driveway. Be reasonable. I'm sure he'll cruise by this afternoon."

"Probably La Hag Gonzales didn't want him seen with me in public."

"If I had a son, I wouldn't let him date you either." I found I could take the cordial down in bigger swallows, now that I was used to it. I emptied my glass. "You know, of all Momma's potions, I think this is the best she ever made."

Candy sloshed another shot into my glass. "Do you think Daddy was happy with her?"

"Does it matter?" I was beginning to feel lightheaded;

my thoughts, like clouds, pulling softly apart in the gulf breeze. It was not an unpleasant sensation; drifty, but not at all drowsy. Tender autumn sunshine dappled the garden. Not the destroying stare of summer, but a more uncertain light, diffusely golden and unsteady, ruffled by tree limbs creaking in the warm south wind, leaves shifting, the wheeling birds—the sweet, elusive light that comes at the end of days, and seasons.

I blinked, realizing my thoughts had pulled apart again. Empty spaces yawned between them. Something about the emptiness scared me. "Momma wasn't the sort who made you *happy*," I said. "Daddy was not bored, I guarantee you. And he didn't kill her." Another empty space began to open between my thoughts, but I fought it back. "He got what he paid for."

Candy sipped from her glass. "Well I've about had it with Carlos and La Hag Gonzales. Cut another notch on the barrel. Time for this *chica* to move on."

A concrete-colored Ford Explorer rolled slowly down the street. Birds swirled up like leaves in the wind of its passing, birds doubled by their shadows, swooping and whirling, birds in flight from the cold; passing to some warm, unnamed, blessed country of the South, where winter never comes.

With a little start of terror I realized I had been caught in one of those empty places between my thoughts. There was a whiteness in my head that seemed to keep me from thinking straight; like when you stare at the sun and afterwards there's a bright circle that dazzles you wherever you look. Only this whiteness was behind my eyes, back in my head, and it was cold.

"Can-Cand—?"

I felt a hand close over my hand. "Toni? Are you okay?"

Candy's voice sounded tiny and distant, as if coming through a telephone receiver in another room. A cloud must have passed overhead, for the light in the garden got suddenly dimmer. Silence fell over the world. I could see birds with their beaks working, but no songs came. Acorns fell into the pond without splashing.

"Unh!" I stood up clumsily, knocking my chair over backwards. Where was the sound of the iron chair clattering on the stone?

Then I smelled the Widow smells, of silver polish and scorched cloth, and I knew what was happening.

I stepped back to keep my balance. My right foot came down and froze. A line of cold whiteness ran up past my knee. I cried out and pulled the leg up, and the whiteness drained down a bit.

"Toni! Toni, what's wrong!" I staggered. As soon as my right foot came down on the stone flags it froze again, and I was pinned to the garden path. The whiteness raced up my leg and flowered in me like fire eating through a piece of paper. I tried to scream but no noise came out. I went mad with fear and ran senselessly around in my head but there was too much whiteness everywhere. From a long way off, I heard Candy whisper, "Oh my God. I can smell her, Toni." Then the whiteness exploded in my head and the Widow came.

TWO

Here's the first story I remember Momma telling about the Widow. Imagine me lying in my nightie, too hot to be under the sheets, the balcony doors open so the humid East Texas night steals into the room. It's bedtime. Candy is asleep in her crib at the foot of the bed. I can hear her little baby snores coming through the mosquito netting. Momma is sitting beside me, her face pale and indistinct in the gloom. She has the most marvelous voice, husky and slow.

I don't know if her stories are true, if the Riders tell them to her or if she just makes them up.

Imagine her leaning over me, her special smell of cigarettes and bourbon and hairspray, me with my eyes closed, the baby's snores, and the Little Lost Girl steps into the room on my mother's voice. . . .

. . .

Now, that Little Lost Girl has been a long time walking. She's walked down by the bayou and she's walked up on the Hill where the rich people live. She's walked through Chinatown where the food smells funny and she's walked out late, past the corners where the colored girls wait in their gold shorts to climb into Mr. Copper's car and be carried away. She's been walking a long time, always looking for her own little house with the yellow trim around the door and the white fence around the yard and the swing hung from the limb of the live-oak tree out front, but she never has found that house—until now.

This day, she's walking through a nice homey neighborhood and all of a sudden there it is. She's been lost so long she can't be sure it's the place, but the picket fence is white, there's yellow trim around the door, and wouldn't you know, there's a swing that hangs from two long chains bolted to the limb of a big live-oak tree.

There's a woman out front working in the flower bed, shovelling dirt from a big pile under the rosebushes into a hole the size of a laundry basket. It's as if she's filling in a little grave.

"Momma!" says the Little Lost Girl. "Is that you?"

The woman stops shovelling, but when she turns, with a heap of dirt still resting in her spade, the Little Lost Girl sees that it is not her mother standing there but the Widow. The girl is scared of her cruel old eyes. "Oh. Excuse me. I been lost a long time, and I thought this might be my house," she says. "Say, what might you be burying there under that rosebush?"

The Widow looks at her for a good piece. "How did you come to be lost?" she says. She's got a voice like a steam iron hissing down on a shirt.

"My momma told me I was sick and took me to the doctor. The doctor said I was well, but when I got back to the waiting room my momma wasn't there. I waited for her until the office closed, but she didn't come back, so I've been trying to walk home by myself."

The Widow looks at her for even a longer time. "That's a long walk," she says. Then she turns back and drops her spadeful of dirt into the little hole under the rosebushes.

"Are you for certain this ain't my house?" the Little Lost Girl says. "It surely does look like it."

The Widow turns back to her. "If ever it was, it isn't now."

"Oh," says the Little Lost Girl. Then she cries. Cries and cries for all that lonesomeness. For all that walking.

When she's done crying she says, "What have you got down in that hole?"

"What's your name?" says the Widow, real quick-like.

The Little Lost Girl does not answer.

"Cat got your tongue?" the Widow says. "I asked you what your name was, girl. We'll do a trade. You tell me your name, and I'll tell you what I've got at the bottom of this hole." The pile of fill dirt is nearly flat. When the little girl does not answer, the Widow sets to tamping it down with the back of her spade.

"My momma said not to tell my name to strangers."

The Widow puts her shovel aside and steps onto the fill dirt, tramping it down until it's level with the rest of the flower bed, and you can hardly tell there ever was a little hole beneath the rosebushes. "No little girl lives here anymore," she says.

Then she closes the gate in front of the Little Lost Girl, and latches it, and walks back up to the front porch, and goes into the house, leaving the Little Lost Girl outside.

When darkness falls, a yellow light comes on in the living room, but the front door never opens. Finally the Little Lost Girl starts walking on, looking for her very own home, where there would be yellow trim around the door and a white picket fence and a swing hanging from a live-oak tree outside. And if she hasn't found it, she's walking still.

"Toni?"

I was lying on my back on a tile floor and someone was supporting my aching head.

"Toni?"

Ah, Daddy's voice. I recognized it now. That would be his hand under the back of my skull. My eyelids fluttered open, then fell shut again, like butterfly wings too new and wet to stay unfurled. *Ow!* I meant to say, but only a weak grunt came out.

"What? What was that?"

"Ow. Ow."

"I'll bet. Just take it easy there, kiddo. You aren't fixing to go anywhere soon."

Candy's voice came from off to one side. "It was the Widow, Toni. She mounted you." I opened my eyes again, with more success, but Candy was not in my field of vision and there was no way I was going to turn my head. I settled for looking up at the ceiling fan, watching the slow sweep of its long wooden blades. Even when it isn't hot we keep the fan going on low, just to move the air around. Momma always thought that was healthful.

"Ow," I said, more vigorously. I had a brutal pulsing headache, my stomach was queasy, and my whole body felt like a fried egg someone had just slapped into a hot skillet sunny side down.

I remembered the Widow's smell and prayed Momma's demons wouldn't get me.

Candy said, "This better not turn out to be your idea of a joke."

"Oh, hysterical," I said. "Fuck off."

"Your sister's a little jumpy," Daddy said. "The Widow put a scare into her."

"Are you laughing at me? It's not funny! Toni, the Widow said I had to marry Carlos! *Marry* him! And pump out a few little bambinos afterwards!"

"Congratulations. I look forward to your pregnancy. It will be nice to see you fatter than me, for once."

Candy nudged me in the side with her foot, none too gently.

I straightened out my shaking legs. "Most people have to buy a bottle of cheap tequila to feel like this. Guess I should consider myself lucky. S'okay, Daddy. You can put my head down. I'll just rest here a second or two longer." Daddy remained squatting behind me, holding my head in his hands. I loved him for it. "Anyway, Candy, you don't have to do what the Widow said."

"Yeah, right." Candy started to pace again.

Another throb of pain made my vision wobble. "God, sis, it should have been you the Widow mounted. You *like* this stuff. Oh Candy. I don't want to fight with the Riders. It can't be the Mockingbird Cordial; we both drank that."

"Um—well . . . To be honest, Toni, you were the only one who drank that stuff. My glass had Dr. Pepper in it."

"What!"

"Momma said so! She said the cordial was only for you." More quietly Candy said, "Her last gift was only for you."

"Oh, great." A wave of nausea made me gasp and close

my eyes. The pain in my head went on and on. "You jealous?"

Candy's footsteps stopped. "To the heart," she said.

Apparently I had been possessed for about thirty minutes. The Widow had inspected the house, looked through some of Momma's photographs, and informed Candy that she was to marry Carlos. Eventually she had returned to the chifforobe on the ground floor and opened the doors so the dolls could look out. At that point she must have considered her work done; she left my head so fast, Daddy barely managed to catch me as I crumpled to the floor.

By the time I was able to sit upright at the table with my face in my hands, nearly an hour had passed and we were expecting the condolence calls to start at any moment. Candy ran out to pick up some coffee and cakes. At my request, Daddy got one of Momma's bottles of Evan Williams seven-year-old sour mash bourbon and unhurriedly poured me one shot. "You sure you want this, Toni? You're not much of a drinker."

"I'm thinking of taking it up," I said. He gave me the glass.

I don't think I ever saw Daddy in a rush. With his sad eyes and his patience and his careful, measured speech, I always figured God had meant him to be a career minor league baseball manager, a quiet mentor to eager young bucks on their way to the bigs. Instead, the Lord had unreasonably chosen to make him a traveling salesman for American Express. He spent a lot of time on the road, getting places to stock the Travellers Checks. Physically he was smaller than Momma, with a fine-boned frame, a small head beginning to show jowls, and rounded shoul-

ders, but she flew around him like the wind swirling
around a stone. Many was the time Candy and I had hidden in his lee.

The shaking in my limbs was gradually fading. The
bourbon tasted vile and made me cough until my eyes
watered. "If this is Momma's idea of a gift, if now, after
thirty years I'm supposed to take on her bad debts—"
Once the bourbon reached my stomach, it flowered into
a warmth in my blood. "I don't see why she has to always
get her way. I mean, good Lord, Daddy, why did you let
her, let her be that way with us? Why didn't you ever
stand up to her?" My father looked at me. I was horrified
to find myself saying these things, today of all days. I
started crying. "You can't let her do this to me!"

Daddy pushed his chair back from the table and walked
into the kitchen. In a moment he came back with a bottle
of Dos Equis from the fridge and a bottle opener. He was
fond of Mexican beer. Dew was already beading on the
cold bottle from the warm, humid air. Daddy said, "Imagine there's a man who needs a job done. I say I'll do it for
a hundred dollars. When I finish, I go to collect my money.
But the fella says, 'Thanks, but I'm only going to pay you
seventy-five.' I say, 'We had a deal. What makes you think
you can cheat me out of twenty-five dollars?' Then he
pulls a loaded gun out of his desk and puts the barrel to
his temple and pulls the hammer back and says, 'If you
won't do it for seventy-five, I'm going to shoot myself.'
And I know he means it."

Which was always the kicker, with Momma. For all the
lies she told, she never had to say a thing about her own
desperate unhappiness. None of us had ever doubted she
wanted to pull the trigger. That was for real.

"Why me?" I said. "Why don't the Riders come for

Candy? She'd like them. She'd invite them in. Oh God, Daddy." The tears were running out of me faster now, I'd lost the knack of holding them in. "It was so awful. It was like being killed. The Widow came into my head and murdered me so she could ride around in my body. I was so scared."

Daddy drank some of his beer. "Your momma always said it was like being run over and left for dead . . . I imagine that's why it was you the Riders came for."

"Meaning?"

He looked at me. "Your sister only sees happy things."

"Ha."

"It's true."

I scowled into my shot glass. "If Momma thinks I'm going to start now, with all the spookery and horseshit— No ma'am. You can't have everything your way. Not after you're dead. It's one of the rules. If she wanted to pass along her nasty little presents, she should have done it while she was still alive. I am no kind of mockingbird. I've got one song to sing and that's my song, Antoinette's song."

"There are some gifts that cannot be refused, Toni."

I drank the rest of my bourbon. "Horseshit. I refuse. I refuse!"

My father put down his beer, fitting it exactly onto the ring the bottle had left on the table. "I'm going to give you a piece of advice. I love you dearly, girl, but don't try to muscle a fastball through your momma's zone. She'll drill you out of the ballpark. You're AA crazy at best, Toni, but your momma was an All-Star in the majors."

The Friesens were the first to come by with condolences that afternoon, Bill Sr. with a squat eight-sided bottle of Blanton's Single Barrel, Penny carrying a beautiful lasagna from The Olive Garden.

(I am nine and sulky. My mother is cooking food to take to Mr. Hierholzer at the end of the block. His wife has just died. She dumps a fat tablespoon of butter into a dish of yellow squash poached in cream. Across the street Candy and my friend Greg and Greg's cousins from San Antonio are playing Batman, but Momma has made me stay inside and cook all afternoon. First it was an apple pie and I nearly cried because the air was so humid my crust wouldn't hold. Then chili rellenos. My fingertips are still burning from handling the poblano peppers. Now we're making poached squash. I hear Candy laughing from across the street, she's five and never has to do anything, and I ask why we can't just buy Mr. Hierholzer an ice-cream cake at the Dairy Queen.

"When I die, we'll see who brings store-bought and who brings homemade," Momma says. "Then you'll know who my real friends were.")

"We were just so sorry when we heard." Penny Friesen held out her lasagna. I used to think Penny looked down her nose at us—Momma said it often enough—but after I grew up I decided she was just shy and awkward, particularly in the shadow of her big affable husband. Penny always wore the uniform of her class, the white linen blazers, pink lipstick, gold hoop earrings, and white hair spun into a round ball like a puff of bleached cotton candy, but she wore it without conviction, like an impostor.

I forgave her the store-bought lasagna. "Daddy's out back."

Bill Sr. nodded and waggled the bottle of Blanton's. "I'll bring out some glasses," I said. Daddy would nurse his Dos Equis, of course, but Bill would want to try some of the expensive bourbon he had brought. I showed them to the French doors and let them into the garden.

The younger Friesen, Bill Jr., was the next to arrive. He was a blandly ugly man: a big head topped with curly brown hair stuck on a big loaf of a body that never managed to fit properly into his very expensive suits. He had inherited his mother's white complexion, turned pasty and running to freckles, along with watery hazel eyes and an unfortunate mouth that was too wide and full-lipped for his face. He was rather a good argument for makeup for men, actually; a bit of foundation and some careful management of his lips would have done him a world of good. I had known Bill Jr. since he was in diapers, and made him show me his wee-wee when we were six. At the time I thought it looked like something you would put on a hook to catch catfish.

Since then, Bill Jr. had graduated from the Fuqua School of Business and returned to take up his part of the family business, the investment division where I worked. He was an okay boss. Now that he was in Management, he never called me anything but Ms. Beauchamp. He never closed his office door when talking to a female employee, which was appreciated, and he never raised his voice. As a boy he had often fantasized about being an admiral in the Navy; he saw himself in a commanding, rather than fighting, role, though he carried the ideals of honor fully in his chest. His version of a glorious death was going down with a ship. He was also greedy and a bit of a sneak, as long as he wasn't caught by anyone, including himself. "I'm just so sorry," he said. "Don't, ah, don't worry about that oil prospectus we were talking about. You just do what needs to be done for the family right now."

"Thanks. As Momma would say, I'm about worn to a frazzle with Daddy and all." Not to mention having the Widow creep like a spider into my head.

I showed Bill Jr. into the garden and started putting together a cheese and cracker plate. I was cutting the cheddar into very thin slices to make it look like there was more of it when I heard the Muertomobile drawing up to the house. It was not a sound you could mistake; its engine rumbled like the organ in Satan's front parlor.

Houston is a funny town; superstition and heavy industry have had strange sweaty couplings amid the oil refineries and shipyards, and produced some very weird offspring. There have been spirit cars here for twenty-five years, altogether stranger beasts than the regular low riders, but the Muertomobile outclassed them all. Carlos had salvaged a '62 GM-built hearse, dropped the body down to the legal limit for low riders, and then set about patiently encrusting it with artifacts of power. Seven star-shaped clusters, each made from thirteen silver dollars, demarcated the Muertomobile's zones of power. Its white staring eyes were ringed with polished shells, and a bleached calf's skull served as the hood ornament. The body of the car was coated in photographs of Carlos's ancestors; hundreds of them, all in frames of wood or bronze or plastic or porcelain or pewter or silver, most glued down flat, but some dozen propped to stand upright, such as the great gold-framed portrait of his maternal grandparents that stood proudly on the roof of the hearse, just over the driver's side of the windshield.

Inside the car every surface was swathed in crushed red velvet of the sort you imagine in the bottom of Dracula's coffin. The red air was full of dancing men; skeletons and crucifixes of every description hung from the ceiling, trembling and bouncing on a spider's forest of thin black threads. It was not at all comforting to have Carlos driving behind you, late at night. His souped-up halogen high beams were a white, annihilating stare; he himself was only a black shadow surrounded by a deep red light that welled from the windshield like the afterglow of hell.

"Candy! Carlos is—"

"I know, I know." She stomped in from the garden. "That damn car is scaring all the grackles up out of the trees. I hope they cover it in birdshit." She pursed and puckered her lips, brushed back her hair, and checked to make sure her slip wasn't showing. "How do I look?"

Like a centerfold for the Funeral Home Girls of the South pictorial, I didn't say. Outside, the bank-vault doors of the Muertomobile swung shut. "Not bad. A little too pretty, I think. La Gonzales would like to see you a bit more crazy with grief, but—"

"Screw the old hag, I don't care—shit, there they are!" Candy checked the coffee and boxes of pastries set out on the long table, smoothed her dress, and opened the door.

"*Buenos días*, Señora Gonzales," she said, gravely bobbing her head. "Carlos."

"An' what's good about it?" asked La Gonzales, stepping heavily through the door ahead of her son. She had a figure like Queen Victoria in her later years. Her forearms were the size of loaves of bread, her knees were hardened from a lifetime of kneeling at early morning Mass. La Gonzales had raised nine children and buried two husbands. Her hair was still as dark as a widow's veil, her crow's eyes black and bright and sharp. "Carlos, put those dishes on the table."

"*Sí, Mamá.*" Carlos cleaned up rather well. His mother had bullied him out of his usual undershirt and jeans; in-

stead, he wore an old double-breasted black suit of his
father's. His beard was trimmed and the line of hoops had
come out of his left ear. His only remaining piece of jewelry was a necklace on which was threaded a spark plug
from his first car, which he had crashed into a bayou at
age seventeen. Miraculously he had escaped nearly un-
hurt, and ever since then had carried the spark plug as a
lucky charm.

The platter he carried over to the table was laden with
four deep casserole dishes and a red clay Dutch oven.
Astonishing scents crept out from under the covers and
made my mouth water. La Gonzales, who had the virtues
as well as the vices of the old-style Mexican mother, was
an incomparable cook. "We have brought just a little
something, *chica*," she said, coming over to me. The hands
that clasped mine were firm and soft and warm as dinner
rolls. "You poor thing, with your mother passed away,
now you must look after everyone, *sí*? We have just a few
chili rellenos, and a plate of tamales, a chicken mole and
some rice and in there a little pig," she said, pointing at
the Dutch oven.

Her eyes rested a moment longer on the table, and a
frown settled over her face. She let go of my hands. Her
frown deepened. She reached out to the three boxes of
beautiful cakes and pastries Candy had picked up, and
poked one with a finger fat and mottled like a breakfast
sausage. "Store-bought?" she asked, looking at Candy.
"Your sainted mother is dead, your sister is making the
plans, the calls, is a comfort to the father, *and you have
only store-bought on the table?*"

"*Mamá!*" Carlos said.

"*La madre fallece, ¡y compran panecillos!*"

"*Entre ellos, no es igual, Mamá.*"

*"Y cuando paso a la más allá, ¿que vas a traer a la mesa?
¿Una caja de Kentucky Fried Chicken y un Milky Way?"*

Candy looked murderously at Carlos, as if this were
somehow his fault. "When you die, Señora Gonzales," she
said, "I promise I will cook a feast."

Slowly the garden began to fill up. Visitors continued to
arrive on our doorstep, more than I had ever imagined.
Women who had come to Momma for advice or winning
Lotto numbers or for curses on their cheating husbands,
a couple she had helped elope, a woman she had hidden
in our house for a month to escape her abusive boyfriend,
the manager and stylist from her beauty shop, friends of
Daddy's, people from Friesen Investments, and many others I could not place. Everyone brought flowers or, more
often, food, and soon our long farmhouse table was laden
with potato salad, devilled eggs, coleslaw, barbecued brisket, chicken and dumplings, chicken sopa, meatloaf, pecan
pie, lemon pound cake, sopapillas still warm from the vat
and sprinkled with icing sugar, green beans with sautéed
almond slivers, mashed potatoes with cream and brown
gravy both, shrimp étouffée and red beans and rice, a rust-
red jambalaya seething with okra and onions, and a growing array of spreads and jams and jellies put up in Mason
jars by the older women of Momma's acquaintance: plum
preserves and apple butter, pickled onions and banana
peppers, and from Momma's oldest friend, Mary Jo, an
extra jar of the things she gave us every Christmas: jala-
peño jelly for Daddy, the special chow-chow that I loved
on burgers and hot dogs, mustang-grape jam for Candy.
Last of all, a pot of the Mexican mint jelly Momma used
to love to slather on her pork chops and lamb. "For your

mother, wherever she is now," Mary Jo said to me, and gravely I accepted it.

Mary Jo had known Momma forever. Her secrets were the only ones Momma ever kept, and I suspect the opposite was also true. Mary Jo's husband had left her and his eight-year-old son for his secretary when I was eleven. If Mary Jo heard from him after that, we girls did not know of it.

Mary Jo had worked at Sears for a time, but now stayed at home stuffing envelopes. The last time we had taken her for dinner, before Momma got too weak to go out, Mary Jo had claimed to be able to tell the astrological signs of our fellow diners from the thickness of their ankles. Later on she had remarked, in a loud voice, that a gentleman two tables away gave clear evidence, in the set of his neck and the shape of his ears, of mental retardation.

We loved Mary Jo to death, but we didn't show her to strangers much.

I let her help me set out some more plates and silver for the guests and then took her outside, still talking, around the edge of the house to an area of the garden away from the main throng. All Mary Jo could talk about was the will. "Did you ever notice that she changed it, Toni?"

"Not that I know of."

"Never told you to call a lawyer for her in the last month or two?"

"No."

"Dagnabbit," Mary Jo said glumly. We stood together in the shadow of the west fence, looking up at the leaves of the small palm tree that shaded the kitchen window. Our palm trees aren't like those willowy, anorexic things you see on TV shows shot in Los Angeles. In Texas we grow them short and plump and pretty, like the waitresses in a good Tex-Mex joint.

"I told her I was going to need me a piece of change to get my roof fixed," Mary Jo said. "Darn thing leaks all the time now. Every time it rains, the drips come down the insides of my walls."

Having the Widow mount me had taken its toll; even hours later I felt tired and empty inside. "I guess we'll just have to wait to see what's in the will, Mary Jo."

"I know what's in the will," Mary Jo snapped. "'Less she changed it, anyway. Ain't any of us going to know. She had her lawyer put it under court seal. She told me she didn't want anyone looking at it, even us."

"You're kidding. No, you're not. That would be just like Momma. Lord only knows what secrets she thinks she has left," I said. "Well, she's welcome to them, and any money too. I wouldn't get your hopes up, Mary Jo. Momma wasn't the saving kind."

"Well, you're right and you're wrong both, Toni." She looked at me. "Aren't any of you children going to miss her like I do," she said. I started to speak but she held up her hand. "I ain't saying you didn't love your momma, you especially, Antoinette. But you won't miss her like I will. You got your sister and your daddy. I got nobody. Not one soul."

"Mary Jo. I—" She held up her hand again, and I stopped because she was right. Her husband was lost and her son never wrote, and I could not pretend to be lonelier than her.

"So what did the Widow have to say, honey?"

I stared at her, shocked. "How did you know?"

"Smelled her on you. You think I don't know that

smell, the number of times I picked your momma up after the Riders dropped her on her fanny?''

''Oh.'' I hadn't thought of that. ''I don't know what the Widow said. I wasn't there. Ask Candy.''

But Mary Jo shrugged, losing interest. ''I doubt the old horror told how to fix my roof,'' she said.

Greg, our childhood friend from across the street, showed up just after dark. ''Sorry I'm so late,'' he said. Typical Greg, that: apology without explanation. He dropped his linen jacket on the coat tree and tapped the door shut behind him with one foot. Greg had spent a lot of energy learning juggling and stage magic in his early twenties, and though it never made him a living, I always thought it suited him well, physically. He moved in lovely, graceful, unexpected ways, frequently doing different things at once; for example, leaning forward to kiss me on the cheek while pulling a bottle of red wine from behind his back. ''What stage are you at? Fear, denial, depression? Bargaining?''

''I thought acceptance was supposed to be in there.''

''Nope. Too soon. Don't kid yourself.'' He held me by the shoulders and studied my face. ''You look dreadful.''

''Gee, thanks.''

''No, I mean it. You look like you ran a marathon. Have you not been sleeping?''

''I'm okay.'' If having your dead mother's gods crawl into your head is okay.

Greg walked over to the chifforobe and stood a long minute, staring up at Momma's dolls. ''She used to scare the shit out of me, you know.''

''Momma?''

"Oh man, did she have my number." He reached up and scratched behind Sugar's pointed cat ears.

"Don't touch that. It's not a toy." Greg hopped back from the chifforobe. "Um. Sorry," I said.

"No, no. My fault." He shook his head. "I remember once, I must have been about sixteen, I met her in the pharmacy there on Yoakum. Have I told you this story?" I shook my head and he grinned. "I was dating this girl, Cindy Sanford. God, what a body. So there's Cindy and me in the drugstore, loitering around trying to get up the courage to buy a pack of condoms. I'm just reaching for the Trojans—not the ribbed kind or anything, we weren't ready for that—when your mother swoops down on me like a buzzard from a blue sky, smiling the biggest smile you ever saw. Cindy does the smart thing and pretends not to know me. If there'd been a drain in the floor, I would have gone down it.

"This is bad enough, but it gets worse. Instead of chatting and then moving on, or even just giving me a wink, which would not be beyond your mom, she puts one claw on my shoulder and draws me aside. Then she whispers, only she whispers very loudly, so I'm sure Cindy can hear, and she says, "Oh Greg, she's so *pretty*! Now listen, honey, the cost of a good, safe abortion is about two thousand dollars. Call me if you need one, okay? You know, later on. I know some good people. Don't be embarrassed. Promise?"

"Oh my God."

Greg cackled. "Then she swoops off down the aisle and never says another word about it."

"Did you ever sleep with the girl?"

He grinned. "Never even held her hand again. I was a virgin until I was twenty, swear to God."

"Good Lord, Greg. You? *I* would have fixed that for you at seventeen."

"Yeah, I know. I mean—"

Yeah, I know. And I had been so careful never to let him know I had had a crush on him. Tore the pages out of my diary and flushed them down the toilet so Candy wouldn't find them and tell. Only apparently he had known all along. And hadn't even tried to take advantage of it or anything. Which was good, but I hated him for it just at the moment. A horrible hot prickle of embarrassment crept over me before Greg could save the situation. "Um, what I mean is, I think your mom was warning me off you and Candy, too."

You could have lit paper by touching it to my face. "Good old Momma," I said.

I showed Greg into the garden and then crept upstairs to compose myself. The party didn't seem to miss me much. I pulled open the balcony doors and lay down in my old bed. The smells of perfume and cigarette smoke drifted up from down below, mixing with the sounds of ice clinking in glasses and laughter and lies being told while birds sang and fluttered darkly in the night. I could hear the plips and pats of live-oak acorns dropping onto the roof, and the parked cars beyond our fence, and into our ornamental pond, steady as rain.

All the serious eating, drinking, and entertaining at our house was done outdoors among the monkey grass and oleanders. How familiar this all was, the company-night smells of cigarettes and hibiscus and charcoal briquettes; ropes of smoke coiling around the crepe myrtles; candle flames shaking, their reflections burning like stars in our little pond. Other nights the small mop-headed palm trees would have been shaking with laughter as kids dove for them, calling out "Home Free!" Mary Jo might strum some chords on her beat-up guitar while Momma sang old Mexican songs full of people who died for love; and over everything the black, thigh-wide branches of the live-oak beyond our wall.

And when we could stay awake no longer, and the guests with children had gone, Daddy would take us upstairs and brush our teeth, and after I got Candy into her pajamas Momma would come up, humming and smiling, and she would tuck the baby in and touch my cheek with her hand, and sing to us always the same lullaby

Hush little baby don't say a word,
Momma's gonna buy you a mockingbird.
If that mockingbird don't sing,
Momma's gonna buy you a diamond ring.
If that diamond ring don't shine . . .

The shock of Momma's death and the Widow's possession must have been greater than I knew, for I found I had fallen asleep. The clock said an hour and a half had passed since I came upstairs. Voices still murmured in the garden below, though fewer of them, and they spoke more quietly. I struggled out of bed and switched on a lamp. I passed my fingers through my hair and then sat for what seemed like a long time, looking at my face in the hand mirror on the bedside table. Daddy never let us buy a full-length mirror after Momma broke all the old ones.

Momma always said I had her eyes, but I didn't believe her until I saw her in her casket, surrounded by carnations and calla lilies. Sure enough, there they were. My eyes with her wrinkles around them.

I looked at my face for a long time. Looking for her.

When I crept downstairs I found Penny Friesen standing
at the long table nibbling on a piece of cornbread. At
twenty she had been prettier than Momma, I suppose, in
a bland white-bread way, but her looks hadn't lasted, and
she had never blossomed as Momma had. Momma at forty
and fifty and even sixty had so much life in her, the room
got bright and dangerous when she walked in. But Bill
Sr.'s big shadow had left Penny pale and starved for sunlight.

She held a glass of Greg's red wine in her hand. "Having a rest?"

"It's been a long few days."

"Hm." She took a sip, and gave me an odd look. "You
know," she said, "the hardest thing about having someone
die, I find, is forgiving them."

"I beg your pardon?"

"You can love them or hate them, but when they die
they've gotten the last word, and now you'll never be able
to even the score." Penny drank a little more of her wine.
"That's hard to forgive, isn't it?"

"Yes it is," I said.

After the last visitor had left and the dishes had been
brought inside and washed, after Candy had gone home
to her apartment and Daddy had gone upstairs to sleep, I
went back to the little bed at the top of the house and lay
down. The whole jumbled day turned and twisted in my
thoughts, falling away piece by piece, until, just before
sleep took me, I was left with only the grim spare figure
of the Widow staring down at me. "What's your name,
Little Lost Girl?" she said in her steam-iron voice. The
smell of burnt cloth and silver polish made my head swim
as she loomed over me. *What's your name?*

THREE

For some reason—maybe it's the magic in Candy, some remnant of the Riders' touch—my sister has always had her own special smell, a faint, beautiful scent of burnt cinnamon. All my early memories have that smell. I suppose there must have been a time when I did not have a sister, but I cannot recall it. My memories start with the new baby in the cradle at the foot of my bed, as if I didn't really have a life, didn't have a story worth telling, until there was someone else to tell it to.

My earliest clear memory of the Riders is actually about Candy. It's late on a summer afternoon. The Preacher has mounted Momma downstairs, so I have taken the baby up to our room to play where we will be out of the way. Candy has short fat little legs, and stumps happily around the room pulling out drawers. I must be nearly six years old. It's much too hot to keep the balcony doors closed, but with them open, Candy has found a wonderful new

game: taking clothes out of our chest of drawers and dropping them off the balcony into the garden. Two of her
little dresses go overboard before I realize what she is doing. Now I will have to sneak out and get them before
Momma sees them or else she will slap the baby, which
makes Candy cry and then I have to shut her up. Or
Momma will yell at me, and then I will have to shut myself up or get slapped too.

So I'm watching the baby, and every time she makes
for the balcony, I chase her down and lug her awkwardly
back into the room with my arms around her chest so she
dangles from her armpits. She thinks this is hilarious, and
starts running back to the balcony as soon as I put her
down, knowing I will come chase her again.

I have just picked up her giggling fat body for the fourth
time when there is a terrific crash from my parents' room,
a horrible glass-smashing sound. I am so frightened, I drop
the baby, who falls *bump* on her bottom. There is a long
aching moment of silence. Then another smash from
downstairs, and a reek of jasmine and roses. The Preacher
is smashing Momma's perfume bottles.

I remember thinking that Mr. MacReady and any customers in his Garage Mart next door must be hearing this.

I stare at Candace Jane, willing her to silence, praying
she won't do anything to draw the Preacher's attention.
The baby looks at me with huge eyes, and then—she
laughs! Laughs at the drop-go-bump game, and holds out
her arms to be picked up so we can play *that* again. The
baby grins hugely with her sprinkling of teeth and I love
her so much, so desperately. She is everything good in this
life and I wish dumbly and hopelessly that I could be like
her. The love I feel is so fierce and hurt and huge I have
no words for it, I can't see around it or even remember it

most of the time, but it's always there. And sometimes I catch that faint cinnamon smell of her, and then I remember.

I got pregnant.

I decided the day after we buried Momma. I made an appointment with a fertility specialist on Monday and started plowing through his literature on artificial insemination. Interestingly, the part where they actually squirt you only costs about a hundred and fifty bucks, plus a surcharge if you use their sperm, as I did, rather than bringing your own supply from home. The real charges mount with the ultrasounds. These are internal rather than external ultrasounds. They are not great fun. The internal monitor is, frankly, penis-shaped. I guess there's no point in reinventing the wheel, but I have to say that when the technician slathered that thing with lubricant and then approached me, I was filled with serious misgivings about the whole procedure. She also banged one of my ovaries while probing around in there. If you are a guy reading this, try giving one of your testicles a sharp rap with a tack hammer to see how that feels.

The purpose of the ultrasounds is to pinpoint the exact time of ovulation. The closer you get, the more ultrasounds they take. It's a lot like playing Battleship. Since each ultrasound runs about a hundred and eighty bucks, charges can mount up. My egg was a bit elusive, so the whole go-around cost nearly thirteen hundred dollars, but the doctor said that a thousand dollars a month was pretty typical. Happily, either my eggs were seething with desire long denied, or else the Widow approved of an increase in the gene line. Whatever the reason, I caught a baby on the very first try.

Why? Why did I rush out and get pregnant? Um, I'm
glad you asked me that. Um . . .

Is it too clichéd to say that time was passing me by?
From the moment Momma died I had felt time blowing
past me like the gulf breeze. I had put off *so many things*,
waiting for my life to be perfect. Marriage, kids, family.

Or maybe—does this make sense?—I had been afraid
to have a life while Momma was alive.

I didn't like to think about that too much.

So here I was, carrying a baby of my own, and scared
as a sinner in a revival tent. The doctor had promised me
that sperm donors were screened for genetic problems,
but what about subtle things—alcoholism, a curse in the
family, dyslexia? What could you expect from a man who
jerked off for money? What if he was the sort of guy
who—

No. No. I willed myself not to think about it. It was
my baby. Nobody else's. Only mine.

It was ridiculous, I guess, to try and keep it a secret,
but I did. I used up bereavement leave at work and then
pleaded illness when the ultrasound frenzy heated up. I
said not one word to Daddy or Candy. Unfortunately,
having a sister who can see the future makes it hard to
keep a secret. Two months after we buried Momma I
asked Candy to help me do some shopping, but the moment I saw her in the mall I knew I was in trouble.

I had asked her to meet me at the ice skating rink in
the Galleria, Houston's most expensive shopping district.
Hordes of Japanese tourists and Saudi oil barons and rich
trashy blondes in concubinage to assorted South American
despots troop through the Galleria on a regular basis, looking for outrageously expensive merchandise in the same
spirit that drives successful West German businessmen to

go on safari in Africa and gun down bull elephants with automatic weaponry.

Candy was sitting on a bench next to three teenagers lacing on skates. She was mad. "You're *pregnant!*" she said, jabbing me in the chest with one accusing finger. Her black hair was done up tight behind her head, with a couple of wispy ringlets framing her face. "You think I need this right now? I have a wedding to plan, Toni. How am I supposed to fit you being pregnant into that?"

"You finally proposed?"

"Well, not yet," she admitted. "I keep hoping Carlos will think of it himself."

"Candy!"

"Okay, okay, I'll do it. Anyway, I've already picked the date, September twenty-first. The autumn equinox. I had a friend do a chart for me and it's got great signs." She paused. "Are you okay? You sort of choked there."

"I'm fine."

"Toni? Toni, don't lie to me. What . . ." She hissed. "You're *due* then, aren't you?" She stood with her hands on her hips. "Oh, sure! Go into labor in the church. It has to be a church wedding, of course. La Hag will strangle herself if we aren't married in a church. So what's the date, Toni?"

"The twentieth," I said weakly. "But with first babies they're usually a week late. Ten days even."

Candy eyed me coldly. Out of respect for the blue norther that had brought freezing temperatures to Houston that January weekend, she was wearing her version of cold weather gear: soft red leather ankle boots with a one-inch heel, jeans, a black tank top, and over that a bulky black leather bomber jacket with a Sacred Heart of Jesus embroidered over the left breast. The entire back of her

coat was dominated by a huge head of Saint Jude, patron
of lost causes, from which arrows of angel-light darted
forth in every direction. **Carlos** was stitched on the shoulder with scarlet thread. "How are you going to help dec-
orate the church, Toni?"

I backed out of the skate-lacing area, pretending to spot
something of interest in the dreadful Baubles & Bijoux
across the atrium from us. Candy stalked after me. "You
never even told me you were seeing anybody!"

"Bad enough I should have a sex life. But to not tell
you! Boy. What nerve."

"Damn right. You go so long between boyfriends, I'd
like to give up hope. You could at least throw me some
crumbs."

A pregnant woman waddled by and I stared at her
tummy, mesmerized. "Even normal women get bowlegged," I said. "What's going to happen to me? Did you
know your cartilage actually loosens when you're pregnant? The ligaments and stuff get all wobbly so the baby
can get through your pelvis without breaking your hip
bones."

"Don't be gross, Toni."

"Don't blame me. I didn't design the system. And did
you see the flush on that woman's cheeks? That's the
'glow' people talk about. What it means is that her blood
volume has gone up by about forty percent. If she's hot
now, what is it going to be like for me in August?"

Candy made a face. "Where did you learn all this
stuff?"

"Baby books."

"Of course." She looked at me. "You didn't even buy
them, did you? You took them out of the library."

"There's no point in spending money on books you can

use for free. What? What! Look, I refuse to be embarrassed about something so stupid."

Candy laughed. "Then refuse to blush."

A stroller went by. "Is there a baby convention in town or something?" I muttered. I caught Candy grinning at me. "What is your problem, anyway?"

"Congratulations." Candy hugged me and kissed me once on each cheek. I hugged her back, wondering what it would feel like to do this when I had a belly the size of a watermelon.

"How many weeks are you?"

"Five today."

"Wow, Toni. How do you feel? Are you happy about it?"

"I don't know." The Saturday afternoon crowd had arrived in earnest. Purses jingled, shopping bags rattled, change clattered on counters, children cried and parents shushed them, customers complained and clerks flattered. "Have you ever read a book about being pregnant?" I said. "Do you know how many times you see the word 'bloat'? Bloat, bloating, bloated. 'In the eighth month, you may experience further bloating, along with hot flashes, more frequent urination, hair loss, and difficulty breathing.' "

"*Hair loss?* Omigod."

"Swear to God, Candy, it's like being a Hiroshima survivor."

(A quick memory of Momma, bald from radiation, the skin on her neck shaking. Forget it. Forget it.)

Another young mom came by pushing a stroller. The hapless baby inside looked like something made from plastic and crushed velour. It had the most amazingly black eyes, peering up from under a ridiculous fluffy cap. I felt my own eyes get damp and my throat constrict. Quickly

I turned away. "Anyway, I want to buy some clothes. That's where you fit in."

Candy snorted. "You need my help to buy a few smocks? Don't get anything tight around the tummy. After that, you have your choice: flowered granola tent dresses, or navy jumpsuits with big bellies."

"I don't mean maternity clothes. I want pretty clothes. Sexy clothes."

"You? Why?"

I closed my eyes. "Someday, Candy, I'm going to push you in front of a bus, and you won't even know what you said."

"What did I say?"

"It just so happens I want to look good, for once. Accept it as a miracle from God and shut up, okay? Put your mind to the problem. And I don't mean I want to look . . . 'professional,' either. I want to look attractive. The books all say two parents have an easier time than one. So if I can pick up a dad for this kid, so much the better."

She looked at me, shocked. "But the baby has a father. It's Bill junior's, isn't it?"

"What!"

"But Toni—Toni, I dreamed him playing with the baby! That's how I knew you were pregnant. You and him, and you were still a little fat, you know, from the pregnancy, and he was with you out in the garden. Playing with the baby."

"Bill junior? Are you sure? Omigod."

"You mean it isn't his baby?"

I shook my head. "I got artificially inseminated."

"What!"

Another baby came by: this time a skinned-rabbit-looking kid in a Snugli. He had on the most incredibly

cute little checked tam-o'-shanter. The mom's back was
to me as she walked past, so I could stare as much as I
wanted at the little goggle-eyed alien wobbling on her
shoulder. I must have smiled, because the baby smiled
back and then burped up a teaspoonful of white slime,
just for me.

I tore my eyes away. "It makes perfect sense. I want to
have a baby. But if I try to wait for a good father first, I
might run out of time before Mr. Right comes along. If I
get the baby first, then even if I never find a suitable guy,
I've still got a family." I trailed off as I saw Candy staring
at me. "Half a loaf is better than none, right?"

"You've gone crazy," Candy said. "The shock of
Momma's death has thrown you into a midlife crisis."

"I'm not crazy, I'm an actuary. It's different. This
makes perfect sense."

Candy began to smile. "What's really cool about it is,
you genuinely think you're being reasonable. When in fact
you're bent as a three-dollar bill."

"Candy, I'm thirty years old. Maybe you can get a husband in New York if you're thirty. But here, I'm an old
maid. And not an especially pretty one. It's time to play
the odds." I made for the Galleria Directory in front of
the stairs. "Bill junior? Are you positive? Maybe it was an
ordinary dream that didn't mean anything."

"Fat chance. Mind you," Candy added, "it wasn't like
I knew you were married. I don't remember a ring or anything. I saw you and him and the baby, and I assumed . . ."

"Maybe he was just visiting over business."

Candy shrugged. "You looked pretty friendly to me.
Pretty happy." Which was no big surprise; as you remem-
ber, all Candy ever saw in the future were happy things.
Apparently a time would come next fall when I would be

tickled pink to be sitting there in the garden with Bill junior handling my baby. But at the moment all I could think of was his ugly mouth and damp handshake.

Candy shrugged "*Quién sabe?* Well, it's a good omen. Someone like you could do a hell of a lot worse." I stopped dead and Candy bumped into me. "Ow. What did I say?"

We reached the store directory. I looked at my dumpy reflection leaning out of the dark glass toward me. Round head, round face, stocky limbs. The nicest thing you can say about my face is that it's "amiable." And that's only in my rare good moods. High-school gym teachers looking to praise me used words like "dogged." In softball, I played catcher. In track—no, let's not even talk about track. I always walked with my head down, looking at the floor, which was just as well, as I had a tendency to trip over things. Unkind classmates had told me I was bowlegged. My fifth-grade teacher, Mrs. Harris, used to fuss at me for "stumping" and "trudging" and "clomping." I was the only woman wearing Doc Martens in the Rice Mathematics Department, and this was years after they weren't cool anymore.

I considered trudging over Candy's toes by accident. Or stumping on them. Or clomping. Unfortunately, I needed her. "Okay, fairy godmother. Make me beautiful." I scanned the directory of stores. "Or a reasonable facsimile thereof."

"Okay, Cinderella." Candy started up the stairs, then looked back over her shoulder. "Don't take this the wrong way, Toni, but I can't honestly promise Prince Charming, okay?"

"Prince Breathing will do."

"Gotcha."

She led me into the strange regions of the Galleria's third floor. I have to say I felt stupid to be there. First, because I had always despised the kind of women who spent all their time hanging out in the Galleria trying on glamorous clothes. Second, because I was afraid the glamorous clothes weren't going to look good on me. Go figure.

"Help! We've crashed on the Planet of the Babies," I murmured as we left the stairs. There were babies in strollers, babies in backpacks, babies in Snuglis on their fathers' chests. Babies tucked into Mom's tummy, waiting to come out. A snot-nosed toddler gimballed by, dragging a crying sister behind him like a teddy bear. If the kids weren't crying or peeing or drooling or actually throwing up, their noses were running, or a sort of thin cottage-cheeselike substance was hiccuping from their tiny mouths. "I never realized how *damp* children are."

"Buy permanent press," Candy said.

"Hey—Versace," I said, stopping in front of a shop window. "I've heard of this guy, haven't I?" The mannequins were all incredibly thin and had this Italian arrogance to them and sported clothes that looked like what Jackie O. would have worn if she had been a streetwalker: pleated stirrup-pants, or little sleeveless lemon-yellow dresses that came a third of the way down their thighs, or tall leather boots in black and white checks.

Candy winced. "You could never wear this stuff."

"Why not?"

"Toni!" She waved at the models. "You, you've got, oh . . . too many knees or something. Trust me on this."

"Too many *knees*?"

"Here. Definitely more your speed," she said, stopping in front of the Gap.

"Candy, you're patronizing me. No. No! I told you. I

want something new. Something different. Something with some style, not just . . .''

Candy tried to smile. Candy with the great tits and the little waist and the ass men would pay to slap with a Ping-Pong paddle. "Toni . . . let's keep the training wheels on for a bit, okay?"

Unlike Candy, whose figure you could appreciate from the front, I only had contours when viewed in profile: a little slope forward on top, a little shelf down on the bottom. In the middle, only a dictionary would call what I had a "waist." "All my parts function," I said. "What's this fascination with topology, anyway? If I had a great pair of breasts stuck to my elbows, would that be a turn-on?"

"*What?*"

When I told Momma I didn't care about makeup or hairstyles or what dress I was going to wear, she used to say to me, "Honey, I've been pretty and I've been ugly, and ugly's worse." Another one was, "Beauty is only skin deep, but ugly goes clean down to the bone."

I stared through the Gap window at racks of sensible cotton pants and comfortable casual sweaters and cheeky girl-next-door vests of the sort you wore to spruce up that old blouse you were getting tired of. "Oh, Candy. It's so . . . me."

My sister regarded me. "You're a mess, aren't you?"

"I know," I said humbly. "When did I get to be an old maid? You know, lately I've been having this fantasy. I'm at a party, like an office Christmas party. All of a sudden, across the room, I see a man."

"I know the fantasy. He sees you. Your eyes lock."

"And I know, I know at that instant, it's . . . it's . . . *it's Mr. Anybody!*"

Candy sighed. "You're not making me look forward to

turning thirty. Okay. Are you really sure about this style thing? You're in the Galleria. Style is going to cost."

"Let it. I *want* to spend money. You know what *Time* magazine rated the best job in America? Actuary. Most money for the least risk. And by God I spent seven years with no life, taking my damn exams, and now I'm making some money and I deserve to spend it. I deserve to."

Candy grinned. "You sound just like Momma."

"Don't ever say that."

"You do, you do, you do," she said, making a face. "Nyeah nyeah. Okay, then: thumbs down on the Gap. Keep walking."

The next store was full of lingerie. Gorgeous cantaloupe-breasted models in black underwire bras gave us their best sultry looks from seven-foot-tall posters. "Victoria's Secret Supporters," I said, reading the display. "What are those?"

"Girdles," Candy said briefly. "Come here."

I joined her at the next shop entrance. "Bebe?"

"They're out of San Francisco. And I guarantee you can spend some money here."

She was right. I left the store forty minutes later and six hundred dollars poorer, but in possession of the most beautiful jacket in the world. It had the New China look, small square shoulders and tailored at the waist and it was made of this incredible stuff called silk shantung that shimmered and changed color when you looked at it because all the warp threads were brilliant gold-green, while the weft ones were sapphire blue. That's what the sales clerk said, anyway, and she said that silk shantung was in all the magazines, and that this season you could wear it over a casual blouse for lunch or at work, and then throw it over a dress for the classiest evening wear. It was beautiful stuff, soft to the touch, and also textured with little knots and tufts of this sea-foam thread. I loved it. I also got a pair of slacks to go with it, and then we sailed off to a shoe store to buy a pair of pumps in peau de soie—I made the clerk spell it for me—which is French for "silk shoes" and I loved everything I bought very, very much, as I had not ever allowed myself to love clothes before.

Momma was dead. I didn't have to be the plain one anymore.

"I feel this incredible energy these days," I told Candy as she led me to the Starbucks coffee joint at the end of the floor. "This freedom. As if I had spent my whole life holding back my natural strength, and finally it's come bursting out like . . . like a kinked hose when you straighten it."

She laughed at me. "Splash!"

"Exactly! I used to drag myself out of bed after eight and a half hours of sleep. Now I'm staying up until one every night." I had moved back into my parents' house for the last six months of mother's illness and was sleeping once more in the bedroom Candy and I had shared as girls. I had pulled up the blinds on every window because I couldn't bear to miss a minute of daylight, and by six-thirty every morning I was sitting on the balcony watching the garden resolve out of the darkness, developing like a Polaroid from a mass of humped shadows into trees and monkey grass and palm fronds and ferns, and every now and then the cobalt flash of a bluejay.

I slept less and I ate less. After years of turning down cheesecake in public and sneaking to the Empire Café for a furtive eclair, I didn't even want dessert. "Half the time I was eating, it was like a bribe, this way of killing time, of dulling my spirit."

"Are you sure you're not in love?" Candy said.

I hugged my jacket in its crinkly paper shopping bag. "Not yet, but here's hoping."

At Starbucks I let Candy examine the tags and turn the shoes over, plotting makeup, while I sipped my cup of Jamaican Blue Mountain coffee, the recommended special. I felt giddy and lighthearted, watching the ice skaters three stories below, bumping and circling. Putting an ice-skating rink in the middle of a mall in sweltering Houston was a stroke of genius, I thought, a perfect way of saying that at the Galleria, you really could get *anything*.

Most of the skaters were hapless: eight-year-old boys trying it on a dare, or thrill-seeking visitors from Panama in rented skates. An elderly couple I judged to be transplanted Canadians did better. But the class of the field was one young woman who had clearly trained as a figure skater. While the rest of them milled and slipped and tottered their way about, clinging to the boards or creeping gingerly along, she swept around the rink backwards, her head cocked over one shoulder to see where she was going, controlled and wholly beautiful. The hair she wore in a short swing was the same beautiful auburn shade Momma used to get out of the Clairol box. She was going terrifically fast, but her strides were long and smooth, nearly motionless, so that she seemed to glide swiftly and effortlessly among the other skaters, soaring like a gull among pigeons.

("You will never be as pretty as your sister." We're at Candy's junior high-school graduation. Momma has leaned over and whispered it to me, so softly that Daddy, on the other side of her, can't hear. "It's not just the dress and the smile," she whispers. "She is pretty and you are plain." I sit stiffly in my chair. "O baby," she whispers.

Her breath is warm against my neck. I can smell her hairspray. "Oh, baby, and I'm just so sorry." Something wet and hot touches my neck. It's one of her tears. I know the way they feel, oh yes.)

"Candy."

"What?"

"I got lost for a minute," I said carefully. "In my head." The whiteness was back, the whiteness that had eaten my thoughts away just before the Widow mounted me the day we buried Momma. "Candy. Candy, help me."

"Oh shit, Toni, what can I do?"

A cold whiteness, like the ice below.

The light in the Galleria's atrium dimmed, as if it were a movie theatre and the show was starting. Silence fell over the two Mexican women who had been bantering at the table next to us. Down below, the skaters faltered and looked up, all except for the young woman with auburn hair. The light failed and darkness came on, but still she soared and circled, gathering speed, weaving between the boys cluttering the ice and their parents and the teenaged girls and the elderly couple who stood still, looking up at the darkening sky as if suddenly afraid. A silence stretched out, carved by her skates cutting into the ice. She gathered herself and then she leapt, high, high in the air, arms and legs spinning, and her auburn hair.

I didn't see her come down. Blindness washed through me, and I smelled peaches.

"Sugar!" I tried to push back my chair, tried to stand up and keep moving, tried to look away from the ice and the skaters circling, circling. My right foot froze to the carpet, ice racing up it from the rink far below. I wrenched it up, pulling with both hands. People were staring but I didn't care. All I cared about was living, living, not letting the goddess come for me, not letting her blot me out.

The smell of peaches suddenly redoubled and my head spun with it. Heat, flies, fruit and liquor. Secrets. Sex. "No," I whispered.

It didn't save me.

"Toni? Toni—come sit out here with me for a minute. I'm going to tell you a story." I am eighteen. It's later on the night of Candy's junior-high graduation. I am still angry, so angry at what Momma said to me, whispering that Candy was pretty and I was plain.

Momma is sitting in the garden with her back to the French doors, but somehow she has sensed me tiptoeing barefoot across the kitchen tiles. I could pretend not to hear her, but I don't. I have come to dread Momma's stories, but living in this family has made me honest. Bitterly, resentfully honest. I scorn to lie.

Momma has the most beautiful voice. Sometimes she claims to have been an actress in her younger days. I can't prove that, but no one who hears her speak can deny the power of her voice; not clear at all, but worn soft with smoking and tears and bourbon, and laughter too. I don't think I've told you how much my mother laughed, or how much her laughter sounded like crying.

When I was a little kid, I use to love it when she told me her stories. If she was lying propped in bed in her pink nightgown of Chantilly lace I would come curl up with my head on her lap while she stroked my hair. On summer nights out in the garden I would sit next to her and close my eyes to listen better. Texas folk legend has it that Skin-So-Soft moisturizing cream works as a mosquito repellent, so we spent all summer wiped down with it, and

I would breathe in the skin lotion and cigarette and hair-spray smells that drifted from Momma into the lilac-scented night. As I grew up I began to suspect that her stories had a point to them. Maybe they always did, and I just hadn't noticed.

"Come set yourself over here." Momma pats the arm of the wrought-iron chair next to hers. Her voice is lazy, calm as a slow creek in dry weather. "No, I'll tell you what. Get us a couple of those little Cokes out of the fridge and bring them here, would you, honey? It's a night for it."

"Yes, ma'am."

She's right, the Cokes are cold and taste pretty good. She always buys the little ones, the six and a half ounce ones in the old-style glass bottles that stay cold to your touch long after they leave the refrigerator. It's been dry for a spell and the mosquitoes aren't so bad with our Skin-So-Soft on. We talk a while about nothing in particular. She never mentions Candy's name. I give short, sullen answers. Finally the effort to make small talk becomes too burdensome and Momma says, "Did I ever tell you the story of the time the Little Lost Girl took Sugar to be her mother?" Which is a lie because I know she's just now made it up.

"No, ma'am," I say. Not wanting to encourage her; not willing to leave and miss hearing the story.

"Would you like to hear it?"

"I reckon you're going to tell it to me."

She has a little more of her Coke. "I reckon I am," she says.

Well, she's been a-walking and a-walking, that Little Lost Girl, trying to get back to her momma's house, but the longer she walks, the lost-er she gets, and never has she found that house where she was born, with the white paint on the fence and the yellow trim around the door and the big live-oak tree with the swing outside.

Finally one day she sees Sugar sittin' out on a step. " 'Morning, ma'am," she says. Real polite, like she was taught.

"Well, hello, sweetie," Sugar says, with a tired smile. "How is it with you this fine day?"

"'Bout that poorly," says the Little Lost Girl. "I been all this time a-walking and I ain't ever found my home. I reckon I could walk the rest of my life and not find it, neither. My momma left me and now I'm lost for good." And she sets herself down beside Sugar and starts to cry. "Can't I just stay with you? You're the only one that's nice to me, and I am so tired of all this walking on my lonesome."

"Oh, honey-child,' says Sugar, "I don't think that's such a good idea."

Well, the Little Lost Girl starts in to crying and blubbering and holding on to Sugar's arm, piteous as a baby bird, until finally Sugar, whose heart is soft as tar in summer, agrees to let her tag along. "Well all right," she says, "but there's one rule you'll have to mind if you want to come with me, and that is No Crying. I can't ever cry, and if you come with me, then you can't neither."

"Why can't you cry?" asks the Little Lost Girl.

"Sweetie, ain't nobody wants to see Sugar cry. Okay?" The little girl nods. "I have to warn you, we ain't done walking yet. I haven't had me a bite to eat in about a day or maybe two. We're gonna have to find us a friend."

. . .

(Just here Momma stops and looks at me to make sure I'm paying close attention, which I am.)

So Sugar wipes the tears off that Little Lost Girl, and brushes her hair, and rubs the spots out of her dress. Then she puts her lipstick on, and her earrings, and smooths out her little red dress, and bites her lips a few times until the pink comes up, and then they set out together to find a friend who might give them something to eat. The first person they meet is Pierrot, standing on a corner juggling apples. Sugar gives him her prettiest laugh. "You must be the most talented fellow alive, I do declare."

"Hey, sweet thing! Do you want to have some—oh. Too bad about the kid," he says, with a wink. "We might have had a little fun together, you and me."

"Maybe I could come back later?" Sugar asks, a little desperate.

"Oh, well. Sure. Try around about lunchtime," Pierrot says, and he saunters off. But when lunchtime comes and they go back to Pierrot's corner, he isn't there anymore. A shopkeeper says he went off with a real cute young lady not so long ago, and he hasn't been back since.

"Thank you," Sugar tells him, and gives him her pretty smile. She stands outside a minute, fussing at her reflection in the shop window. It's been a while now since she's eaten, and it's hard to get the color into her lips and face the way she likes it.

"Sorry," the Little Lost Girl says.

"Don't you worry, honey," Sugar says. "We'll get us a bite here sometime soon."

But they didn't. They walked all afternoon and by quitting time they still hadn't found Pierrot, and Sugar was beginning to look a little shaky.

They're just walking down the boulevard when the Little Lost Girl smells this smell of hot dust and gasoline, and Mr. Copper's car rolls up beside them. "Sugar," says a voice from inside. It's so dark inside that car, the little girl can't even see Mr. Copper, but she can hear his dry, smooth voice. "Sugar," says the voice again.

Sugar pretends not to hear.

"You look a mite hungry," says the dry, smooth voice. Still Sugar doesn't turn around. "I have food for you." The car keeps creeping along beside them. "I have food for the little girl too."

Without turning Sugar says, "What do you want for it?"

"Come here and I will tell you." The car rolls to a stop. Sugar looks down at the little girl, and then slowly walks to the curb and leans into the open window.

A minute later she stands straight again, and Mr. Copper's car drives off into the night. "No food?" says the Little Lost Girl.

"Not from him. Not yet," Sugar says.

"What did he want for it?"

"I reckon that's none of your business," Sugar says. The Little Lost Girl doesn't ask again.

Well, they keep on, walking into some pretty sorry neighborhoods, until about sunset they find themselves at the Preacher's mission, a little white church with a cross on top that stands out among the shacks and tenements like a bleached skull with a hundred candles burning inside. The church is crowded with a long line of women waiting. At the back there's tables covered with every kind of delicious food, brisket and sausage and fried chicken and mashed potatoes and fresh green beans and yellow squash and on and on. Standing before the pulpit is the

Preacher, with his long black coat over his long white bones, and his two eyes burning in his head like train lamps far down a tunnel. As each woman comes forward he says, "Daughter, have you climbed into Mr. Copper's car?"

Mostly the women say yes when he asks them this question. Some do it real quick and soft, but he makes them say it right out loud, where everyone can hear it. And after each woman confesses, the Preacher grabs her chin in one white hand, and with a brand in the other he presses the image of a snake onto her forehead. It doesn't seem to hurt exactly, but the Little Lost Girl can tell that afterwards many of them are crying. Once a woman is branded, the Preacher waves her over to the tables of food. There are clean clothes over there too, and clean white panties and hose and sturdy shoes.

Once, not long after Sugar and the little girl get into the church, a pretty, red-haired woman says, "No." At that the Preacher shakes his head, and asks his question again, and then once more, and each time she says no. The Preacher says, "And if ye not repent, how can ye be saved?" and he sends her away without any food.

"Sugar?" the little girl whispers. "What should we do? He won't give us any food if we say we didn't go with Mr. Copper. But if we do, we'll be fibbing."

"Sometimes you have to tell a man what he wants to hear," Sugar says, a little sadly. "It's not your fault for telling a lie, then; it's his fault for hearing it."

The Little Lost Girl wasn't sure what her mother would have said about that, but her mind was made up by the sight of all those candles and all that food, and the thought of the darkness outside, and the men sitting on their porch steps watching her go by.

When they get to the front of the line the Preacher glares at Sugar. "Daughter, have you climbed into Mr. Copper's car?"

"Well, hang it all, I must have done," Sugar says, good and loud, so he won't make her say it again. Then the Preacher reaches out and grabs her chin with one cold hard hand, and with the other he presses the snake brand into her forehead.

Then he points at the table and pushes her and the little girl along. He doesn't even look at them again, like he doesn't care a lick about Sugar except for getting her confession. The food is wonderful, and the Little Lost Girl is grateful for the clothes, especially the shoes, as she has worn hers about down to strings. Sugar helps the Little Lost Girl load up her plate with cornbread and ribs and black-eyed peas and stewed okra and a big slice of sweet potato pie. Then, when they are done, they go together to a little room at the back of the church to sleep.

The next morning, when Sugar wakes up, the Little Lost Girl says, "Thank you so much for having me along, but I b'lieve I'll make my own way from here."

"Well, if you must," says Sugar, who doesn't seem any too broke up about it.

"I don't think your days are any much easier than mine, and if I'm going to be always walking, maybe I better look for my very own house with the yellow trim and the white picket fence," the little girl says.

Then Sugar kisses her on the cheek and gives her a hug and wishes her well, and the Little Lost Girl goes back to walking on her lonesome, where she doesn't have to care so much about Pierrot and Mr. Copper and the Preacher, and she can just think about getting back to her very own home. And if she hasn't found it, she's walking still.

. . .

My mother takes another sip of her Coke.

"Is that the end of the story?"

"Nearly," Momma says. "Not quite." She reaches over and to my surprise she takes my hand, the one holding my Coke, and brings it to her lips and kisses the back of it, on my knuckles, and lays it against her cheek. "The only other thing to tell is how some time later—I don't know how long; a few weeks maybe—the Little Lost Girl is out walking in the middle of the night. It's late, really late, but she's too scared to fall asleep, she's back in a bad part of town, so she just keeps walking. Finally she sees a building up ahead that looks empty and she thinks maybe she could find a little corner inside to sleep in. But when she gets closer she sees there's light coming out of one solitary window. So she creeps up to that window and stands up on her tiptoes and peeks inside.

"There she sees the strangest thing. She sees Pierrot and the Preacher and Mr. Copper in the same room together, playing dominos. From the cigarettes in the ashtray and the empty bottles on Mr. Copper's side of the table she can tell they've been playing together for a long time. The dominos are white as bones, and click together at every play. And the strangest thing is, the tablecloth they're playing on is brown and black and red and gold, all kinds of soft colors. When the Little Lost Girl squints a little harder, she sees that's because it's woven up from real girls' hair." Momma presses my fingers to her cheek and kisses my hand. "Do you understand, baby?"

I realize I have been holding my breath. "No, ma'am."

Momma kisses my hand again and looks at me. "It's all made from beautiful, beautiful girls' hair."

And that's the end of the story.

• • •

Some time after Sugar mounted me in the Galleria she walked out of me again, leaving my head pounding. My breath came in great whooping gasps and I sobbed helplessly, completely unstrung. Every part of me was trembling with exhaustion. The crying jerked my whole body, making my shoulders jiggle, and my thighs and my feet, limp as a jellyfish.

"Oh, thank God," Candy said. "You're back."

I tried to nod, but it came out as more crying. I hadn't been able to open my eyes yet, but there was crushed velour under my cheek and we were moving. Candy was driving me around in the old Oldsmobile Momma had given her. The car slowed and gave the kind of rolling nod that Candy uses to recognize stop signs. We turned a corner and drove on.

I had forgotten how soothing it was to lie in the back of a car. Momma told me any number of times that I had been a colicky baby. There was many a day when she had lost her temper with my fussing and shoved me into Daddy's arms after dinner and he would take me out in his old Chevy Impala and drive around Houston, and I always went silent as a lamb, they said, as soon as the car started up, and would go to sleep before he drove a mile.

Candy must have remembered the same stories. I opened my eyes. "How long was it?" I asked.

"About two hours."

Sugar had mounted me for two hours. I knew it had to have been her from the peaches smell. Momma always had the same smell on her when Sugar was in her head.

I squeaked and tried to sit up. "Two hours? With Sugar? *In the Galleria!*" My legs felt cold. I looked down and gasped. I was wearing a skirt so short it showed the top of a black stocking at the hem. Stupidly I tried to tug it down, but there wasn't any more to tug. And garters. I was wearing garters. I could feel the cool elastic against my thighs. And a pair of panties you could mistake for a Kleenex. "Omigod."

Candy glanced at me in the rearview mirror. "I must say, Sugar is a lot of fun to shop with. Wait'll you see what's in the trunk."

I whimpered. "How much?"

"I couldn't keep track, to tell the truth. I just put it on your gold card. American Express," she intoned. "Don't leave your body without it."

"I'll call them up. I'll cancel the purchases and return everything."

"You'll do no such thing," Candy said. "Hey, I had to sign for it all. You want me to get in trouble for faking your signature? Besides which, they aren't your clothes to give back. They're Sugar's."

"Shit. You're right." A new thought occurred to me. "Oh no. Candy, did she . . . ? I mean, she didn't go off with anyone, did she? Not in two hours."

"Not really. Mind you," she added, smirking, "there was a very pretty salesclerk in Victoria's Secret she was flirting with. Carmelita. Finally she called her into the changing room to help with a garter belt. Now, I'm not saying anything happened—but they took fifteen minutes at it, and pretty Carmelita came back fairly flushed."

I considered. "Could have been worse."

Not that I would ever, ever show my face in the Galleria again. Ever.

"First the Widow, now Sugar." Candy turned left onto a stretch of Westheimer that I recognized, not far from

Momma's house. "Girl, you've got a bad case of the ghosts."

"Mockingbird Cordial," I said.

"What?"

"What's a Mockingbird? What does she do?"

"Sings. I don't know," Candy said. "The Mockingbird can be anyone, I—Oh."

"Yeah." I pressed my hand against my forehead but it didn't seem to help. "I think she let the Riders into me. I think that's what the cordial did, Candy. Damn it."

Hush little baby don't say a word,
Momma's gonna buy you a mockingbird.

There are some gifts that cannot be refused.

"Is there any more left?" Candy asked.

"No, you may not drink the stuff. It wasn't meant for you, Candy. Momma left it for me, damn her. Anyway, I flushed the rest of it down the toilet after the Widow mounted me."

"Oh." It was hard to read the tone of her voice.

I sat upright and took a deep breath, which pulled the hem of that ridiculous skirt up to about my navel. "Candy?"

"Yeah?"

"It's not your fault you're pretty."

"Oh, Toni." She didn't turn around. "Thank you," she said.

F O U R

I wasn't at all happy about being afflicted with Momma's gods. Then the IRS called up and made me even less happy. It turned out that Momma owed them a lot of money. A *lot* of money. We couldn't see the will itself. That was under court seal, but to make a long story short, it took all of the (not much) money Momma's estate had left, plus most of my savings, to square our family's accounts. (As Mary Jo had feared, there was no money for her roof either; just some old photographs and a handful of Momma's paintings.)

Luckily, I was used to paying off Momma's debts. Was I mad about having to pony up thousands of dollars of my own money? Sure. Furious. But I had known Momma all my life, and ever since she died I had been waiting for the other shoe to drop. There was just bound to be a nasty surprise waiting for me. To have it be something I could deal with by cashing in a mutual fund and writing a check seemed almost too easy.

And even if money was suddenly a bit tight, I had an excellent job and, for the first time, a real sense of direction. I had a plan. Momma was dead and I was going to have a family of my own. For the time being I had a good job; the next trick was to acquire an equally good father for my baby.

It sounds cold-blooded, put like that, but statistically, children who come from two-parent homes do better in school than those from single-parent families. Obviously there is a confound there, as plenty of single moms are dirt-poor. And of course lots of kids from one-parent families turn out fine. Still, I saw no reason not to stack the odds in my child's favor. Candy might be the sort to draw to an inside straight, but as an actuary I preferred to stick to the percentages, and the percentages were better with a father figure in the family.

Sex never was one of my strong points. I was self-conscious on dates, confused, ashamed of my appearance. I wasn't a teenager anymore, I didn't stammer and blush, but like a lizard or a roach, I had developed a dry protective coating. At my best I could be funny; but dating me, as Candy said unkindly, was still too much like going out with your high-school librarian.

Failing to be friendly, flirty, and engaging when it was only my Saturday night on the line was no big deal. Now that my baby was at stake, I no longer had the luxury of embarrassment. I owed it to my child to get a mate, and there was no excuse for not doing it as calmly and rationally as I would go about managing my mutual fund or stock portfolio.

Which meant I had to date. To this end I dressed up in my best Single clothes and shouldered my way into Cabo's Mix-Mex Café, which I knew from reading the *Houston Press* was *the* singles spot in town.

"How on earth are you supposed to meet someone when you have to scream your order over the jukebox?" I said to Candy the next day. "I lasted about four minutes. I swear there was blood in my ears."

She hooted with laughter. "Toni! You can't go to Cabo. Go to the Bookstop on Shepherd. That's the best pickup spot in the city for, you know, people like you."

People like me? I didn't ask.

And the Bookstop *was* better, much better. The Shepherd store is a converted Art Deco movie house. Down at the end where the screen used to be they have a huge magazine stand, perfect for loitering and friendly chitchat. The first time I went there, however, it took me so long to work up my nerve to talk to someone that the store clerk pointedly asked if he could help, obviously thinking I was planning to shoplift a copy of *Architectural Digest* or *Crank!* I slunk out in shame.

The following week I tried again. This time I fell into a perfectly lovely conversation with a beautiful man in his mid-twenties with a gorgeous smile and one unexpected gold tooth. I followed him, still chatting, to the checkout counter, where he bought his copy of *Out! The Magazine of Gay Liberation.*

We parted amicably. It is a strange but true fact that gay men are way easier to talk to than straight ones. I toyed with the idea of finding a paternal queer for a marriage of convenience, but that would mean giving up any hope for sex inside my prospective marriage. It seemed defeatist. Also, it would be hard to explain to a kid why

Daddy and Mommy were always fighting over their boy-friends.

With two strikes in the count I shortened my swing and just tried to put the ball in play. Good things happened, up to a point. I met a guy named Tom who was riffling through *American Photographer* examining telephoto lenses. His eyes lingered, but did not fixate, on the Artistic Nude inside, which seemed like a good sign. We made it as far as the cash register, still chatting. I started to ask him if he'd like to go for a drink, remembered that I couldn't have alcohol because I was pregnant, changed to ask him out for coffee; remembered I couldn't have caffeine either; realized further that even a Coke was out of bounds, and was too flustered to think of anything else.

Three strikes and out.

So it was some relief when a date came to me, from an unexpected direction: Bill junior, damp palms and wide mouth and all.

It seemed like fate. Just before Sugar possessed me, Candy had predicted I would marry Bill. Three weeks later, completely out of character, he asked if I could come to lunch with him. *Mrs. Bill Friesen, Jr.* Well, I supposed I could get used to it. Maybe I could practice writing it out on the bottom of his checks. There would be a certain justice in having the money Momma had made come back to her daughters after all.

Here it was Friday, and we were standing together in the elevator of the Downtown Hyatt, heading for the Spindletop dining room where he had reservations. My only problem was that I desperately wanted to throw up. It wasn't Bill's fault. I had morning sickness.

Take my advice: if you are ever out on a date when you are violently nauseated, don't go on any long elevator rides. The first sickening lurch as you start up is a test for the strongest esophagus. The back wall of the Hyatt elevator was made of glass and looked out on Milam Street, downtown, so you couldn't miss how fast the ground was dropping away. I looked away from the window. I looked up at the burnished bronze light bar above the elevator doors. I glanced at Bill Jr., standing beside me, and gave a little smile. He gave a little smile back.

The street plummeted away from us.

I refused to throw up on this date. I was wearing my beautiful silk shantung jacket over a pair of slacks and a rather dressy white silk blouse; I was determined not to get that outfit dirty.

"Morning sickness." The words seem to promise that you'll be okay in the afternoon, don't they? Fat chance. I hadn't had an appetite for five days. It wasn't just like having the flu either; my body was engaged in a much weirder betrayal. Food didn't *smell* like food. I could pick up a cookie and the smell of the baking soda in it would be overpowering. The ketones in bananas nearly made me faint. And that acrid, sap-green taste in lettuce! You might as well ask someone to gnaw twigs. There was a chemical stink on cabbage; a strange, industrial stench bound to anything canned; a rotting-garbage odor coming off fruits and vegetables. My books assured me that the thing to do was to have little meals as frequently as possible, so I started each day with a soda cracker. If you want to know what it was like to get that cracker down, go to your bathroom and eat a bar of soap.

One thing I found which did help was coarse-ground black pepper. For some reason, pepper had very soothing anti-nausea properties for me. If I covered my crackers with pepper I could swallow as many as three of them.

The elevator raced up a seam of clouds between two office towers. "Ever been here before?" Bill Jr. asked.

"No." I stared resolutely at the elevator doors.

"Um . . . Are you afraid of heights?"

"No." More staring.

A sudden shadow chopped down behind me like a guillotine blade falling. We must have entered the top of the shaft. A moment later the elevator stopped with another sickening lurch. (Actually it was the tiniest bump, but any lurch is sickening if you are as nauseated as I was.) The doors opened, revealing a small, tasteful foyer and a small, tasteful hostess. She smiled at me. I didn't smile back. Nor did I move.

"We're here," Bill Jr. said helpfully.

I was going to have to walk out of the elevator. It would have been a splendid time for Bill to offer me his arm, but he didn't. With great dignity I stepped forward on my own and forced back a rush of bile by biting my lip, hard.

"Reservation for Friesen."

"Yes. Right this way, please."

Although Bill didn't know it, he was interviewing for the job of Mr. Toni Beauchamp. I can't say his initial rating was high, but I did give him points for his choice of restaurant. Nice enough to be *nice*, but not *too nice*; not the sort of stuffy, swanky establishment I had feared, with gloomy oil portraits on the wall and young men named Gustav offering selections of 14-ounce steak for thirty dollars a pop.

There was a bit of affectation at the Spindletop—antique marbletop sideboards for serving stations, sprinkled with a variety of breads, rolls, French knots and baguettes which had all been dried and sprayed with plastic sealant—but the antique furniture had been left with the dints and scratches unfixed, and the glass walls let in a great deal of light, making the seating area pleasant and cheerful. One other oddity of the restaurant was that it was circular: a ring of tables around a central hub which housed the kitchen, foyer, and elevators.

"Will this suit y'all?" the hostess asked, leading us to a table next to the window. There was a booth on one side of the table and chairs on the other. Bill looked at me.

"This will be fine," I said. My voice came out strangely high and gushy, as if I were enthusing over somebody's baby pictures. Nervousness. I noticed that Bill waited for me to choose, chair or booth. Score another point for him. I chose the chair side. Easier not to have to struggle out of a booth if you have to run to the Ladies to throw up.

We sat down. Bill was looking at me rather intently, I thought. I tried to see beyond the wide mouth and doughy face to the person within.

"Nice view," I offered. Our window looked nearly due south. Some thoughtful person had lettered the names of the office buildings outside on the glass. We were seated opposite 1100 MILAM. Beyond the little cluster of sky-scrapers in the downtown core, Houston looked very flat. Well, it is flat, of course, relentlessly flat. There are few buildings more than two or three stories tall, but there are trees everywhere, particularly live oaks. Viewed from the Spindletop, Houston looked like a a flat expanse of broccoli crowns stretching to the horizon, interrupted some miles away by the white mushroom cap of the Astrodome. Occasional pale apartment blocks bobbed above the broccoli, like lumps of tofu.

I closed my eyes and counted to ten while a wave of nausea subsided.

"I come here for luck," Bill said.

"Pardon?"

"Spindletop. You know."

"Oh. Right." Spindletop was the name of the first East Texas gusher. "The oil partnership. How's that coming?" I said, to be polite. Bill had gotten Friesen Investments heavily involved in some hideously risky oil speculations. Because I always wanted everyone to be more cautious, nobody in the office could tell when I thought something was risky and when I thought it was insane. Bill's oil deal verged on the insane.

"I know you think it's a risky investment, but you do have to admit that our first well was a bonanza. It wasn't 'just a fluke,' as you said."

In my new capacity as potential encouraging soul mate, I nodded understandingly. "I'm sure it just looked that way from the outside. I know you went over the geologicals very carefully."

Bill looked at me, surprised. "You do? I mean, yes, I did."

I wondered if a sip of ice water would settle my stomach. It didn't.

"When my father was a young man, he built this company on oilfield exploration."

"When your father was a young man, he had my mother guessing which land to buy and which wells to drill," I said. "You don't have her. You have me. I don't dowse for oil. I read stock quotations. I research companies. I estimate risks and calculate buy-out costs. Not as glamorous, but it's what I do." With a really commendable burst of willpower, I manufactured a fetching smile, one part sly humor, one part self-deprecation. The effort made my eyes water.

Bill's tongue peeked out from between his lips, slid furtively around his mouth, and then pulled back into hiding. The inner man, I told myself. Concentrate on the inner man.

(Momma is watching me do the dishes. Technically she is drying, but in fact she's smoking a cigarette and propounding her theories of marriage. "The trick to keeping a husband," she says, "is to let him understand that you know, and tolerate, and in a goofy way even love, the little flaws and imperfections that would *shame* and *humiliate* him if anybody else were ever to discover them.")

"Ah. Yes. Look, Ms. Beauchamp—"

"We've known one another since we were in diapers, Bill." Still holding that smile like a pearl diver holds her breath. "Outside the office, Toni would be fine."

"Um, okay." Bill Jr. leaned forward over the table, his shoulders hunched, brow furrowed in an expression of Serious Intent. "Well, Toni, you're probably wondering why I asked you here today. The truth is—"

I shrieked. Bill jumped back as if he'd been shot, bumping the table hard with his large knees. Ice water slopped from our glasses and ran briskly over Bill's side of the table onto his lap.

"Omigod, I'm so sorry, I didn't realize—" I grabbed the cloth napkin from my plate and dabbed at the spilled water on his side of the table.

"No problem."

"It's just, oh damn, I'm sorry—" My pregnancy-enhanced sense of smell picked up the oily, dirty-pipe odor of Houston tap water.

"That's fine, I can mop up over here."

"The restaurant . . . I just realized the restaurant is *moving*," I said weakly, sinking back into my seat. I bit my lip, hard. "It's a *revolving* restaurant."

"Of course. Didn't you know?"

"A restaurant that goes around and around." My stomach was whirling majestically around the hub of the Hyatt Regency. The next set of letters on the glass crawled toward me, informing me that the green skyscraper hoving into view was the Enron Building. "No," I said. "I didn't know."

"My dad used to bring me here when I was little. I thought it was neat." Bill put his sopping napkin back on his salad plate. "It's funny how what you notice changes. When I was a kid, I always used to look for the Astrodome, especially when we came here for lunch and I knew the Astros were playing a day game. When I got older, in business school, I started connecting the skyscrapers to the businesses inside. There's Tenneco. There's the Allen complex. There's the Pennzoil Building." He looked out the window. "You know, I don't pay much attention to the buildings anymore. Now I see the trees. I've stayed in a lot of hotels, in America and Europe too, and there's not another city in the world for trees like Houston. No town on earth looks so green from above. We take that for granted. Now I often find myself thinking, if for some reason everyone were to leave, there was a neutron bomb or something, I think the trees and the swamp would be over this city in a second. The Hyatt here, the other skyscrapers, they'd stick up out of the jungle like mysterious ruins in an old Tarzan movie."

I blinked. "Wow."

He laughed, embarrassed. "Maybe it's from watching *Planet of the Apes* too many times when I was a kid."

"Yes! On the Dialing for Dollars Movie at three!"

"That bit at the end when they're going to blow everything up—"

"And the monks take off their masks and they've got this white skin and blue veins and these horrible transparent heads!" I said. "Exactly! . . . Oh God."

"Are you okay? You look a little green."

Sand, I told myself. Think about sand. Black pepper. Newspaper.

My stomach subsided.

A perky blond waitress came to our table. "Hi, my name is Susan and I'll be your server today. Would you like any drinks to start?"

"Ms.—ah, Toni? Wine? They have a Louis Jadot Pouilly Fuissé that's very nice."

Sneaking a glance at the wine list, I saw that this was the most expensive item on it, forty-five dollars a bottle. Should I give him a point for subtly indicating that I could order whatever I would prefer, or subtract points for trying to show off? Hard to call. "No thanks," I said. "Not before dinner for me." Or, in fact, until next October. "Water will be fine."

"Are you sure?" Bill said. "In that case, um . . . I'll have a Peachy Keen, please."

Susan sparkled brightly at him and perked off in the way of blonde waitresses everywhere. I wondered if she was pregnant. It's the eeriest thing about pregnancy: you can have a baby in your womb, your whole life about to change, your body turning itself inside out, sucking the calcium from your very bones, morning sickness leaving you weak and dizzy with hunger, your fingernails blue and your concentration shot, *and no one can tell.* Time and again over the last couple of weeks I had found myself staring at the young women who passed me in the street, or the girl working behind the counter at McDonald's, or the salesclerk who rang up my purchase, and thinking, Is she pregnant? Is she? What about her, over there?

And you can't tell. You just can't tell.

"So what's a Peachy Keen?" I asked.

"Peach cordial, ice cream, and Kahlua," Bill said. "They make these great frozen drinks here. You sure you wouldn't like one?"

Yuck. "No, thank you." I wondered what Louis Jadot would think of his pouilly fuissé losing out to a Peachy Keen. "Anyway, you were just starting to say something when I yelped."

"Oh." Bill's mouth worked for a moment. "Let's, uh, let's just order. I'll get back to it later."

Another set of letters came around, announcing the approach of the Kellogg Building and the YMCA. "For some reason I always thought a revolving restaurant would turn so slowly you could hardly tell it was moving," I said. "But this one just . . . *rockets* around, doesn't it?" I tried looking away from the windows, toward the hub of the restaurant, but we had just come even with a tank of lobsters. They sat there like so many political prisoners in the blue-tinted water, their claws held shut with rubber bands, waiting numbly to be boiled alive and then served with creamed butter and port—

I took a few quick panting breaths, as the books advise, and stared very hard at the pepper shaker on the table. The stuff in it was fine ground, not coarse, but the shaker had a gold top and it was something to cling to.

"Are you sure you're all right?"

"Absolutely."

Bill stared at me for a longer time, caught himself, and looked around. "Nice view," he tried.

"Mm."

"Um—Terrible thing about that woman in Phoenix," Bill said. "You hear about that?" I nodded. "Inconceivable. That any mother could take her own child and step off a building. She must have been on drugs."

"No."

"What?"

"No drugs. They did an autopsy. There were no drugs."

"Oh. I hadn't been following the case that closely." Bill shook his big head and reached for his menu. "Just shows that some people don't need drugs to be stupid. See anything you like?"

"Oh, well," I said, staring blindly at my menu. "Everything looks so good."

(Momma dries a coffee cup and puts it up. She is taller than me, always, until the last six months of her life, when she shrinks terribly. She is smoking two packs a day and doesn't give a damn about the effects of secondhand smoke on the rest of the family, no matter how often I bring it up. "One good tip about how you pick a husband," she says as I hand her a bowl to dry. "The reason you leave a man is the same as the reason you married him.")

If I could say why I would leave Bill Jr., would I see why I should marry him? He sat across the table from me, looking awkward in his expensive suit, and all I could see was his clumsiness. Him suggesting the most expensive wine on the menu. The dreadful peach and Kahlua drink. How big and sure and comfortable he was dismissing Mary Keith, the woman in Phoenix who had killed herself and her child, this woman he knew *nothing* about, nothing . . .

And it seemed to me, seeing him there, that Momma was right, and that if I were to love him, someday, it would be because he had his clarity to offer, his certainty.

He might sneak a cookie or a bowl of ice cream to gratify his small greeds, but he would never deceive me. The obtuseness, the Dignity I disliked, were also a sense of honor that compelled him to do right, and I knew, I just knew, that when he found his woman, he would treat her well, because it would dishonor him to do less.

And maybe a man like Bill Jr. needed a mate like me to see around a corner or two for him. Well, that was probably a fantasy. "Men don't change," Momma used to say. "They grow, but they don't change."

Bill's Peachy Keen arrived and he set to, sucking down great streams of dirty orange alcoholic Slurpee. Whether he changed or not, I was pretty sure Bill Jr. was going to grow, all right.

"Are you ready to order?" Susan the waitress asked. (Are you sick with nausea behind your bright smile? I wondered. Do you lie awake at night wondering how you're going to cover daycare on your waitress's salary?)

I forced my eyes to focus on the menu, wondering how little I could order without Bill noticing. I decided to go for a salad. Eat a couple of pieces of lettuce and a lot of the bulk goes away, making it look as if you've really tucked in. "Grilled chicken caesar, please. And could I have lots of cracked pepper on that?"

"Sure!"

"Lots," I said.

"I think I'll try the Cobb Spindle," Bill said. According to the menu, this was a delicious combination of romaine lettuce, smoked turkey breast, Gorgonzola cheese, provolone, egg, tomato, olives, white beans, roasted pepper and red wine vinaigrette. I nearly passed out from reading the list of ingredients.

"Is there something peculiar about that pepper shaker?" Bill said. "You seem very taken with it."

"What? No! No, no. It looks like one we have at home," I babbled. "Maybe Momma stole a pair from here. She would do stuff like that. I used to think you could buy Hilton brand hand soaps at the store."

Bill closed his menu. "Your mother was quite a character."

"Several of them. Um, would you excuse me?" I said, easing out of my chair and walking as steadily as I could to the ladies' room.

There is something extremely soothing about a really clean bathroom. Bright, clear light, clean fixtures, mirrors if you want them, cool tiles, and silence. And unlike the restaurant proper, the bathroom, being in the central hub, wasn't careening gaily around the Greater Houston Metropolitan Area. I wet my face with cold water and stood for a couple of minutes with my head hanging over the washbasin. At home, when the nausea was really bad, I had taken to lying on the floor. There was something quite perfect about the hard, cool tiles pressing against my back. I couldn't bring myself to lie flat in the bathroom of the Hyatt Regency, not in my silk jacket and nice blouse, but I was sorely tempted.

The nausea receded and I made it back to the table much refreshed. I even took out a disused smile, polished it up, and gave it to Bill.

His answering smile looked, to my eyes, a little unfelt. I was beginning to lose some patience with Bill Jr. A good fellow, basically, but here I was, having accepted his date, doing my level best to make sparkling conversation. He could at least try to be a little more entertaining himself. In the long run, I suppose, it's not terribly important that your husband be a great romancer, but, like being hand-some or rich, it's one of those little attributes that a man really ought to cultivate if he possibly can.

I sat down, and he gave me a long look. "Ms. Beau-champ—"

"Toni, please."

"—Ms. Beauchamp, you are no doubt wondering why I asked you here today," Bill said. He took a breath and met my eyes. "I'm afraid we're going to have to let you go."

Once again I felt the sensation of the elevator starting up; the dizzy earth falling out from under me.

"In recognition of the good work you've done for the company, my father and I have agreed to give you twelve weeks' severance pay. We won't be filling your position, so you won't be required to train a replacement. I should make it clear that this move reflects the direction of the company, and is not intended as a slight against your pro-fessional qualifications." He reached into the breast pocket of his suit. "I have already written a letter of ref-erence." He handed it to me. "You can review it this af-ternoon and tell me if there are points you would like to have clarified."

"You can't do this."

Bill regarded me across the table.

"You can't do this. This is wrongful dismissal."

"You are not being dismissed, Ms. Beauchamp. The po-sition you currently hold has been eliminated."

"I'll sue."

"You are certainly welcome to speak to legal counsel, if you think it appropriate," Bill said. "I think you will find Friesen Investments is acting well within its legal rights."

"Legal rights. Legal rights! What about moral rights, Bill? Your family owes us every goddam dime," I said hotly. "If it wasn't for my mother—"

"I agree," Bill said. He looked out the window. "But you aren't your mother, are you? Ms. Beauchamp, the . . . special relationship between your mother and my father has been very productive. But your mother was an exceptional woman. To be perfectly frank, I very rarely need an actuary. And when I do, I can always hire a far more experienced one as a consultant." He met my eyes again.

"You had this scripted out, didn't you? You read it in one of your magazines: 'How to Lay Off an Employee: Make eye contact. Be unemotional. Don't be drawn into arguments.'" I looked down at my beautiful silk shantung jacket and felt outraged that he should ruin the first occasion on which I'd worn it. "You'll be hearing from my lawyer this afternoon."

"I think you will find you have no case, Ms. Beauchamp. Don't waste your money."

"Oh, I'm not filing for wrongful dismissal," I said. "I'll be naming you in a sexual harassment suit."

"What! I've never—"

"You invited me out to lunch. I couldn't very well say no, could I? Not to the boss. We came here, sat down, and then you made it clear that if I wanted to keep my job, I would have to sleep with you. When I turned you down, you came up with this 'downsizing' scam."

Bill's doughy face got blotchy and congested. "That's ridiculous. No one would ever believe I'd force myself on you. Why not Maria, or that pretty secretary down the hall?"

I smacked my forehead with my hand. "Gosh, Bill, you

sure know how to flatter a girl. I don't know, maybe you have a thing for bowlegged chicks."

He started to flush. "Toni, I didn't mean—"

"It's too late to be a Southern gentleman now."

"I can't believe you'd . . . You'll never win that suit, you know."

"Probably not. I'll make sure to get it in the papers, though. Often and I'll be especially sure to tell your mother, Bill. Gosh, how upset will she be to think that her son—" He slammed his hands on the table. "My momma used to call me the hatefulest child there ever was," I said. "You oughtn't to mess with me, Bill."

"Go ahead," he said, white with anger. "Try telling my mother. While you're at it, you can tell her how your mother was screwing my dad nearly up to the day she died."

The instant he said it, I knew it was true. Oh, Daddy. "What did you say?"

"You heard me."

Momma, you lying, lying bitch.

"He told me the night of the funeral," Bill said. "He had a few too many bourbons in him. Wanted to stay up talking after we got home. Mother went to bed. 'Just between us,' he said. 'Man to man.' " Bill looked down at the table. "You are exactly right. Your momma made us. She made our money, and she made fools of us too. She made a fool of my mother, all those years. The Friesens have to make it on our own, Toni. Can you see that? We just . . . we can't have our families joined together like this. It's not right. It's dirty. It's a bad, dirty story, and we have to stop it."

Another wave of dizziness swept over me. Houston kept sliding, sliding, slipping away from me as we spun.

"Yeah, well, it's one thing to call the game over when all the chips are on your side of the table, isn't it, Bill? You've made your profits off Momma, so now you get to cast her off. But what about me? I'm—" I bit it back. "I'm not in a very good position right now. Financially."

"It's a really good severance package, Toni. Really generous. And the letter I wrote is embarrassing. It's a great letter. I looked it up in one of those magazines of mine you were talking about. 'Winning References, and How to Write Them.' "

I wouldn't do the bastard the favor of smiling.

Bill said, "When you're trying to convince my mother that I'm a sexual predator, don't mention about Elena and Dad, okay? She doesn't know."

"Okay."

But I was remembering how Penny Friesen had looked when I came downstairs the night of the funeral and found her alone by the kitchen table. *The hardest thing about having someone die, I find, is forgiving them.* Oh, she knew about Momma and Bill Sr., all right. She had known all along.

I wondered if Daddy knew. God, I hoped not. That too, on top of everything else he had put up with. Too much. Too much.

"Are you going to file that suit?" Bill asked.

I looked at him across the table, a great lump of a man sitting there, greedy and pompous and well-meaning and a prick. "Funny how it always works out like this, isn't it? The rich guy's son goes to business school and has a nice suit and when the axe falls it's somebody else's head bouncing in the street." Susan the perky waitress was approaching with our orders. "No, of course I'm not going to file any damn lawsuit."

"Thank you. I really think—"

"But you know what I am going to do, Bill? Let me tell you, as my mother's daughter. I'm putting the curse of the Beauchamps on you and your crummy company," I said, shaking with fury. I heard the Preacher in my voice, his iron sentences. "You're going to drill three thousand meters into bedrock and suck sand, Bill. Your partners will get scared, your creditors will all ask for their money on the same day. Strange blips on the world currency markets are going to thin out your cash reserves overnight, costs for your rigs are going to be two hundred percent over budget, and stains will appear on the office carpet that no amount of shampooing will remove. *Are you listening to me?*"

"Here we are!" Susan said, setting down our lunches. "Y'all enjoy now."

Rich steam rose from Bill's Cobb Spindle, heavy with the smells of provolone and Gorgonzola cheese. "Thank you," I said, and rising with all the fury and dignity I could muster, I walked proudly to the bathroom and threw up.

I didn't go back to my office at Friesen Investments. I drove to Slick Willie's instead, the swanky sports bar-cum-billiard hall where Candy worked as a waitress. I had promised her I would report back about my date.

"He *fired* you?"

"Yep."

She pulled a beer for a customer. "Wow. Bad date."

"Yep."

The black bicycle shorts of the Slick Willie's uniform made her legs look chunky, but the white peasant blouse emphasized her excellent breasts; as, presumably, it was supposed to do.

The real action at Slick Willie's was always on the pool tables and at the jukebox, which played an assortment of my generation's rock 'n' roll favorites VERY LOUDLY. **Just an . . . exCITable BOY!**

"Did you tell him you were going to have another mouth to feed?" Candy shouted. "For that matter, why didn't you tell him earlier, and skip the restaurant gig entirely?"

"He was—I . . ."

"Didn't want to scare him off?"

"Yeah."

She hugged me and pathetically I started to cry. "Oh God, Candy. What am I going to do? Baby coming, no job, no money from the will . . ."

"You know that for sure? The lawyer called?"

"Yeah. It gets worse. It turns out that Momma owed the IRS a lot of money. A lot of money. I went and talked to my accountant about it last week. To make a long story short, it took most of my savings to keep them from putting a lien on Daddy's salary."

"Oh my god. Can I, uh . . ."

"No you can't," I said. "You haven't got any money, right? Of course. I still have some stuff stashed away in my IRAs. I figured I'd be okay in a year or two. But now I don't have a job . . ."

Two college-girl types next to us laughed, billiard balls cracked, and the jukebox continued to thunder around us.

"Isn't that just like her?" I said. "Spend everything and then skip town, leaving me to clean up."

Candy shook her head and held a finger up to my lips. "You can't take care of everybody, Antoinette. You can't cover all of Momma's debts."

"Yeah? If I don't, who will?" I said bitterly. "That's my job, picking up after Momma. If she hadn't been—"

I stopped myself. Candy didn't need to know I had lost my job because of Momma's affair with Bill Sr. Candy, pretty Candy—she saw happy things. And she did her job. She cheered us up, she laughed and joked. She pulled her weight. It was my job to pay the debts, to hold the bitter things. And I was going to pull my weight too. Because if there was one thing Momma taught me, it was to endure.

I shook my head and changed the subject. "So, have you proposed to Carlos yet?"

Her face fell. "Almost. Very nearly. We were supposed to go out last night, and I was going to do it then."

"He cancelled?"

"No, I did." She grimaced. "Jeez, Toni! I'm not supposed to have to do this! He's supposed to go through the whole humiliating down-on-one-knee thing. What if he says no?"

"He won't say no."

"Then what if he says *yes*!" she cried. "You know what that means, don't you? I'll be married! To Carlos! I'll be La Hag's daughter-in-law!"

George the bartender finished polishing a couple of glasses. "I think those beers should have nicely hit room temperature, Candy. You can deliver them any time now."

"Kiss my banana-flavored butt," Candy yelled over the music. Two patrons volunteered. "Shit, I gotta go or we'll both be looking for work." She kissed me quickly on the cheek. "You'll be all right. The Widow is looking after you and that kid, you know. The old bitch will take care of you, whether you like it or not."

· · ·

As soon as I got home I went to sit out in the garden. After the roar of Slick Willie's it was very quiet. The temperature was back up around 60° now, but there had been a frost the night after Sugar possessed me, and ferns lay dead everywhere. The banana tree had been pruned back to an ugly stump. So winter came, even to Houston. Even here.

I was pregnant. On some mad whim I had conceived this child. I had no father for my baby. I had lost my job and God only knew if I would be able to find another one with training as specialized as mine. Maybe I should have been like Momma after all. Maybe the real money was in fortunetelling, palm reading, casting the Evil Eye and blessing little children.

What was I going to give my baby? What kind of love could she expect from me, the hatefulest child who ever was? Maybe we could sit down and work out mortality tables together. That would be fun, wouldn't it?

Or maybe, a little voice whispered, you will mother in the only way you know how. You will be another crazy Beauchamp woman, driven half-mad by Riders, only this time there won't be any Daddy to shelter your baby. It will have no protection from you at all. You used to be sane, you used to be in control. But now the Riders can get into you. Maybe Sugar will whore you out next time, or the Preacher will beat your child for its sins. You are out of control, Antoinette. You're no safer than Elena now.

I closed my eyes and squeezed them tight, trying to cry, but no tears came. I couldn't even do that right, I couldn't even cry.

. . .

Her name was Mary Keith. She was a secretary in an insurance office in Phoenix. She had stepped off the roof of an office building with her six-year-old daughter in her arms. The little girl's name was Kirsten.

The story had haunted me since the first report on the TV two nights before. The door to the roof of the building should have been locked. God, I had lain in bed with my hands over my still-flat belly obsessing about it. Had Mary known the rooftop door was open? Had she taken her daughter up there, knowing what she was going to do? Or had it been pure chance that they had wandered up the wrong stairway?

Was it something the little girl said, or did, that made Mary Keith snap? Was she on medication, had she just lost her job, was her husband leaving her? Or was it "only" depression: a black animal that ate at her and ate at her, as it had always eaten at Momma. Only Momma was too tough to kill, she was a tough bitch and not even her gods could break her. Not everyone could be so strong.

We had this secret, Mary Keith and I, this bond, because I was going to be a mother too, and she needed someone to defend her. That's why I was mad at Bill for passing judgment on her. Because there is no way of knowing whether that black moment will break you until you are in it. You can't ask everyone to be like Momma. You can't ask every woman to be so strong.

Thinking of little Kirsten, her first-grade photo on the nine o'clock news, I remembered a fragment of one of Momma's stories. In it Sugar says, "Now tell me again, honey-child, how did you come to be on your lonesome?" And the Little Lost Girl says, "My momma sent me to the store to buy a sweet potato for a sweet potato pie, but she give me the wrong directions. I did what she told me, but there weren't no store there. So I went on a piece, looking for another store, but I couldn't find one that had a sweet potato in it, and when time came to go home, I couldn't find my way back.''

"Now wait a minute," Sugar says, and she puts her hands on her hips. "That ain't the same story you told me last time. Last time you said she dropped you at a movie and didn't pick you up. And now I come to think of it, I recollect one time you said she took you to a softball game and went for a soda pop but never came back. Now, how can you be lost all these different ways?"

The little girl looks up at Sugar with big, solemn eyes and says, "I been lost pretty bad."

Poor Mary Keith. Poor Kirsten. Sweet Jesus, protect my baby.

I sat in a wrought-iron patio chair trying not to think about Mary Keith, trying not to think about being fired. I had eaten nothing since throwing up in the Hyatt Regency bathroom, and though the day was not cold, I was starting to shiver. I shivered and shivered, I couldn't stop. As I sat shaking in my chair, a mockingbird dropped down from the live oak and landed on the stump of the banana tree. It perched there and it stared at me. It stared at me for the longest time, and then it opened its beak and rang— a long, trilling dingle. It must have chimed three times, opening its beak to let out the sound, before I realized that the rings were coming from the telephone in the kitchen.

I scrambled out of the chair and made it to the phone on the fifth ring. "Hello?" I gasped.

"Oh—I was just hanging up." A woman's voice on a long-distance connection.

"Hello?"

"Ah, is this the . . . Bow-shawmp residence?" There was no trace of a Texas twang in the caller's accent, nor anything of the South.

"Beech-um, yes, that's us. Sorry."

"Ah, yeah. Beech-um? Okay." There was a pause. "Look, I know this is going to sound kind of strange, but I think we might be related. My name is Angela Simmons. I'm calling from Calgary, Alberta. That's in Canada."

"I know." Calgary was another oil town; lots of Houstonians had been there in the course of business.

"Oh, okay. Ah, when the lawyer contacted me about Elena's will—that was her name, wasn't it? Elena? Anyway, I hired a detective to find you. Shit, I'm starting in the middle, aren't I? My mom and dad came up here when I was real little. He had a job in the oilpatch. Only my mother didn't stay. She went back south. Elena. That was her name, Elena Beauchamp."

"Oh my God," I said.

"Yeah." The woman on the other end of the line laughed. "Kind of a shocker, eh? Are you one of her kids? The detective said she had two daughters. Two besides me, I mean. So I guess you and I are related. Half-sisters. All my life she would send me money. I'm thirty-seven, by the way. My name is Angela Simmons. Actually it's Angela Jarvis, but only until the papers come through, then it's back to Simmons. I'm just finishing up a divorce. Anyway, a few weeks ago this lawyer calls to say my mother has died and left me a bequest. That's when I hired the detective. He found this number . . . Hello? Hello?"

"Yes?" I whispered.

"Look, I'm kind of embarrassed here. Have I got the

right place? Did an Elena Beauchamp used to live there? Did she ever talk about having a daughter up in Canada?"

"No. Never."

"Oh. Well. I must have the wrong—"

"Oh my God no. No, you don't have the wrong number." Everything was falling into place for me. The scenes and the drinking. The way Momma went over to Mary Jo's to cry sometimes. The way we never had any money, even in the years when Bill Sr. was good to us.

Now the tears that wouldn't come when Momma died flooded into my eyes, and my throat cramped. I couldn't see and my whole body was shaking. "My God, my God, you see? You are the Little Lost Girl," I said. "And your name is Angela. You are the Little Lost Girl. Only now you've found home."

I talked to Angela several times over the next few weeks. I kept the calls short, not wanting to put more weight on our relationship than it could stand. But I really liked her. She was tough and funny and she laughed at my jokes. Finally I asked if she would like to come and stay with me and Daddy for a few days, just to visit. She said she would. She had a divorce to finalize, she said, and a daughter named Monica whose high-school graduation she really ought to attend. School in Calgary didn't get out until the end of June, but after that Monica could stay with her father for a couple of weeks while Angela came down, maybe sometime in July.

Wanting her to come, I did not dwell on what the weather would be like in Houston in July.

"The only thing wrong with Angela is that Momma left her all our money." I said that to Candy the night we played pool together at Slick Willie's. She was stone-drunk at the time because of what had happened with Carlos, but I'll get to that later.

Candy had just beaten me for the fourth consecutive time. "Make his head," she said, which was her way of telling me to rack the balls up so she could break.

"Sorry, Carlos," I murmured, and racked for Candy. I finished and she exploded his head into fifteen rolling pieces. My sister has a howitzer break and she was really outdoing herself.

"Speaking of money—" Candy said.

Had she been sober and paying attention, she would have known this was the last topic to bring up. "No!" I said. "I can't lend you just a few twenties until you get your paycheck, or cover your last parking ticket, or make the payment on your Visa card."

Candy blinked. "What the shit?"

I stalked around the table pretending to look for a shot. "I'm so sick of you hitting me up. Don't you get it, Candy? I got laid off. I bought eight hundred dollars worth of stuff for Sugar in the Galleria and spent six hundred more on that stupid jacket and shoes. I made a thirteen-hundred-dollar downpayment on a baby, remember? I've got responsibilities of my own to look after. Only that isn't all. Now I've got all of Momma's responsibilities too: I'm supposed to look after Daddy and Mary Jo and my little sister who at twenty-six years old still can't live on a budget like an adult."

Candy looked at me. "Shoot the three. Or else the ten for the side pocket. Do you think a quick couple of beers would really hurt your baby? Because you could surely use them, Toni. Don't go postal on me here. I'm the jilted drunk, remember? *You're* supposed to be holding *my* hand."

"Were you going to ask me for some cash? Were you?" Candy didn't answer.

"I swear, Candy. Giving money to you is like pouring water in a lace bucket."

"Yes, Momma."

I grunted and shot at the three so hard the cue ball jumped the rag and went rolling under the table next to us. "That would be a scratch," Candy said.

But I'm getting ahead of myself. That night at Slick Willie's happened when my panic over money had become crippling. In the first days after Angela's call I wasn't thinking about money yet; I was grappling with the idea that suddenly, at the age of thirty, I had inherited an older sister.

Momma had married before she finished high school, a man named John Simmons who worked for Texaco. Together they had a daughter, Angela. John was transferred to Calgary when Angela was only three months old. He went to work downtown; Momma stayed home to look after the baby. Two months later John Simmons came home to find his daughter in the care of a next-door neighbor. Momma had paid her twenty dollars to watch the baby for the afternoon, saying she had some shopping she needed to do. She never came back.

She did not lose touch entirely. From time to time, Angela said, an envelope would arrive, stamped with a Houston postmark but no return address. There would be cash inside, or Treasury bills; never a check or anything listing the sender's name. Momma never wrote letters, but sometimes in the envelope there would be drawings in

charcoal or soft pencil, or watercolor paintings of cats
or ponies or shells. These kept coming long after Angela
was grown; her daughter, Monica, had grown up with
Momma's pictures in her room. Like gifts from a fairy
godmother, Angela said.

Ever since I was a teenager I had despised my mother
for drinking up our money. I didn't know exactly how
much she took in from old Mr. Friesen, but I knew it was
more than we ever saw. I blamed her for the weeks Daddy
had to stay on the road for American Express instead of
being home to look after us when the Riders or the booze
mounted Momma's head. Now I knew where the money
had gone.

It hurt, oh it hurt to find out there was another little
girl she had loved more than us. Well, maybe not more,
and maybe it was guilt, not love; but suddenly Candy and
I weren't so central to Momma's life as I had always believed. My whole notion of my childhood was adrift. At
fifteen I thought I understood my mother to a T; now at
thirty I found I hadn't known her at all. Not really. She
hadn't been daydreaming, those long afternoons at home
when she told me to hush and cried to herself. She had
been looking north to Canada. It was Angela far away she
was thinking about, not Candy and me playing quietly at
home.

I always thought things would be better if Momma
would only go away. But when Angela said, "I spent my
whole life wishing she would come back," I was filled with
a strange, aching jealousy and confusion, and could not
speak.

(I am holding my mother and patting her on the back
while she sobs in my arms. She is crying because she has
hit me. I am fourteen. "I never wanted to be bad to my

girls. I never wanted to. I'm so sorry." She cries with the crazy abandon of an actress on TV. Her guilty tears make me strong and I feel nothing for her but contempt.)

Except now I know those tears weren't all for me; they were for the Little Lost Girl most of all.

I went to Daddy with Angela's story. "Your mother didn't much care for the cold up there," he said.

"So you knew. You knew about this all along."

He got a Dos Equis out of the fridge and brought it back to the kitchen table. "It was January. Thirty-five degrees below zero, she said. She couldn't take the baby outside in that. So she was all day, every day, trapped in that apartment. You can imagine how well that set with your Momma. The sun didn't get up till nearly nine and it was dark again by four. One day she was feeling pretty sick, and the baby was fussing and fussing, and finally she went to attend to it. . . . Next thing your Momma knew, she was waking up on a Greyhound bus at the border."

He looked at his bottle, not at me, but I heard the story he wasn't telling. I saw Momma half-crazy with boredom, crying and lonely in her little box of an apartment in a cold, alien land, the baby wailing, and maybe Momma hit her, or picked her up to shake her, or maybe she started to take her up to the roof of the building, as Mary Keith had. Except something had stopped her.

"The Widow," I said. "The Widow drove Momma out. She put her on the bus back home and she never let her see that child again."

Daddy said, "I can't speak to that."

"But why?" I asked. "Why would Momma never tell us? My God, to all the time be thinking of that baby she had left behind . . ." A foolish thing to say. As if she hadn't told us every day of our lives, with her tears and drinking and slaps and lies.

Daddy looked into the garden. "She was afraid you'd think poorly of her."

Daddy drank a little more beer. "I hear you're bringing up a rookie." He glanced at my abdomen.

"Candy told you? That little brat. Don't you worry, I won't make you raise it. I'll handle it on my own."

"You and yours are always welcome in this house."

"You're not mad at me, are you? Please don't think I'm crazy. I worked it all out, and I'm not going to be like—I mean . . ."

Daddy held up his hand. "Seems to me like the organization could use a little fresh blood," he said. I looked at him with my eyes wet and grateful. "Where you figure on playing this rookie in the line-up?"

I laughed. "Oh, lead-off, I expect."

He nodded. "Let's hope this 'un can learn to take the occasional base on balls. The last lead-off hitter we had through here," he said, looking at me, "got on base all right, but led the league in Hit by Pitch."

"Ouch," I said.

" 'Worry never climbed a hill, worry never paid a bill.' " Candy, this was, drunk as a skunk that night at Slick Willie's. She had just won her sixth game of eight-ball. She was quoting one of Momma's favorite slogans. "Don't worry, Toni, as soon as I sober up, I'll start missing shots."

"Easy for Momma to say. She never even balanced a checkbook."

" 'Ooh, baby, who sewed those pleats between your eyebrows, Antoinette?' "

"Shut up, Candy."

Candy burped and laughed. " 'Who tacked your mouth down at the corners?' "

("Here come the scissors," Momma would say, and then she would tickle me under the chin with her long red nails and I would shout "No!" and squirm to get away.)

Momma never worried, least of all about money. She grieved and she despaired, but Momma's problems were always in the past. The future did not trouble her, the future was a place not yet marred by her mistakes.

I always thought the future was my only hope of heaven. I needed it to be perfect there. I spent all my time worrying and working for some distant tomorrow. The only thing I knew about happiness was that it was still a long way off. I meant to build me a bunker there, in the future. In it I would stash financial security, a decent house, and at least one healthy child. A doting husband and a winning Astros team would be nice ornaments, but were not essential. And when I had this bunker ready, I would crawl into it and slam the door, while life's war raged overhead.

Now I had not even a hole in the ground to fortify. I was stuck in my parents' house with no husband in sight and careening toward bankruptcy, while the Astros were coming out of the grapefruit leagues with grave questions in their bullpen and infield defense.

Worrying about money is the worst kind of worrying, because it is the most demeaning. To be concerned about your health is reasonable; to care for a loved one is laudable. Worrying about money is only humiliating.

Mr. Copper says, "Cash is cold." What he means, I think, is that money is simple. Money is inert. But we surround it with this haze of our desires, our fears, our hopes. Even business people are frequently much too emotional in their dealings with money. The standard actuary's joke goes:

Boss: What are the numbers on that project you were looking at?

Actuary: What numbers do you want?

Okay, it's not a side-splitter, but actuaries are notoriously boring. Go into an office and trust me you will find the joke apt. Even working two-thirds time at Friesen Investments (I had two hours a day to study for my actuarial exams) I must have had dozens of conversations with Bill Jr. where he would say, "Shouldn't we be making more? What return are you assuming?" and I would say, "Seven percent a year over three years." And he would say, "Oh, I'm sure we can make ten percent," despite the fact that guaranteed securities like bonds and T-bills were paying in the five and a quarter range. Sure, you might get ten percent . . . but to assume it?

Unfotunately the day I cleaned out my desk I lost my head for money. With the baby on the way, financial worries were eating me alive. The job-search experts say to allow yourself at least a month of looking for each $10,000 a year you want to earn. With my qualifications, it was not unreasonable to think I might get a job starting in the $40,000 range. Actuaries are rare and expensive. After getting my math degree I had to take four hundred fifty hours of exams to become a Fellow. My salary ought to reflect that.

Did my baby care? No. My baby would want a place to sleep, food to eat. My baby would not be interested in my pride or my qualifications. And—let's be honest—I desperately did not want to be a stay-at-home mom. I knew, I knew deep inside me, that I could never risk my child in the care of a woman growing bored and lonely in her apartment. I did not dare leave my baby with a woman who might turn into Mary Keith or Elena Beauchamp.

And so what should have been easy became hard. I sweated blood over resumés and then threw them out afterwards. In my suddenly abundant leisure time I went to the library and read book after book on finding a job—and then failed to submit any applications. I started imaginary stock portfolios that made a 23% annualized return over the month I followed them and I didn't dare to invest a cent. In the same notebook I made hypothetical killings trading commodities futures but never called a broker.

I had been fired. I hated that.

Instead of daring to make more money, I started spending less. I felt my fingers crimping like claws around my pennies. Weeks went by in my parents' house. When I had moved back home, it had been clearly understood that I was staying only to help nurse Momma through her last illness. Now I couldn't think of giving up the free rent and looking for an apartment. I stopped going out to movies and then I stopped going out at all, staying home to eat crackers and watch the little green lizards creep across the tile floor and clamber up the white plaster walls.

The last three weeks of morning sickness were a calvary. I don't think I could have functioned at my job even if I still had one. I lay in bed and watched TV. I could not read the newspaper, as not a day seemed to go by without a Crushed Baby story. Locked Car Baby Dies of Heat Stroke. Baby Savaged by Pit Bull. Young Child Slain in Gun Mishap. Infant Twins Die in House Fire. Toddler Strangles on Playground Equipment. Abducted Child's Last Words—no, I cannot say them.

Do you know how many child abductions are perpetrated by strangers? One third of one percent. One in three hundred. We spend all this time streetproofing our children these days—but you know what? If you don't want your child abducted, don't get divorced. Because that's who steals children. Estranged husbands, bitter ex-wives, righteous in-laws. It's love that is the problem. Passion. Romance. In the movies and on TV we are constantly told that love, love, love is the thing that will make us happy, that it's the strongest force in the universe. But in the real world, love can eat you alive.

Read the headlines. Pay attention to the beating, the stalking, the stolen children, the shots fired in anger. Love is a wild magic and cannot be controlled. The next time you see a Just Married car with tin cans tied to the back, look at it with an actuary's eye and admit just once that sometimes the very worst case will come to happen.

My mother loved Angela. My mother loved me.

Better to have a child without a mate, the way I did, and eliminate one variable, one wild factor: the abusive husband or the divorce down the road, or the gentle man who to the shock of his neighbors comes home one day with a gun and—

My way is safer.

I lay in bed and watched TV. Not the news, of course: should a child die horribly anywhere on the globe, CNN's crack investigative staff was there to report it every half hour. Little boy drowned in a well in Maine. Six-year-olds used as slave labor in Madras sweatshops. Eleven-year-old girls contracting AIDS and fucked to death by tourists in Thai brothels.

But there is one safe haven on daytime TV, if you have cable: CNBC, the Business Channel. I recommend it. It's very soothing. Watching the business news is like watching a really complicated weather report. The Nikkei jumps, the S & P drops, lumber is unsettled in the wake of the latest NAFTA ruling on Canadian softwood. Trust me: if you can watch baseball, or follow Paris fashion trends, you can spend some deeply relaxing hours keeping up with the business world, and you might be better informed on where to stick your retirement money into the bargain.

Like baseball and fashion, business has players, some colorful, some stodgy. It has daily scores and won-lost columns. It has established teams like IBM and General Electric, as well as rising stars, jokesters, and cagey veterans. It even has baggy-eyed managers delivering the time-honored cliches: "This was the hardest decision I've had to make since I took this job, but we felt we had to do what was best for the (ballclub) (shareholders)."

I was completely hooked on CNBC by the time my morning sickness finally began to ease. A day came, not far into April, when I padded downstairs in my nightgown and found myself thinking how nice it would be to fry an egg for breakfast. I fried that egg like a clean-up hitter taking his home-run trot. I showered it with coarse black pepper until it looked like someone had dropped it in the sand, and then I added a shot of Pickapeppa hot sauce for good measure and wolfed it down, feeling my spirits lift.

That Thursday I went in for my fifteen-week ultrasound. I put on a blue clinic smock and lay on an examining table. This time at least it would only be an external. The technician pushed up the smock and pulled my panties halfway down my hips, exposing a thin fringe of pubic hair. Before getting pregnant I had always felt uncomfortable when doctors saw me naked, but the whole process

of pregnancy, particularly if you get artificially inseminated, involves so much routine exposure you get a bit
numb to it. My advice, by the way, is to have nurses or
techs do the vaginal examinations. For some reason
M.D.'s, even the women, seem not to understand the pa-
tient experience very well—the value of warming a spec-
ulum, for instance, before giving it the brisk medical
shove.

My technician, Laquisha, was a young black woman
with purple lipstick and bleached gold hair, worn wavy
and flat to her head like a 1920s flapper. Over the years
the nail-care cult has really taken hold among the black
girls in Houston. Laquisha's nails were very fine, two
inches long and indigo, with seven tiny silver stars on the
index fingers, and a thin gold crescent moon on the nail
of each thumb. Momma would have loved those claws.
They passed, clicking like hard-shelled insects, across the
face of Laquisha's machines and instruments.

She brought out a pot of pale blue lubricating slime
and rubbed it over the bottom of my abdomen. It was
lighter and less greasy than Vaseline, more like K-Y jelly.

"Is the baby going to look all right, or will it be gross?"

Laquisha smoothed more slime on the bottom of my
belly, grinning. "It's gonna look like a lima bean with a
head."

"A lima bean with a head?"

"Only it's blue."

"How many do you get with extra toes or tails?"

"Hardly any. We had a mom come in with two heads,
just las' week. But the baby was fine," Laquisha said. She
grinned wider and gave me a little poke in the tummy.
"Do you b'lieve that?" She finished sliming me. "Don't
be nervous, sugar. It's going to be fine."

Usually I despise the way people talk to a pregnant woman as if she had the IQ of her fetus, but just then I was scared about what the ultrasound might show—terrified, really—and I could have hugged Laquisha for being so nice to me. She left and came back wheeling the ultrasound machine in front of her. She turned it on and the screen flashed for a moment and then went blank. "Do you want to know the sex of the child?"

"You can tell when they're this little? Gracious. Um, no. Don't tell me."

"Some people like to know what kind of clothes to get, you know. What kind of name to think up."

"No thank you," I said. I realized I did not wish to see the future. My mother and the blessed Isaiah had not been made glad by prophecy, either one. Anyway, Candy would tell me the sex of the child soon enough, if I really needed to know.

"All right, then." Laquisha pulled a paddle from the machine, pressed it to my abdomen, and began to rub it slowly across my belly.

Up on the screen I saw my child for the first time. "Oh," I said. It was blue, digital readout blue, and its tiny arms and legs were pulled in. Its head was huge compared to its limbs. The image on the screen flashed and shivered as Laquisha moved the paddle around, as if I were seeing my child's reflection in a windblown pond.

"There—see that? That's the heart. Beating jus' fine. Two arms, two legs, one head, no tail. You sure you don't want to know the sex?"

"I'm sure," I said.

It did not have a sex for me. That thing in my womb was not yet a baby, much less a child. That was a secret being hidden inside me, on a great voyage alone in its submarine world. What an epic there was unfolding within me! How strange that its heroic journey would be forgotten; that this tiny sexless voyager would disappear at the moment of birth, witched into a squalling, ignorant infant boy or girl, its memories of its mysterious beginnings falling away, away, away.

I found my eyes were wet.

Sail on, lima bean child. Sail on, hidden voyager.

Only when the ultrasound was over did I realize how much of the first trimester I had spent worrying that I might miscarry. That's another thing no one ever talks about, how common miscarriages are. Mary Jo miscarried five times, the last at twenty-six weeks, before she and her husband quit trying to have a brother for their baby Travis. It wasn't long after that their marriage broke up. Still, the majority of miscarriages occur in the first trimester, when the body discovers there is something wrong with the fetus and decides to scrap it and start over. I wasn't home safe yet, but I could breathe a little easier. The morning sickness had largely faded, and the ultrasound showed no signs of abnormal development.

Filled with new strength and resolution, I determined to go over to Mary Jo's house. She had been pressing me to come for weeks, no doubt to inspect the state of her leaky roof. I had been so stressed out I couldn't face dealing with someone else's problems, but now I decided to stop shirking.

I didn't just love Mary Jo the way you love, but avoid, your more eccentric relatives. I *owed* her. She had rescued me and Candy a ton of times when Momma was on the rampage, or when she and Daddy were fighting. Just as important, she had taken care of Momma when nobody at our house could.

But beyond that, Mary Jo was the first woman to tell me some hard truths about what real life was like. When I was fifteen years old, just before I went out on one of my early dates, Mary Jo came over to visit. She said she'd heard my boyfriend had a driver's license and was going to pick me up. When I confirmed this, she took a twenty-dollar bill out of her purse and pressed it into my hand. "What's this for?" I said.

"Cab fare," she said. I started to say I wouldn't need it, but Mary Jo held one finger across her lips to shush me. "Toni, every woman needs her own cash," she said. She fumbled in her purse for a cigarette, lit it, and gave me a long, considering look over her first drag. "I'm going to tell you something now, but you have to promise not to tell Travis." Travis was her son. I promised. "Chester and I hadn't been together three years when I knew I wanted to leave him," Mary Jo said.

I was shocked. I never guessed she was unhappy with Chester. When the split came, I assumed she had been devastated.

"But I couldn't leave him. I was afraid to. I was at home with Travis, and Chester made all the money. If I'd had money of my own, I would have gone. I would have had a happier life. Instead I stayed with that man, miserable every day, until he left me. Then I got my job at Sears. It's not a good job. I didn't go to college, I didn't have a lot of work experience, because I stayed home and let Chester make the money. Are you paying attention, hon?"

I nodded. She wrapped my hand around that twenty and gave it a good squeeze. "Don't do like I did, Toni.

Don't think you're being greedy. If you want to find true love in this life, you make sure you have your own cash on hand. You got that?"

To make a long story short, I used that twenty-dollar bill.

When Mary Jo told me her story it was as if a grown-up had pushed back a curtain and let me look at real life for the first time. I was deeply touched that she would talk so honestly about her weakness and her failures. I felt I owed it to her not to waste her unhappiness by ignoring her advice. In college I despised the artsy girls whose idea of romance was living in a fashionably appointed garret and who thought that caring about a good income represented the death of the soul. Mary Jo taught me that making money wasn't frivolous. It wasn't something I did because I wanted a new car or a fancy stereo. It was about freedom and independence and love.

I drove straight from my ultrasound appointment to Mary Jo's house. She only lived ten blocks from us, but they were the wrong ten blocks. The charming, quirky houses of affluent Montrose faded into a neighborhood of small bungalows all built during World War II, long before insulation or central air conditioning made it to East Texas. Houston is essentially built over a swamp, which plays havoc with our houses. The soil is so liquid that septic tanks, pipes, and other buried conduits tend to float up out of the ground and must be periodically whacked back down again. Foundations in Houston are a nightmare; every house on Mary Jo's block had been re-levelled at least once.

I parked along the curb behind a Chevy pickup with a rifle rack visible through the back window and a COM-MANDOS FOR CHRIST bumper sticker on the tailgate.

I saw the Commandos at a summer camp once in my teenage years, a bunch of muscle-bound guys in combat fatigues who smash bricks with karate chops and do powerlifting demonstrations to magnify the glory of Jesus. Most of the other kids thought it was a bit weird to seek Christ by breaking cinderblocks with your head, but growing up with Momma as I had, I did not feel in any position to call the kettle black.

The paint was peeling on Mary Jo's house and a grass fungus had killed much of the lawn. The rest was pitted with fire-ant hills. Worse yet, I could see at once that the roof was beginning to sink like the back of a spavined mare. My spirits fell. I had been hoping Mary Jo was fussing at nothing.

I opened the screen door and knocked. "Mary Jo? It's me."

"That's what you think." A flurry of small noises came from inside; I thought of startled rats bolting for cover. The chain lock clinked and rattled. Moments later the door opened and there was Mary Jo's pale white face and ringed eyes glowering at me from the interior gloom. "Get in, honey, you're letting all the cool out."

Mary Jo closed the door behind me. Hers was a small, dark, stuffy warren of a house. Many of her neighbors had fat evaporative air-conditioning units hanging from their back windows, but Mary Jo despised them. Instead she kept her heavy maroon drapes closed at all times, so even in the middle of the day there was barely light enough to see inside. As a girl I was forever tripping over some unseen pile of books or porcelain doll or "antique" stool that Mary Jo had collected and left lying on the floor.

The house smelled badly of mildew and wet cloth, window mold and damp paper.

"Would you please examine this?" she said morosely, jabbing something at me in the murk.

"I can't look at anything, it's pitch-black in here. Give me a minute."

As always I could hear the whirring of fans in the darkness: the thin electric hiss of the new Sears fan back in Mary Jo's bedroom; the whine of the tiny oscillating fan she kept on top of the refrigerator; the great black iron fan, built near the end of World War II, that still patrolled her living room, sweeping his head from side to side, making the drapes and doilies shiver. Above my head, the chopping wooden blades of her ceiling fan swept into eternity.

"It's ruined, is my point."

My eyes had adjusted to the dim light enough to see that she was holding out an old children's book. "It was on a shelf next to the wall and the rain come in and ruined it." Mary Jo thrust the book at me again. The cover was damp and warped out of shape. Bubbles had crept under the cloth cover. "*Little Black Sambo*," she said, opening it. "Fine story, a fine story for kids. A real collector's item. Now they've took it out of the school libraries 'cause it's got a black child in it. Prejudice, my aunt!" She opened the book to the place where the Tiger is chasing Little Black Sambo around the tree and turning into a pat of butter. "What's prejudiced about that? I'd think they'd want stories with black children in them. Cute kiddo, too, like a little blob of molasses. When I was a girl we called black people niggers, and they did too! Didn't mean anything by it. Like calling you a, a . . . I don't know. Nothing bad. This one old fella name of Nigger Joe used to give my brother a ride on his horse every Sunday and a pinch of tobacco. That old nigger was the kindest, most dignified fellow you ever met. A natural gentleman. Loved us kids to death. They had their own schools then. Churches too. We all got along. Look at him turning into butter. Isn't that the darnedest idea? Your momma used to think of stories like that. I never could. Used to you could find that story right on the menu at the Big Boy, you know."

"I thought it was Denny's."

"Was it? I don't recall." Mary Jo shook her head. "Took it off, of course. Prejudice, my aunt. Got this for fifty cents at a garage sale the year they impeached President Nixon. I hear they built him a statue in California. Can you believe it? You build a statue of a president who broke the law, but you can't have Little Black Sambo on your menus anymore. Gosh he looks like he was made of chocolate cake in these pictures, you could just eat him up. The artist who did this sure knew how to paint."

Humps of clutter littered Mary Jo's armchair and the dim regions of her sofa, so I eased myself down on the piano bench where she used to make me sing "O Tannenbaum" and "The Star-Spangled Banner" the year I was in fourth grade. (My Christmas solo at school had convinced her I should be a child star and sing on the radio.) Above the keyboard, blotched with water stains, yellowed sheet music stirred and fell still as the wind from the fan passed across it.

"Never find another copy for fifty cents." Mary Jo's mouth crimped shut like a change purse closing.

The smell of mildew rose powerfully from the damp carpets and curtains.

I sighed. "Mary Jo, you need to get your roof fixed."

She said, "I had been meaning to mention that." She laughed, a hoarse smoker's laugh. Not like Momma's, though. Nobody laughed like Momma could. "I got a good banana pudding in the fridge if you want it, Toni. I'm gonna get me a Coke. Want one?"

She came back with one of the little six and a half ounce glass bottles, like Momma favored. "This is the real deal, you know. Not that watery Coke Classic stuff. I wanted that, I'd drink Pepsi. They used to sell that for a nickle cheaper, you know. Nobody would buy it. They must think we're all born idiots to believe that Classic's the same as old Coke before they switched." She tapped her bottle. "These are imported from Mexico. They never did the switch there. If you get it bottled from a Mexican bottler, you get real old Coke. You can feel the difference in your nose."

"That's really old Coke?"

"You bet."

I headed for her fridge. We take our cold beverages seriously in Texas. Half the memories of my childhood (the ones that don't include Momma, anyway) are cold-drink memories: the sound of ice clinking in a glass of iced tea when you're stirring in the sugar; sweat beading on a bottle of Coke; the metallic taste of those big steel milk-shake canisters; the way you had to open a can of Dr. Pepper in that brief era between pull-tabs and the current modified pull-tab, when there were two little raised nubs on the top for you to push in, a big one to let the pop out and a little one to let the air in. Daddy explained the whole physics of that to me.

"I buy them at the Mexican grocery down the street. You know, the lady who runs that store had a cousin who just had a third breast removed. It was growing right down from her armpit. Can you imagine?"

"I'm trying not to." Mary Jo kept her Cokes in the side door between the Pickapeppa Sauce and a jar of Rio

Grande green olives stuffed with jalapeños. She didn't seem to be eating any worse than usual: besides the banana pudding, topped in true orthodox fashion with a handful of 'Nilla wafers, I saw about sixteen little Tupperware containers full of yesterday's salad and last week's meatloaf, a package of pimento-loaf sandwich meat, a bag of Wonder Bread, half a bar of rat-trap cheese, three cans of Miller Lite, a bowl of pink marshmallow salad, and of course jars and jars of homemade salsas, jams, jellies, and relishes. There were also Giant Economy Size jars of pickles and applesauce and mayonnaise. "Mary Jo, I'm throwing out this mayonnaise," I said, dumping the giant jar in the trash beneath the sink. "The best before date is from last Thanksgiving."

"It ain't like I don't check it, Toni."

"Uh-huh." I checked the date on the pickles and applesauce. They were still good for a few more months. On top of the fridge sat a bag of Fritos closed with a chip-clip.

"The doctor said it was entirely normal to have three breasts. If you think about it, a sow has teats right down her ribs. Apparently we can too. There's a switch in your DNA turns them off."

"Turns what off?"

"Our teats."

"Oh. —I'll be darned. This does taste like old Coke!"

"You stay in school, honey," Mary Jo said with her hoarse laugh. "You bound to learn something."

I brought my little Coke back into the living room and sat on the piano bench. "The thing is, Mary Jo, I don't have the money to fix your roof. *No tengo dinero. Nada. Solamente* zip."

"Don't whine, Toni. You always were a whiner. Do

you see the roof's got to be fixed? Just answer the question."

"Yes, ma'am."

"Let's us stop making excuses, then." Mary Jo went rummaging through a drawer in the tall glass-fronted cabinet she used to show off her prized knickknacks. "I have here a cashier's check in your name for eighteen hundred and twenty-seven dollars. It's all I can spare. It's all I've got."

"I can't take that!"

"I made it out in February, so you best cash it directly."

"Mary Jo!"

Mary Jo coughed. "I really am going to quit smoking. Did you ever see a picture of a smoker's lung? They had one in the *Reader's Digest*, looked like bathtub sponge soaked in motor oil. I tell you, that's it for me. I'm gonna quit." She folded my hand around the check.

"What am I supposed to do with this? You need your whole roof fixed. That's going to be, I don't know . . . ten thousand dollars, maybe."

"Baby, you have to look after me." She held my hand tightly, tightly in her own. "You think I don't wish I could cover it? I make my money stuffing envelopes, sugar. It's all I'm good for. But I always came through for your momma, and she did the same for me." Her mouth shut tight and her jaw worked. The skin of her face was pale and unhealthy-looking. "Don't make me beg, kiddo. Don't you make me a beggar."

"We'll look after you, Mary Jo. I promise you that."

"She left all her money to that baby. Angela. She told me a hundred times she wouldn't forget me when it was time for her to go, but she did after all. She said she was sorry when she got out of the hospital. Every blessed dime to this girl she never seen in nearly forty years, what a crazy thing. And the people here, you and Candy and all of us, not one nickel. Not one dime. All that Friesen money, and where did it go?'' Mary Jo gave my hand a squeeze. ''Your daddy said you knew about Angie now.''

I nodded, unable to speak.

''Ma-maw would spin in her grave if she saw me living this way,'' Mary Jo said. ''Pappy would have tanned my hide. Letting water get on the books. He loved his books. I haven't ironed since I don't know when.''

''Mary Jo—''

''There were times your momma would have lost her mind if it wasn't for me,'' Mary Jo said fiercely. ''If she didn't have someone who knew. Someone she could talk to. Your daddy never wanted to hear about little Angela. She didn't blame him, he was good to her, so good to her, even after he didn't love her anymore.'' Mary Jo was crying, a couple of tears on the old soft sallow skin of her face. ''She wasn't the easiest friend in the world to have, you know.''

''I know it,'' I said.

''That Angela. Hah. I'd like to meet her just one time before I die.'' Slowly Mary Jo let go of my hands.

I put the crumpled check in my purse. There are some gifts which cannot be refused.

That was the afternoon before I had my fight with Candy in Slick Willie's. The house was empty when I got home. Daddy was on the road for American Express, swinging through the northern loop of his territory: Waco, Dallas, Texarkana, Little Rock, Pine Bluff, Monroe, Shreveport, back across the Texas line into Longview, Tyler, and home. Seemed like the older he got the harder they worked him. Now at sixty-two he was covering a territory three men used to handle. Sometimes they made him go as far north as Oklahoma City, or as far east as Jackson, Mississippi. I told him they were trying to force him to retire early so they could cut down on his pension and benefits, but Daddy wouldn't complain.

(I'm in the kitchen helping Momma do the dishes. She turns on the radio on top of the fridge. The Astros are batting in the sixth with one out and one on. She catches me looking at her. "I know. It makes no sense." She shrugs. "When Daddy's on the road I like the company. It reminds me of him." She cocks her hip and gives an up-from-under smile, imitating how she is when Sugar is riding her, and switches to Sugar's sweet, husky, playful voice. "But when he's at home, I want him to shut the damn thing off and pay attention to *me*!")

It still surprised me not to find her in that kitchen.

But the kitchen was mine now, if it was anyone's. I meant to live up to it. During the two months of morning sickness I had lost some faith in my pregnancy books for telling me, in tones varying from jolly to menacing, that I had better be eating ten small portions of whole grain starches per day, five or six portions of fruit or fresh vegetables, three portions of hard protein, and enough milk to drown a cat. To a woman living on a handful of Saltines a day it seemed a tad fantastical. It was especially hard to care once I read the fine print, which said that it was only me, not my baby, who would suffer if my diet went to hell. Apparently evolution had its priorities straight; the baby would suck the needed nutrients from my body, leaching the vitamins from my skin and the calcium right out of my bones if necessary. I read this with a sigh of relief and, since I couldn't possibly feel worse than I did already, pushed all thoughts of food away like a bowl of steaming chicken's innards.

But now that I was officially into the second trimester my appetite had returned, and with it my determination. After all, once the baby was born and weaned, I really would be cooking for two. Between college, work, and studying for my actuarial exams, food had been a low priority since I left home: something that came in a disposable cardboard package, soon forgotten. Now, back in the kitchen of my childhood, surrounded by ropes of peppers and bulbs of dried garlic and herbs blooming along the window sill, I was determined to do better.

I flipped on the radio. The Astros were playing their first afternoon game of the year, a businessman's special against the Dodgers. We'd just gone to our bullpen for a jittery rookie southpaw from the Dominican. "This fella's so jumpy—" said Milo Hamilton, the play-by-play man, "—he'd make coffee nervous," I chorused out loud, keeping Milo company. It was Milo Hamilton who called Hank Aaron's 715th home run, the one that broke Babe Ruth's record, back when he was broadcasting for the Atlanta Braves. Old-time baseball guys have a kind of wit all their own. I think it was Milo who once said, talking about Charlie Hustle, the legendary Pete Rose, "If Pete were to remarry at the age of eighty-five, he'd look for a house near a school."

Our reliever did his job, inducing a pop-up with a riding fastball at the letters to end the top of the seventh inning with the score tied 2- 2. I flipped through a list of Approved Pregnancy Recipes as the game cut away to an ad for Mac Haik Chevy's Good Ol' Boy promotion: buy a pickup truck and they'd throw in a shotgun for free. I had just decided to try a recipe for Wheat Germ Enhanced Lasagna when the phone rang. "Hello?"

"'Bout time."

"Candy? Is that you?"

"Mostly. You were Out. I called knowing you are always In, but you were Out."

"I was at Mary—"

"A few hours ago I could still drive. Not now. Now I'm Way Too Drunk. You're going to have to come here."

"You've been drinking? At five in the afternoon? Where are you? What's wrong?"

Music was blasting away on Candy's end of the phone. "Can you imagine how many times guys have said to me, 'Hey, honey, I got a Slick Willie here for ya!' I don't mind anyone's fun, but it gets Old. You know? It gets Old."

"You have been drinking. You're at work."

"Unless they've fired me and I didn't know, in which case I'd just be a customer." Candy paused, apparently to let someone back a heavy truck over an electric guitar. "Come to think of it, I am supposed to go on shift at seven."

"Oh Lord."

"Oops."

I left a cup of wheat germ on the kitchen counter and drove the six blocks to Slick Willie's. The place was just beginning to fill up with guys on the way home from work, a nicely dressed crowd stopping in for a beer at day's end. Junior account executives practiced their predatory pool-table prowls, circling the helpless balls that clumped like spherical zebras on the green felt Serengeti. The jukebox was in fine fettle, roaring out "Bad To The Bone," reassurance for those young men, who needed to hear that they hadn't traded in their wild sides for nice Italian shoes and jobs at Tenneco and Shell. Every turncoat likes to think he's actually a double agent in deep cover.

When I came in, the bartender jerked his thumb at the bathroom. Candy emerged a moment later, smoothing her hair back and sporting a grim yet glassy expression.

"Are you okay? What's going on?"

She held up her hand for silence and led me to a pool table at the back of the room where she had started a solo game. "He turned me down," she said, folding suddenly at the waist to disappear beneath the table. She returned a moment later clutching the triangle. "Rack 'em."

"What? Who turned you down?"

"Rhymes with 'shit.'"

"Carlos? Carlos turned you down? Oh, sweetie."

Candy stopped and smelled her fingers. "Gross. I tore open a packet of mustard and stuck it into the back of my throat until I threw up. Trying to get the tequila out. Once it's in your bloodstream it's too late, you know. People always ask for coffee when they're trying to sober up, but it doesn't help at all. That's in a training booklet they give us. Can you smell the mustard?" she asked, sticking her hand in front of my nose and wiggling her fingers.

"Candy! Stop it!"

B-B-B-B-Bad!

"Get a cue," Candy said. "It helps me stay straight if I'm concentrating on something. But I don't if I'm playing by myself. I don't want to beat myself bad enough."

I picked out a cue and chalked up while Candy finished racking. "Flip for break?"

"I want to break." She stalked around to the end of the table and placed the cue ball. Candy had always played, and working at Slick Willie's she had played a lot more. For a girl, she had a hell of a break. She sighted down the cue ball and drew her arm back. "Hey, Carlos!" she yelled, and let the hammer fall. Balls blew out in every direction. The nine staggered as if shot and fell face-forward into the right corner pocket. "I'm stripes," Candy said. "You're solids. What else is new."

She had gone to meet Carlos for lunch at the Café Chapultepec and proposed between the chips and the chicken mole, wriggling out of her seat to kneel on the tile floor and look prettily up at him while asking for his hand. He was supposed to laugh and say yes. "He just sat there like a lump, Toni. He actually inched away from me. He was *embarrassed*. He said he'd have to think about it. Think about it! What's to think about? Either you like someone well enough to marry them or you don't!"

"Now be fair." I lined up the four ball for a shot on the corner pocket. "This is all pretty sudden for Carlos. You had no thought of marrying him until the Widow said you had to." I drew my arm back slowly and stroked forward on the exhale. The four plunked solidly into the rag beside the pocket and wandered off in search of some friends further down the table.

"That was months ago," Candy said, blasting the thirteen into a corner pocket and pacing moodily around the table to look at a shot on the eleven.

"Not to Carlos. You've been too yellow to talk to him about it, remember?"

"Whose side are you on? He's had lots of clues. I volunteered to wax his car. I even asked to visit his mother once, didn't I? How blind can the man be?—Shit!"

"Bad luck." I looked around the table for a good shot and didn't see much. "I went over to Mary Jo's today. She wasn't lying about the roof. She might as well run a sprinkler inside her front room."

"Can you imagine how humiliating that is? To be down on one knee in a restaurant, everybody watching you from the other tables, and the guy *inches away*?"

"She gave me a check for eighteen hundred dollars. It'll never be enough. I should just put it into savings bonds and use it for groceries when the baby comes." I shot the five and missed by a mile, only to have it kiss two banks and drop in a side pocket. It is better to be lucky than good, as my mother was given to declare. "Give him a few days, Candy. You're pretty, you're young. He'll come around." I shot at the four ball again. He stepped gracefully aside as if letting someone pass on a crowded train and then returned to chatting up the six. "I'm going to be showing in another month."

"Ten in the side pocket," Candy said.

" 'Single White Female, pregnant, broke, living in parents' house, bowlegged and getting bow-leggeder, seeks financially secure co-parent. No photograph necessary.' "

The ten clutched his heart and stumbled back through the swinging saloon doors into the side pocket. "Live fast, die young," Candy said. The table was now largely populated by my solid citizens. " 'Single White Female seeks weedy Mexican car sorcerer for lifetime enslavement. No in-laws. Send picture of mother's grave.' " She bent down to draw a bead on the twelve. "Toni, what if he doesn't come around? What if he says no for good?"

"Then you have two options." My sister looked up at me. "Chemical, and nuclear."

She laughed and shot, but the twelve didn't fall.

The juke box had moved on to Washing Hands, the best of the eighties postpunk evangelical bands. **Hungry Hungry Hungry Hungry, Hungry for *vinegar*** . . .

"If I was a guy, I would be a highly desirable commodity," I said. "I am well educated. I can be funny. I make good money, when I'm making any money at all. I am no princess, but I am not a frog either."

Candy leaned earnestly across the table. "*I'd* fuck you."

"You're my sister. You have to say that."

"No, really." She shook her head. "Nobody wants to marry me. Do you know I've never had a guy ask? Go figure. I haven't spent a Saturday night alone since I was fifteen years old, but for some reason nobody wants to see me Sunday morning. Well, not past lunchtime, anyway. Hell, even *you've* had a proposal, right?"

I missed my shot badly, nearly ripping the felt, and glared at her.

"What? What did I say? Steve What's-his-face, with the zits. He proposed to you."

"Watson. His last name was Watson."

"Exactly! So what are you doing right? You must be batting about five hundred and I'm zero for my existence. God, I want a beer."

"No, not until your shift is over." I stood for a moment leaning on my cue, overcome with the injustice of Life. "I know what a pitcher's ERA means and why you don't try to steal third base with two out in an inning. I know how to calculate slugging percentage. How many women can calculate a slugging percentage?"

"It's a life skill," Candy said solemnly. "That's our problem, Toni. I have all the Saturday night skills, and you have all the Sunday morning ones." She stopped and blinked. "Between us, we make a hell of a woman. We ought to be able to get at least one husband."

I chalked my cue. "Like a time-share."

"Exactly! Only it would have to be Carlos."

"I was imagining someone taller."

"He's great in bed. I mean—" Candy blinked and then ran her hand down the length of her cue. "Really great. We do a lot of sex magic. He doesn't know the tantric stuff exactly, I've taught him some of that, but there's a Mexican equivalent, he says. You wouldn't regret it."

I snickered and blushed. "Well, maybe. Is he good with kids?"

"Bound to be. Look at all those brothers and sisters."

"We could keep him in the kitchen," I suggested. "In a rabbit hutch."

"Feed him lettuce through the screen. He wants meat, he's got to perfom in bed."

"Or change diapers."

Candy looked at me. "This is a great idea."

"What about his mother?"

"La Hag? Oh, that's easy," Candy said, eyes gleaming. "We'll keep *her* in the oven."

An hour later we had the fight about money. Sisters are like that; you can't spend too much time with them without fighting about something. Anyway, I stayed with Candy to the beginning of her shift and then went home. On the way in I checked the mail, which I had forgotten to do, and found a letter waiting. It was hand-addressed to "The Beauchamp Household." The postmark was from New Orleans. Curious, I opened it, and watched as the solution to all my money worries fell out.

It was from a man named Dr. Richard Manzetti, an anthropologist with some connection to Tulane University. Folk magic in America was his field and he had heard of Momma. In fact, he had even published a paper on her. He was in touch with various collectors, both institutional and individual, and had been asked to investigate the possibility of purchasing some of Momma's memorabilia. *"I have been authorized to make offers well into the five-figure range,"* the letter said.

Well into the five-figure range.

There was a phone number at the bottom of the letter. I dialed it.

One day that Little Lost Girl is walking, walking, walking through the city, when she comes across a big crowd that has gathered to watch Pierrot perform. He is grinning and juggling and talking with his audience when suddenly he sees her. "Well well well! Just who we've been waiting for!" Quicker than she can blink, he handsprings over to her and lands with his long sharp nose touching her nose, and his long sharp chin touching her chin. He grins his long sharp grin and says, "I'll bet you a dollar I can bite my eye."

"I don't have a dollar."

"How much have you got?"

"Eleven cents. I found a dime and a penny in the street this morning."

"Then I'll bet you five cents I can bite my eye," Pierrot says. "What have you got to lose? Eleven cents won't buy you anything, but if you win, you'll have sixteen cents. If you find another dime, you'll have enough money to call your mother from that pay phone on the corner and ask her to pick you up."

"Okay," whispers the Little Lost Girl. "Five cents."

The crowd gasps and then laughs as Pierrot pulls out his left eye, which is made of glass, and pops it in his mouth. Then he stuffs it back into its socket.

The Little Lost Girl slowly opens her grubby palm. Pierrot snatches the dime from her hand and crams it into his ear. From his other ear he pulls out a nickel and hands it to her. "I'll bet you a nickel I can bite my other eye," he says.

"No. You'll just trick me again."

"How could I bite my other eye? Look, if I win, I'll take that nickel. But if you win, I'll give you twenty cents, and you'll be able to call your mother from that pay phone on the corner."

The Little Lost Girl looks from the grinning Pierrot to the phone and back again. "Okay," she whispers.

Pierrot opens his mouth and takes out a set of false teeth, which he gently closes over his other eye. The crowd shrieks with merriment. The Little Lost Girl begins to cry, very quietly.

"There there, poppet, it's not so bad." Pierrot plucks the nickel from her hand and pats her on the back. "I'll give you one more chance. I'll bet you I can pee in your shoes and make it smell like rosewater. If I win, I get your last penny. But if you win, I will show you your very own house with the white picket fence and the yellow trim around the door and the swing hanging from the big live-oak tree out front."

Tears are trickling down the Little Lost Girl's cheeks. "Okay," she whispers, and she takes off her shoes that she's been wearing ever so long while she's been walking, walking, walking through the city.

"You sure now? You are actually asking me to pee in your shoes?"

The little girl nods.

Pierrot picks them up with a flourish and brandishes them at the crowd. "You are actually *asking* me to pee in your shoes?" The crowd snorts and giggles.

"Yes, I said yes." She is still crying.

Pierrot turns his back to the audience and stands against a building. His bottom waggles as he makes a great show of unzipping himself. Silence falls in the intersection, and then everyone hears a faint trickling hiss. It goes on and on, and Pierrot leans further and further back from the building, until his sharp chin and his sharp nose are pointing directly at the sky. "AaaaaaaAAAAAaaaahhhhh!" he sighs, and then he pulls up his zipper so hard he does a backflip.

A moment later he returns to the Little Lost Girl, holding her shoes by their edges and making faces of disgust.

"It smells like pee," the Little Lost Girl says.

"So it does."

"But why? Why did you make the bet if you knew you were going to lose?"

Pierrot drops the shoes on the pavement with a splash and gestures behind him. "You see that crowd? I bet every person in that crowd one dollar that you would ask me to pee in your shoes." The crowd cheers and people begin to reach for their wallets, laughing and shaking their heads.

"My shoes. They're ruined." The Little Lost Girl looks at Pierrot. "You promised me you would show me my house."

"So I did, and here it is!" Reaching beside the girl's head, he draws a photograph out of her ear. It is a picture of her very own house with the white picket fence and the yellow trim and the swing outside, and there is a dim shape you can half see in one window that might be her mother.

"But this isn't my house," the Little Lost Girl cries. "This is only a picture!"

Pierrot is making his way through the crowd, collecting his winnings. "Don't whine, kid. You're lucky I left you that penny."

"But—"

He turns sharply and leans down so the tip of his long sharp nose bumps against hers. "What did you expect? Something for nothing? Don't you see I'm trying to teach you a lesson? Once you lose something, you never get it back. That's *life*, see?" And before she can react he plucks the photograph from her hand and tears it into a hundred tiny pieces and throws them into the crowd like confetti.

The Little Girl gasps. The bits of her home scatter in the wind.

"Want my advice?" Pierrot's face is suddenly weary, with no trace of a smile. "Hold on to that penny."

The Little Lost Girl turns away. She does not say good-bye to Pierrot and she does not pick up her soiled shoes, but starts walking again, barefoot now, looking for her own house with the white fence and the yellow trim and the swing hanging down from the live-oak tree outside. And if she hasn't found it, she's walking still.

Cash is cold. That's what Mr. Copper said. That's what I tried to remember. I did not think he would disapprove of me selling Momma's fetishes to Dr. Manzetti. But as for the other Riders . . . In the days after I called Professor Manzetti, I tried not to look at them. I did not dare close the chifforobe doors, not after the Widow had opened them, but I did my best never to look inside. For all that, I could still feel the Preacher's hard gaze on my back when I was sitting at the kitchen table, or the Widow's pinched and malevolent stare. Worst of all was Pierrot's leer. I could not say whether he approved or disapproved of what I meant to do. But I knew that I amused him, and that was no good feeling.

Richard Manzetti said he couldn't come the following week to view Momma's memorabilia as he had a conference to attend. I vetoed the week after that, so as not to look too desperate to sell. Finally the appointment was set for May 1. For the first time in months I felt able to relax.

"You want to sell your mother's things?" Daddy asked when I told him about Dr. Manzetti's offer.

"You bet. We can split the money three ways."

"I don't want any of it."

"Daddy. Be reasonable." He didn't answer. "Daddy, I really need it. I'm out of a job and I have a child on the way. This is a miracle. This is like maternity leave from God. After the baby is three months old, or maybe six, I can put it in daycare and go back to work."

"Sounds like you've got it all figured out."

"Daddy! Are you superstitious, is that it? Are you worried the Riders will be mad?"

"If the Riders don't like it, they will not need my help to deal with you," he said drily.

"Hunh."

We were quiet for a spell.

"Your momma always did like easy money too," my father remarked.

Your parents always know how to poke your bruises.

Still, things were looking up. Morning sickness was past and I had an appetite again. If Daddy disapproved of the idea of selling Momma's papers and fetishes, at least he had not forbidden it. For me, the cash would be a godsend. While money was still flowing out of my bank account instead of in, the rate had slowed since I started living on the cheap, and the prospect of a fat check from Professor Manzetti made things more bearable. I even began to think that it wouldn't be so hard to get a job, which I would do sometime after the baby was born.

Actually it was becoming very hard to think of life after the baby was born. Every parent I talked to said, "You can't imagine what your life will be like!" So I gave up trying. September 20 loomed like a wall on the horizon and I could not think of anything beyond it (other than wondering under what possible circumstances Bill Jr. would be in my garden, playing with my baby. And why would I be smiling about it? Unless I had poisoned his drink a few minutes earlier, that is.)

Not everything was perfect. Carlos was still stalling Candy about marriage, leaving her trapped between her desire never to see his weedy face again and her increasingly desperate sense that there would be hell to pay from the Widow if she didn't do as she had been told.

I worried about the Riders too. Being mounted twice was like being murdered twice. When the gods came into my head, they had obliterated me. Blotted me out. Just thinking about it terrified me, made my heart race and my head begin to pound.

And worse yet, what if I were doomed to be every bit as crazy as Momma? Crazier, maybe. Now that the Riders had come crashing into my life, I didn't think I had the strength to hold them in check even as well as she had. If it hadn't been for Momma's demons, I was sure I could be a good mother. Well, decent. Well, better than mine, anyway.

All my life I had worked so hard to control things. The Riders destroyed that. They did what they wanted and I couldn't stop them. I prayed every night there would be no more possessions. I prayed and I rocked in my bed, holding a pillow to my tummy where my little baby swam, journeying. I was so afraid I might turn into a mother like my mother was.

Then there were the footsteps.

Not heavy ones, not menacing. Light steps, indistinct. The sort of sounds a barefoot child might make. At first I heard them only as I was slipping into sleep, a footfall or two, maybe a light tread on the stair, and then I was dreaming. Finally I decided to stay up and listen for them.

Daddy was out of town, on the road in Louisiana. I was lying in my bed just after midnight listening for phantom footsteps when I felt the baby move for the first time. It was the strangest feeling, a tiny bump, so faint. A few minutes later I felt it again: bump. Light as a cricket brushing against my leg. Light as a moth trapped in my cupped hands. Filled with wonder, I put my fingers ever so gently on my belly. And at that very moment I heard the clear sound of a barefoot child running down the flight of stairs from my parents' floor to the kitchen.

I stayed awake all night with my pillow in my arms. Small noises crept upstairs from down below. The squeak of a kitchen cupboard opening. An hour later, a brief hiss of water from the kitchen tap. I knew it was the Little Lost Girl. Momma used to say you could hear her, late at night, and now I had.

Scared and yet happy, filled with a sense of portent, I drowsed, not daring to fall asleep. And somehow in my drowsing the tiny kicks inside me and the little noises downstairs ran together in my mind, so ever after I remembered them together. Those faint sounds. Those hidden children.

For the first time in my life I was examining every man I saw as a potential mate, and I have to admit my body returned an immediate *Yes!* when I opened the door and saw Richard Manzetti for the first time. He was a small, dark, intense man in his mid-thirties with a lean face, neatly trimmed beard, and very careful eyes. After a couple of brisk pleasantries he went to examine the chifforobe. He stayed there a long time. Finally he turned around. "Ms. Beauchamp, I want you to think very carefully about this decision. The investor who asked me to come here is prepared to offer you thirty thousand dollars for this collection. I would not blame you if you took it. But I would be disappointed."

"I beg your pardon?"

"Right now there are *gods* in that cabinet. By the time they get to the trunk of my car, they will be just puppets. That is a loss."

"If you think that, Dr. Manzetti, then you have never lived with a god."

"Maybe." His black hair was rather coarse. His eyes were very dark brown, almost black, with lots of tiny wrinkles around them. "Maybe you're right. And after all, they swapped Christ for thirty pieces of silver."

"I know you," I said suddenly. "You're the Preacher. You think you're here on your own, but actually it's the

Preacher trying to get to me. I should have known they wouldn't go quietly."

Professor Manzetti looked at me for a long time. "I am not aware of being anyone's instrument," he said carefully.

"On my eighth birthday the Preacher gave me a whipping for caring too much about my presents," I said. "Daddy had to be out of town the whole week and wasn't there to stop him. Momma had worked for two hours to bake me a cake, and afterwards there was a scribble-card from Candy and a new bicycle and a pretty yellow sundress. Momma had painted me the most beautiful card, six wild ponies running together. But the Preacher got her just as I was blowing out the candles. Threw the cake in the garbage to teach me a lesson. Ripped up the card. 'Vanity, vanity.' That's what he said."

"I didn't mean—"

"Don't you dare lecture me about gods," I said. "Don't you ever dare."

"Okay."

"If you wouldn't trade a god for thirty pieces of silver, then you're a damn fool, Dr. Manzetti. I would like to see you one time when your head started to ache and you went dizzy and Sugar murdered you with the smell of peaches. I'd like to see just how much you'd like it. I'd like to see how you would feel three hours later when you woke up and found you had whored yourself to the gas station attendant. That really happened, you know. Me and Candy in the car for twenty minutes and Momma in the bathroom with the gas jockey. We were driving back from somewhere, maybe San Antone, and she was so ashamed when Sugar left her head. Did you write a paper about this, Dr. Manzetti? Do you know this story? How about the part where I wouldn't stop crying so she made me get out of the car on the side of the highway and then drove off saying that was what I deserved? Drove on out of sight. Came back for me forty minutes later. Did you write that up? Is that the holiness you are searching for? Or are the Little Lost Girl stories the only ones you care about?''

Just then I finally realized it wasn't me, Toni, talking anymore. Toni would have sat and seethed, or told Professor Manzetti to screw off. But not daunted him. Not tried to hurt him. 'If you wouldn't trade a god for thirty pieces of silver . . . ' That was purely Momma, in her best Gypsy Bitch incarnation.

It worked like magic. Professor Manzetti stood there at the kitchen table absolutely paralyzed, partly ashamed and partly fascinated and utterly hooked. I almost blew the whole effect of my speech by giggling; I almost lost it at the sight of him, still as a cat in the dog pound, trying to figure out what to say next.

My God, my mother was a bitch. Not your common or garden variety bitch, though. Momma was the Notre Dame of bitches, the Empire State Building. She had range like a B52 and more stopping power than a .357 Magnum. Women like her should only happen in operas. And like any woman in the opera, she had a boundless capacity for love. God she loved us. Me and Candy and Angela, John Simmons and Mary Jo and Daddy too. It's a wonder we were all still breathing.

I decided to ease up on poor Dr. Manzetti. Actually, I found him attractive as hell, even though he was kind of a bastard. I liked the little black hairs on his forearms. I liked his sense of principle, although it was woefully misguided in the case of the Riders. And I like a man who can hold his silence. I have come to see restraint as a great virtue. "You said you wrote a paper on Momma. Did you ever come here to see her?"

"No. I phoned and talked to your mother once, but she said she didn't want to see me or answer my questions. I tried to respect her privacy."

I laughed. "Privacy? Momma loved an audience. She just didn't care for the truth, that's the problem. I can just see her face at the idea of a trained scientist coming to investigate her. It would be like inviting the IRS to come over for a friendly audit. Still, you should have called back again the next day, you know. Momma probably would have said yes. I don't think she could resist any listener for long."

"I wish I'd known that." He walked back over to the chifforobe. Carefully he reached for Mr. Copper's polished fetish. "May I?"

"No." The word was out before I even stopped to think.

"Okay." His hand froze and then retreated.

"Sorry. We just . . . we don't touch those," I said.

"Okay." He took a step back, away from the chifforobe.

"Sorry," I said again, and immediately felt stupid for having told him not to touch the dolls, and doubly stupid for feeling stupid about it. Why are we always apologizing to men when we haven't done anything wrong? "So how did you come to hear about Momma?"

"When I was an undergraduate I went to New Orleans one year for Reading Week. I had a bit too much to drink," he said. "I got lost."

I waited. "And?"

He looked at me. "I got really lost. So lost I wasn't

really in New Orleans anymore. I was down on the east side of the Quarter . . ." He stopped. "I haven't told this story very often."

"Am I supposed to promise not to laugh? Don't worry, Dr. Manzetti. I have a lot more experience believing impossible things than most people."

He smiled. "I guess you do. And please, call me Rick." I nodded. "The short version is that I wandered out of New Orleans and into some other city. It was *like* New Orleans, but it was like New Orleans in a dream, or a story by Kafka. If cities were people, that was what a city might dream. Does that make sense?"

I thought of the long, empty streets through which the Little Lost Girl was always walking, walking, walking, the black girls with their curling fingernails and Pierrot blowing fire on the street corner. "Oh yes," I said. "I know that city well."

"I didn't think I was there that long. An afternoon and most of a night, I would have said. Finally I dozed off on a park bench. When I woke, I was back in New Orleans. Seven days had passed." He looked at me. "You must think I was really drunk."

I laughed. "I guarantee you that few people alive can tell the difference between liquor and miracles more easily than me. Were your parents worried?"

"Hysterical." He grinned. "They made me move back in with them until I finished my undergrad degree. But I went to Tulane for my master's just to return to New Orleans. I never found my way back into that other city, but when I was doing my master's, I talked to some old vodoun women who mentioned the Texas Girl."

"Somehow you heard a story about the Little Lost Girl—"

"And I knew. Yeah."

"Are you religious?"

"Sort of. I guess I'm sort of a twisted Catholic," Rick said. "I don't know. The more I learn, the less sure I feel about what to believe." He squatted, looking at Pierrot. Pierrot leered back.

"Momma never went to church. 'If God wants to find me, He can hunt me down,' she used to say. Which he did, I guess. They did. I don't know much about where she grew up, except that whatever little town it was, it was deep blue Baptist. Momma always said she felt like a lion in a den of Daniels." Rick laughed. I liked that. "Momma didn't call them Riders for nothing, you know. When a god comes into your head he kills you to make room. The Riders hounded my mother all her life. She would have done anything to be free of them."

"Do you think so?" he said. "Really?"

I looked at him for a long time. "No. You're right. She wouldn't have given them up. It was me who wanted the Riders gone." I stood up, suddenly upset. My tummy, just beginning to swell, bumped the edge of the table. "Would you like a Coke?" I said. I'd picked up some of the good stuff Mary Jo had found for Daddy to drink, even though the pregnancy books wouldn't let me have any myself. "It's real old Coke. There's a little Mexican *tienda* where you can still get it."

"No thanks."

I got my Coke—Classic Caffeine Free in a can, of course. Sigh. "Momma used to say, 'Be careful what you wish for; you just might get it.' I think we would all be a lot safer without gods."

At that exact moment I heard a laugh. A tiny, mean snicker, quiet but unmistakable. It came from the chifforobe. My heart stopped; then raced, smashing against my ribs.

"Let's talk about money," I said. I tried to keep the panic from my voice. Oh God, I had dallied too long. I could feel the Riders staring at me from the chifforobe, staring and staring. I had to get them out of the house, out of my life, quickly, quickly.

"That was abrupt," Rick said. "May I sit down?"

"Please."

He sat at the kitchen table with his back to the chifforobe and took a calculator from his briefcase. "Thirty thousand for the fetishes, I said that. They're the keystone of any collection. Would you be willing to sell the cabinet as well?"

"The chifforobe? Sure, yes, please. Everything. Take it all." My heart was still racing and my stomach was tight, as if I were standing like Mary Keith on the edge of a building, holding my baby, my beautiful baby, the dizzy world one sickening step away.

The baby gave a little kick and I gasped.

"Are you okay?"

"Yes, fine. Come on, let's get on with it."

He looked at me. "Are you sure you are feeling well enough? You look quite pale."

"I'm fine! Write. Write, please."

He looked at me again. "Now, you said that there was a whole body of Little Lost Girl stories that went with the Riders, is that correct? I would very much like to record as many of them as you can remember."

"Yes, okay, we can talk about that some other—" The left chifforobe door trembled and then creaked a little further open. A long sharp nose emerged from the gloom, and a long sharp chin with it. Pierrot grinned at me from his shelf and laid one thin finger on his lips.

"Oh my God."

"What was that?"

"Nothing," I whispered.

Rick Manzetti checked his Day-Timer. "I have to be back in New Orleans by the fifth. Would you have time for us to start collecting stories in the next couple of days?"

Pierrot toppled forward, turned a somersault in midair, and landed on the tile floor with a soft thump, like a cat jumping off a sofa. Rick didn't seem to notice. I tried to speak, but no words came out. I wet my lips and tried again. "Fine. That would be fine."

"Good." Rick made some notes on a pad of yellow scratch paper and and punched more numbers into his calculator. I could barely see him. My vision had fled, as if in a dream; all I could see was the tiny doll-sized figure of Pierrot advancing over the tile floor. He turned a handspring, paused, and executed a lordly bow. Then he scuttled across the floor like a crab and fetched up against my chair leg.

Rick noticed nothing. "Can you think of anything to add? Any old potions, old books, family albums, photographs? I'd be interested in any of it."

"No," I said, remembering with despair the two glasses of Mockingbird Cordial that Candy tricked me into drinking the day we buried Momma. I felt a tiny tug on the bottom of my skirt, then another, slightly higher. Pierrot was climbing up the outside of it.

"All right. If you change your mind, just let me know. For the collection we've already discussed, fetishes, cabinet, and stories, I'm prepared to offer . . . um, thirty-five thousand dollars.'' He met my eyes. .

"That's a lot of money," I said. Pierrot was inching his way around my lap, just under the edge of the table. With a sudden jerk he swung himself around so that he was climbing up the back of my chair, still hidden from the anthropologist. I bit my lip to keep from screaming. Over in the chifforobe, the Widow was pacing along her shelf: back and forth, back and forth, staring at me with her black button eyes.

"The collector who first alerted me to your mother's, ah, passing, is very affluent," Rick. said.

Something hard and sharp bumped against the back of my neck, and a small voice said, "I'll bet you your life I can bite my eye."

I screamed. "Oh God! I'm sorry, they're not for sale. Any of it. I have to keep them, I have to keep them all, oh Christ. God damn it, I have to keep them all."

I cried and cried, helpless and shaking.

"You want my advice?" Pierrot said as the door closed on fine, smart, handsome Dr. Richard Manzetti and his thirty-five thousand dollars. *Hold on to that penny.*

After Rick Manzetti was gone, I stalked to the chifforobe and demanded of the Widow how she meant for me to keep my family, how I was to provide for the child growing inside me. Now, when I really needed to hear her, the Widow didn't answer. The gods never do.

For that matter, the Widow didn't seem to be giving Candy much help landing her man, either. The spring dragged on, and when Carlos finally spoke about the possibility of marrying Candy, he was talking with me. It was a few days after my aborted meeting with Rick Manzetti that Carlos asked me to come for a ride in the Muerto-mobile. It was Cinco de Mayo, the fifth of May, always a big day in the Hispanic community, celebrating Mexico's independence from the Spanish. It was also pretty close to four and a half months for me: halfway through my pregnancy. I finally had a bit of a tummy, just a little bulge above the seat belt.

A tiny skeleton—whittled from real human bone, Carlos said—jiggled from the rearview mirror. I wished Carlos a happy Cinco de Mayo and he wished me the same. Then, more delicately, he said, "Candy tells me there will be no money from the professor after all. *Los duendes* drove him away. Too bad."

"You can only be luckier than average fifty percent of the time."

"*Es verdad.*" Carlos had shown up on the doorstep like a man braced to make out his will, saying he had to talk to me. It was just past lunchtime, 85 degrees outside, and Carlos was in his summer uniform, a white muscle shirt that showed parts of his tattoos: red lines radiating from the Sacred Heart on his left breast; the top edge of a Mayan mandala that covered much of his thin back, and black widow spiders, six or seven of them, scuttling along his ropy arms. I had invited him in for a beer, but he shook his head. "No, we should not talk here, *por favor*. Anyplace else you like, or just in the car maybe. I need to talk to you alone."

"I am alone. Daddy's on the road."

"Your pardon," he said, "but you are not." And he glanced at the chifforobe where Momma's gods were watching us.

So it was I found myself in the front seat of the Muertomobile, sinking in crushed red velvet as we rolled solemnly through the residential Montrose streets. It was hot and horribly humid but the hearse predated air conditioning, so all I could do was roll down the window. Sluggish waves of sweaty Houston air oozed into the car. A year before I would have said it smelled like hot grass and engine exhaust, but now my pregnancy-enhanced nose discriminated a much more complex chemical bouquet:

warm asphalt gave off its distinctive scent as it softened
in the sun, for instance. There was the car wax Carlos had
buffed lovingly into the Muertomobile's body, and the hot
rubber stink of its big black tires. Somewhere lilacs were
blooming. And, too, the refineries on the east side of town
added their own aromas to the air, tinctures of sulfur and
diesel fuel and burning plastic. Two days earlier, according
to the radio news, environmental toxicologists had discov-
ered noticeable quantites of xylene, an industrial solvent,
in the groundwater over in Baytown. They had been called
to investigate because kids in the local trailer parks were
waking up in the middle of the night with bloody noses
they got from *breathing*.

Not that the pollution seemed to stop Houston's veg-
etation. Industrial effluent might as well have been vitamins as far as the local flora was concerned. Pecan and
sycamore trees had unfurled their leaves, the monkey grass
gleamed gunmetal-blue and green, and the cardinals and
mockingbirds were feasting on the season's first fresh crop
of mosquitoes. There were frogs and lizards on our patio
every day, so many I had taken to closing the French doors
sometimes.

This year looked to be a season of vines. More ivy than
I ever remembered ran up the brick houses in our neighborhood, beards of Spanish moss hung thick from all the
live-oak trees, and the signposts at the end of the street
had been engulfed by scarlet runner beans so that the
street names were hidden. It reminded me of Bill Jr.'s vision of Houston reclaimed by the swamp, a Lost City in
the jungle. Brown bayou water would seep over the asphalt and alligators would bask on the hoods of cars lying
abandoned on the drowned expressways. Catfish would
nose through the first floor of our house, swimming into

the chifforobe where Momma's gods would lie rotting. A dense canopy of swamp pine, live-oak, and vine maple would close overhead. In the night, infernal yellow fire would still spit and roar from the deathless refineries on the east side of town.

"So. I am not sure I can marry your sister." Carlos made a little clicking sound with his tongue against his teeth. The black widow on his right bicep rose and sank as he turned onto Mulberry Street and cruised down toward Westheimer following a Lincoln Town Car with a *Holy Spirit On Board!* bumper sticker. He glanced at me again. "This is private, hey? *Solamente entre nosotros.*"

"*Bueno.*"

We turned left onto Westheimer, passing Taurian Body Piercing and 2nd To None Resale Boutique and Dragon-Forge Custom Jewelry and Tarot Cards. "Two things. First, Candy . . . Candy is a nice girl. I like her. She makes a good girlfriend. But a wife? I don't know. A wife means a house. A family. But Candy . . . she does not have a very serious mind, no? She is not like you. She works in a bar. Is that enough for a child, I ask myself: a mother who works in a bar?"

"Carlos! You paint cars!"

"This is different."

"I'll bet Candy makes as much as you do in a day, when you add up her tips."

"It is not a matter of money," Carlos said with dignity. "Well, okay, it is a little. I don't think I want my kid in a public school." He shook his head, making the tiny inverted crucifix dangling from his ear bob and swing. "Too many bad kids in the public schools. Maybe we need to send the kids to a private school, maybe a Catholic school—that's a lot of *dinero.*"

I struggled with a vision of Carlos's tiny Mexican witch-daughter with inverted crucifix earrings sitting demurely in a Catholic elementary school with her little hands folded across a workbook.

"Beside the money, it's a matter of dignity. What I do with cars, it's part of my dignity. I'm not saying my wife has to be rich. But what if I have a daughter, eh? The mother of my daughter should have a dignity, you see? She should not be working only for the money."

I felt sweat stains blooming under my arms and along the waistband of my maternity shorts. "Not everyone can be a priest, Carlos. Some people just have to work for a living. They find their dignity in different places."

"*Si*, okay, but where is Candy's, eh?" We waited at the light at Westheimer and Montrose, across from Oh Boy! Boots and Shoes, which I would lay good money sells more pairs of genuine calf, ostrich, and rattlesnake cowboy boots to gay men than any other store on the planet. "I think you grabbed up all the serious mind. Candy is drifting. A mother needs a more serious mind."

Ah. Suddenly I thought I could hear the steely voice of La Hag Gonzales. I patted my tummy. "Carlos, I promise you no woman has a baby without getting a serious mind. You don't drift with a baby in your tummy. It holds you down."

He made that clicking sound again, then nodded. "Okay. Maybe you are right. You know, I was real worried about the money thing, until I found out you were *embarazada*. Pregnant. I thought, well, if she can do it, by herself, no husband, then for sure Candy and me could be brave enough."

We passed Slick Willie's on our left. Only two cars in the parking lot; they would have just opened. I wondered if Candy was on shift. "Uh—glad to be so inspirational," I said. Oh Carlos, if you knew how terrified I was, you would not take courage from my example.

(Momma and Daddy have been fighting, one of those fights where she screams and cries, while Daddy's voice stays calm and level until he leaves the house "to run errands." Momma stays at the kitchen table long after his Impala has pulled out of the driveway and disappeared into the night. "Men call *us* emotional," Momma says. "That's horseshit, Toni. Men are the romantics. They think they can keep everything under control." She lights a cigarette. "I think I want a beer. You want a beer, honey?" I am thirteen. I shake my head. Momma rummages in the refrigerator and pulls out a bottle of Tecate. She comes back to the table and pokes my chest with one long carmine fingernail. Bits of ash from her cigarette get on my T-shirt. "Women see too clearly not to despair.")

Carlos turned right seemingly at random and we were rolling through a neighborhood of faded Southern Gothic mansions, some in lovely condition, with wide balconies and restored porch swings, others falling apart like blowzy Southern belles many years past their prime. We passed a smaller, Georgian affair that cowered under a tremendous live oak. "Momma once said that a lot of Southern history is explained by the fact that every good-sized live oak has a few limbs at just the right height to hang a man," I told Carlos. You could have dangled a score of bad guys from this monster. "You said there were two things that kept you from marrying Candy. Her job was one. And the other?"

Carlos nodded. "*Sí.* The truth is—*perdón,* Toni—I am not so crazy about my mother-in-law."

"*You?* You aren't crazy about *your* mother-in-law?"

He turned right again, heading back west through the residential streets. "What do you mean by that?"

"But—Carlos! She's dead! Candy's mother is in the ground, *comprende*?"

He nodded gloomily. "*Sí*. If she was alive, that would be one thing. But the dead . . . the dead are not reasonable, Toni. You see? Maybe if your sainted mother was alive, she would try hard to get along, you know? She would want to see her grand-babies. She would hold her tongue, as my mother does. But the dead? No. In my experience they are *muy tercos*. Very bossy."

"Your mother couldn't hold her tongue with a spaghetti fork!"

Carlos looked at me. "I am not here to talk about *Mamá*. I am telling you I am not so easy with marrying into this family. This is my point."

"You don't know anything about my mother. Didn't she always make you welcome in our house?"

"Yes, but—"

"Whose family are you going to marry into then, Carlos? Some dour *chica*, get out of your bed every Wednesday for the five o'clock Mass—you think she's going to want you, with your tattoos and your medicine bags and your death car?"

Carlos frowned. "A family is not a game. It's not for fun. It's serious. My kids, I want them to grow up right."

"Listen, you will never find a better wife than Candy, someone who will put up with your craziness, who *feels* why it's important to light the candles on the hood of your car, who can touch those bones and still be happy, can walk in the sunlight. Candy is perfect for you. If you are too blind to see that, you deserve whatever wife you settle for."

Carlos chewed on his mustache. "This is what my mother says."

"La Hag? I mean, Mrs. Gonzales thinks you should marry Candy?"

"Mm. But a man can't choose his wife to please his mother, " Carlos said. "I have been trying to think it through." We were back to Montrose, by the old Carnegie Library. Carlos swung majestically into the center lane, cutting off a Honda whose driver put down his cell phone long enough to flip us the finger.

"So the reason you haven't said yes to Candy is that she had too much support from your mother."

"Maybe. Okay."

Momma used to say, "Wonders will never cease." Just that once, she surely was not lying.

Later that night Candy called to say that Carlos had accepted her proposal. The wedding was set for September 20th. Everything was right in her world.

It nearly killed me.

I had expected to be relieved for her, or glad, or just amused. Instead, the fragile calm I had been trying to hold around myself shattered. There would be no large check from Rick Manzetti; the Riders had seen to that. I was four and a half months pregnant, showing now, with no job and no father for my child. There would be no Daddy to protect the baby from me. It would absorb my every mistake.

No. I couldn't let that happen. I had struck out at the Bookstop, my date with Bill Jr. had been a disaster, but I could not allow myself to quit hunting. Rick Manzetti was back in New Orleans, but I called and left a message on his machine suggesting that I would be happy to tell him some of the Little Lost Girl stories as soon as he could come back to Houston. Then, to make sure I wasn't missing any chances, I called up my old friend Greg, the one Momma had terrorized in the pharmacy as he tried to buy a pack of condoms.

As a potential father, Greg had some liabilities. He was not reliable. He was not a man with a strong direction in life. He didn't have a good steady job, nor did he seem to want one. But he was funny, and charming, and good-looking, and he had said more than once that he looked forward to having children.

I asked Greg if he wanted to see a movie with me and he said yes.

Now I had to figure out how to push our date past the point of just being friends. Any relationship will go on just as it always has unless you work to change it, or one of the parties goes away and comes back a different person. Well, I had changed, hadn't I? Before Momma died, I had never been mounted by a Rider. I had never been pregnant. I had never been unemployed. Hard to call these improvements, of course.

Once again I wished I was Candy. For the first time I regretted spending all that time catching baseballs instead of men. Humiliating, but there it was: I was more comfortable in a mask and chest protector than in a short skirt and nylons. I was the catcher on the girl's softball team, which went to the city finals and lost out to the Bellaire Bullets. Catcher is a good position to play if you're bow-legged but smart.

I don't think girls everywhere know how to play ball quite like we do in Texas. I'm not saying they don't have good teams, but I think sports is closer to religion here than most places. Thanks to Daddy I knew how to call a game. I knew why 2 and 1 with two men out was a running count and I had a good arm for the throw to second base. I knew how to turn my wrists over when swinging to lift a ball over the infield and how to inside-out a pitch on the outer half of the plate and drive it to the opposite field. I could lay down a bunt if the situation called for it. I was a singles hitter, like most girls, but I was good enough to hit third for our team, because nobody was better at advancing a runner.

Was there such a thing as a dating slump? And if there was, I wondered if there were lessons to be learned from baseball. The worst hitting slump I ever went through was in my junior year in high school. The longer I went without a few decent at-bats, the worse my swing got. I started pressing. After we lost the last game of the regular season, I was 2 for my last 17.

"You're thinking too much," Daddy told me after the game. I remember him looking patiently across the steering wheel at me, his round chin stubbled with greying whiskers. "It's your head that gets you in trouble, Toni. The body remembers."

I didn't say anything, but I stopped taking batting practice. I left the kitchen if there was a ballgame on the radio. I even skipped one team meeting, pretending I had a doctor's appointment. When the playoffs started, I knew the other pitcher was going to want to go strike one, and I resolved to swing at the first pitch even if I had to golf it on the third hop. It came straight over the center of the plate and I drilled it off the pitcher's knee and into left field. For the rest of the playoffs I never touched a bat until I was standing in the on-deck circle. I led all hitters, going 10 for 21 with three walks, three sacrifices, and 9 RBI.

I was remembering that playoff run as I was trying to decide what to wear on my date with Greg. I considered the silk shantung jacket, but it hadn't been lucky for me with Bill Jr. Besides, it was fitted, and I was scared that if I tried it on, my little tummy would make it look funny and I would know I had passed the Pregnant Lady line and could no longer be sexy.

I wandered into the kitchen and looked at the reflection staring at me from the window above the kitchen sink. The reflection was half hidden behind the leaves of a peppermint plant. Those Beauchamp women, always half hidden in the foliage. Then something a little bit magical happened. A slow, lazy smile crept over the reflection. I wasn't smiling, but the reflection was. She leaned forward and looked at me. Her bangs fell across her eyes. I pushed mine aside to see her face better. It was my face. And now I could feel that my mouth had curved into just her lazy smile.

She laughed, a low, husky laugh. "Hey, sweet child," said a voice which was not quite my voice. It was deep as the South, lazy as a bayou. I picked up that voice like an instrument left lying for me to find, an instrument I knew but had forgotten. "Hey Sugar," I said, smiling back.

Maybe I was crazy then; maybe it was all the worry that had left me weak, that made me call Sugar to myself. I walked over to the chifforobe, my feet bare and alive to the kiss of the cool tile. I reached into Sugar's cubby and searched among the sweet and scented things there and took the ones whose touch most pleased me: a silk scarf the color of mangoes; a brooch for my dark hair; a tiny crystal thimble of perfume. Then I went upstairs to change. I did not let the goddess all the way in; not wholly. I left her laughing at me from my kitchen window. But *the body remembers*, I whispered to myself as I climbed the stairs and dressed myself and touched the scent to my wrists. In the Galleria I had *been* Sugar, that sweet one who desired. If I could just stop thinking, my body would remember.

There must be some gifts, I figured, that I could choose to accept.

Later on, sometime after midnight, Greg pulled himself alongside my sweaty body and propped his head up on his elbow. I could just see his smile in the faint blue light of the digital clock beside his bed. I stretched like a cat and purred, the last phantom of Sugar like a lazy ghost in my limbs. "My God, Greg. What on earth were you doing down there?"

He grinned. "The alphabet. Did you like it?"

I closed my eyes and surreptitiously squeezed my thighs together. "Oh my. How far did you get?"

"I think I was on *M* when you rolled me over."

Greg had filled out a lot since high school. Back then he had been whip-thin, all bangs and elbows. But over the years he had found his father's blocky shoulders and wide back and hams somewhere—in the bottom of a few bottles of beer, probably, where most Texas men seemed to locate their figures. Even his fingers were big and thick. But quick still, and light. He reached his hand toward my belly. "May I?"

"Mm-hmm."

His fingers settled on the bottom of my belly, light as doves. He ran his hand along the small undercurve of my abdomen. "It's hard!"

"You expected Jell-O? I'm not getting fat, you know. That's pure muscle, being pushed and stretched by this watermelon growing inside me." His hand stopped. "Do you find it ugly?"

"I can barely find it at all. When will you really start to show?"

"Soon, I think. I don't know. I've never done this before." I covered his hand with mine. Now that the sex was over I felt shy about touching him. It was definitely awkward to be there, naked, without Sugar inside me.

"Do you ever get freaked out, Toni? I mean, to have this *creature* growing inside you? I think that would be so strange, to have a whole other animal living in me, and then *fwaroom!* bursting out like those things in *Alien*."

"Shut up, Greg. Yuck."

"Do you remember Mr. Boggs in twelfth grade Biology? I still remember him talking about how the fetus was made from undifferentiated cells, just like cancer cells. I thought it was so weird that a baby was like a tumor, only the baby was better organized." He stopped. "Uh-oh. Forgot about your mom. Sorry, kid."

(It is two months before my mother's death. Her mastectomy was too late. Now the cancer is in the left lobe of her brain, and in her spine and her ribs and the bones of her legs. She is in so much pain that tears of fury are standing in her eyes. "Get me some more of that goddam codeine, Toni."

The whole day has gone like this. "I can't let you have it yet."

"Don't tell me what the fuck to do, I'm your mother you little witch." Momma has been drinking to help with the pain. Not that she has to be drunk to talk to me like this. "Oh God I wish I were dead and buried."

"Then let's make it easy on all of us," I say. "Here's the codeine, Momma. Here is the whole bottle. You really want it? Take it. Take every last one. I'll get you a glass of bourbon to wash it down, how about that? How about that?'' I'm so mad, the bottle of pills in my hand is shaking hard enough to rattle.

Momma stares at me, and crumples, and starts to cry, rocking back and forth in her bed. "I want Candy here. I don't want you. Go away, go away. You just want me to die."

But it was me, not Candy, who nursed her through the last two months.)

"I don't want to talk about it."

Greg took his hand off my stomach. "Okay."

I moved his hand up and put it on my left breast. I didn't feel sexy anymore, I felt cold and frightened. But I refused to waste the chance Sugar had made for me. "Oh, Christ, that felt good," I said. "We should have done this before, Greg. I don't know why we never did this before."

"You were never like this before. You've changed."

I tried to smile. "In a good way, I hope."

"Zat remains to be uncovered by ze analysis," he said Freudianly, sitting up in bed. I pulled the sheet up over my breasts. "Don't get me wrong," Greg said. "The sex was good. Really good. I've slept with sexier women who weren't nearly so good in bed."

"I hear a 'but' coming."

He laughed. "But . . . yeah. Tonight . . . it was fun, but it wasn't really you, was it, Toni? It was you and something else. Your voice—I never heard you talk that way before. Slow and lazy. Never seen you walk that way. But your mother did, sometimes."

"Momma?"

"Not that I didn't like your mother. But I sure never wanted to sleep with her."

"I can understand that."

"Used to scare the hell out of me, to be honest," Greg said.

"Me too," I said.

Momma. Momma in me like a cancer, in my bones and brain and lungs.

All in all, you couldn't call my evening with Greg a success. The sex had been fun while Sugar was in me, but embarrassing afterwards. Worse, the idea of marrying a man who saw so much of Momma in me gave me the shivers. Besides, what kind of father would Greg make? Up at all hours, joining amateur blues bands or practicing stage magic or heading down to Austin to audition for a bit part in an independent movie. No job, no income, no set course in life.

No. Once I had been rejected, it was easy to see I had never really wanted him.

With Bill Jr. and Greg out of the running, that left only the dark horse, Rick Manzetti. Though even he was more interested in Momma than he was in me. He returned my phone message and said he would try to make it to Houston early in June to collect some of the Little Lost Girl stories.

The night after my date with Greg I was sitting in the garden with Daddy and we were talking. It was dark and warm under the canopy of live-oak. I hadn't yet laid in the summer's supply of Deep Woods Off to repel the mosquitoes, so I had rummaged through Momma's drawers upstairs until I found half a bottle of Skin-So-Soft to wipe down with. The first grapefruits of the year had come in from the Rio Grande valley and I had squeezed us a couple of glasses of juice.

"Daddy, why did you love Momma?" I asked.

He was quiet a spell, and I let him be. "Just loved her, I reckon. And she needed me. It's a great pull, to be needed." He took a sip of juice. "I don't guess there's a man on earth could live with your Momma if he didn't love her pretty good." Daddy smiled. "Then we had you and Candy. I sure wasn't going to leave my girls."

I had some of my grapefruit juice. Fresh-squeezed it is so much sweeter than you would imagine if you only ever had the canned stuff.

"Your momma used to say, 'Men! You can't live with 'em, and you can't kill 'em.' "

"Remember her apron?" I said. "The Way To A Man's Heart Is Through His Chest."

"I believe she was about the smartest person I ever knew," Daddy said. "Not school-smart, not like you. But she had a way of looking at things that was different from anybody else. You could walk down a street a hundred times with a hundred different people and see the same road; but when you went with Elena, she'd make you see it new."

"I hate that," I said. "I don't like it when things change. I don't think Momma ever saw a thing for what it was. I mean, which song is really the mockingbird's own? It isn't enough to keep pretending. There has to be something solid and real and true and forever. Momma couldn't hold herself together two hours running. If she was happy, she saw one thing. If she was sad, she saw another. One day she was a good mom to us; the next day she was a failure. Was I a bad kid, a good kid, ornery or cranky or dutiful or what? Every time I looked back it seemed like the land-scape behind me flipped around."

"You were a good kid," Daddy said. "A good, ornery kid."

"She was just so sad, Daddy." Unexpectedly I found myself starting to cry. "She was so sad all the time. I used to hate her so much for getting sad like that. I used to think there was something I could do, if only I wasn't so stupid or stubborn or willful. If I could just be good enough, she'd be happy and then she wouldn't—"

"Baby," Daddy said, "it wasn't your job to take care of us."

"But I never had a chance, did I? It was Angela, it was the Little Lost Girl up in Canada, and there was nothing I could have done."

"A team falls apart when everyone is trying to do the next man's job. You have to trust the people around you, Toni."

"What if you can't?" I wiped my eyes with my shirt-sleeve. Daddy didn't answer.

"Do you think I'm like her?" I said.

Daddy thought. "Some. And I think you're like me, some. But mostly you're like you, and you will cut your own swath in the world." He took my hand and gave it a squeeze. "So don't you blame your problems on me, you hear?"

I sniffled and laughed.

"Your momma even foxed me about her epitaph," Daddy said. "Did you know that? We were talking, oh, maybe six months before she died. She was pretty sick. The night before we were supposed to go into the hospital for her checkup she says, 'George, I have an announce-ment to make. I've been thinking about you tonight,

George, and I have decided to inscribe my tombstone in your honor.' And I said, 'Is that right, old lady? And what are you going to write on it?' And she looked me dead in the eye, very serious, and said, 'She Had Great Stuff, But Struggled With Her Control.' "

I have a confession to make.

The day Rick Manzetti came over for the first time, Pierrot never climbed out of the chifforobe and whispered in my ear. I made that up.

I know it seems like a lie, but I swear it isn't. If I had written down what really happened, that I got to feeling worse and worse, and more and more scared, that I felt the Riders' stares from across the room and chickened out and told Rick I couldn't sell, you wouldn't have understood. You would have thought I was just getting emotional. You wouldn't have felt the animal terror in my heart. I had to make you understand, had to make you feel what it was really like. Because what I wrote back then, about the weight of Pierrot tugging on my dress, his mean little voice in my ear—that's the truth. It didn't happen, but it's the truth, I swear it. I swear it.

—Which is what Momma would say.

Oh God, I don't know, I don't know. Am I turning into a liar, just like her? That's what Greg said, he said I was like her. I let Sugar in, just as she would have.

But *I'm not her.* I know I'm not. I know I'm not.

Is it possible she was right all those years? That all the time I thought she was lying, she was telling the truth, but I just didn't understand it? I didn't want to hear it?

Who was the liar? Who told the truth? Who is writing this, her or me?

I thought when she died that I would be rid of her at last, but I'm not. It's like Carlos said: alive she was a monster, but dead she's inescapable.

Oh God, Momma. Please let me go.

EIGHT

I was turning into my mother. I was living in her house now, I was the oldest woman in the family; it was me who had to look after Daddy, me who had the child on the way. And I, who had been so sure of myself and who I was—not Momma, mostly—felt myself begin to melt in the May heat, my edges running, my outlines less definite. I was not the daughter I had been, for my mother was gone. My job was gone too, and the safe future I had always meant to make with my actuary's money. I had tried to find a lover in Bill first, then Greg; both had seen my mother instead of me. I had tried to give away Momma's gods and her gods had forbidden it.

Even my body was for the first time not wholly my own. There was another person growing in me, who would have a different face and story, and for the first time I found myself wondering what my mother had thought when it was *me* growing in her belly. Could I really have been as strange and different a being to her as the baby in my womb already was to me? Could she have worried so much about my future, wondered whether I would be left- or right-handed, fretted at the cost of college education, tried to decide whether it was best to breast or bottle feed?

It wasn't only my baby that grew within me all through that hot spring; I was carrying my mother too.

We were nearing the end of May, and snake weather had come in earnest: air so humid you couldn't strike a match in it; heat so intense you could see your shadow sweat. The skyscrapers downtown shimmered and smoked in the hazy air. When it rained, the air was blind with water for twenty minutes. Afterwards the streets smelled of oleanders and boiling tar.

The Saturday after my disastrous date with Greg I went over to Candy's apartment to help mail out wedding invitations. I was dreading the visit. My sister has a thing about not using air conditioning. Even Momma, though she left the house doors open, would at least run the a.c. in her Oldsmobile. Candy just drove with the windows down.

Candy lived on the top floor of a shared house. She had no kitchen table because she had no kitchen (she shared the one downstairs). So we sat on the floor on either side of her coffee table to work. Candy wrote up the invitations; I addressed the envelopes. We each had a glass of iced tea with a wedge of lime. Candy, curse her, was sitting cross-legged in a halter top and a pair of panties. I was wearing a Men's Size XL Astros T-shirt and a pair of awful navy-blue polyester maternity shorts that itched on my abdomen. "This is unbearable," I said, interrupting my own story about my date with Greg. "I can't come over here anymore. I feel like a boiled prawn."

"You're hot?" Candy said, surprised. I glared at her. My skin was slippery with sweat under my arms and between my legs and behind my knees. "I've got a fan, Toni. Just a minute."

"Did you know my blood volume is going to go up by thirty percent over the next four months?"

"You mentioned that a few times. Is that why you're hot?"

"No, I'm hot because it's incredibly hot in here. The blood thing is why I'm even hotter." The fan was new and lightweight, a twenty-dollar Target special. Candy set it on the floor behind me, turned it on, and watched all the wedding invites blow gaily off her coffee table. Careful repositioning followed.

She sat back down before her stack of blank invitations. "Tía Gomez next, right?" Sweat glistened on her forehead, and among the nearly invisble hairs on her upper lip, and between her breasts. The skin showing between her halter top and her panties was as brown as her tanned arms. "So Greg really said it was like screwing Momma, hey? Ouch." Candy looked at me. "You put on Sugar, didn't you?"

"How did you know that?"

"Sugar was Momma's idea of sex. Here's the card for Tía Gomez." I stuck it in its envelope, sealed and stamped it. Candy wiped her sweaty hands off on her halter top so she wouldn't get blotches on her next note. "I bet that's your idea of sex, too."

"What?"

"Sugar." I didn't answer. "That isn't sex. That was Momma."

I thought of the silks in Sugar's cubby back at the house, and the tiny crystal bottle of perfume.

"That's the great Texas lie." Candy put down her pen and stood up. Her attic room was small, with a sloping ceiling. She walked to the window at the front and looked out over the crepe myrtle which had not yet begun to bloom. I wondered if anyone passing could see her, standing there in her underwear. Then I wondered if she would care. "The great Texas lie says we trick men, we cheat and lie and trap them. We lure them into marriage. Pink toenails and a ribbon in your hair, like tying a trout fly. That's Sugar's style," Candy said. "I never believed that."

"I guess we don't either of us like to lie, do we?"

Candy said, "If you want good sex, start with Mr. Copper. Don't look so astonished, Toni. Your trouble is you think about money too much. You only think of Mr. Copper's power one way. But he's about seeing things exactly as they are. There's no make-believe when you see through Mr. Copper's eyes—Hang on. I want to show you something." She walked to the dresser beside her bed and pulled open the bottom drawer.

The ice in my iced tea clinked and wobbled as I held the cold glass against my cheek. The fan passed back and forth across my sweaty body.

"Every time you go to the grocery store you see rack after rack of women's magazines trying to sell you the secret of 'How to Get a Man,' " Candy said. " 'What Men *Really* Want in Bed. How to Turn Him On.' All of them full of ads for moisturizer and pantyhose and deodorant and crap. Like Daddy says, when a man is trying to sell you something, be careful." Candy came back and dropped a stack of porn magazines on the table. HOT LEZZIE LICKS! screamed the top magazine. Two naked blondes knelt together to French kiss with their boobs touching. The taller one was looking at the camera. *Want to help us cum?* read the caption.

"Candy!"

"*Hustler* isn't trying to sell anything," Candy said. "Not to you and me, anyway. *Hustler, Velvet, Club International*—they measure their success by how often their readers jack off per issue." She flipped open the magazine. " 'If you want to know What Really Turns Him On, here it is, straight from the horse's—' "

"Candy!"

" '—mouth.' " She grinned and reached over my shoulder, flipping past the table of contents. I had a confused impression of buff-colored skin, blond hair, pouting mouths, large breasts, many kinds of underwear, women holding their vaginas open. Mouths, lots of mouths: red lipsticked ones, smiling ones, tongues stuck out toward cocks, mouths slack with passion, bitten lips, kissing, one mouth dripping with saliva. Little hot needles of embarrassment prickled across my face and my eyes slid off the pages. I couldn't make myself look, and when I did look, I couldn't take much in. The pictures were gone too fast, I looked away before I had time to understand them.

"Go ahead and stare, Toni. It's not like you're sneaking a peek in a drugstore. No one's going to 'catch' you." Candy turned another page and held it open. *Tammy & Sue:* a blonde with a ponytail and a brunette with short hair. The blonde had on a letterman's jacket. The brunette was the smaller girl, a winsome knockout wearing a tweed skirt and glasses. *The other girls think Tammy and Sue are boring bookworms. They go off to a frat party, not realizing that our girls have been waiting for a chance to bone up on each other!!!*

In the first picture the women were kissing, mouth to mouth. The blonde's jacket was open, her white shirt unbuttoned, her bra peeking out. The brunette's eyes were closed behind her glasses. In the next picture, the brunette's tweed skirt was gone. She was upright on her knees on a bed. The blonde had pulled her panties down. They stretched taut across the gap between her legs, a few inches below the curly hair of her pussy. The blonde had the practiced smile of a professional model. The brunette was a better actress. She seemed vulnerable, her smile half-timid, amazed, hardly daring to feel so much delight. She seemed so happy.

In the third picture the brunette was crouching before the blonde, who now wore only white mid-thigh stockings and a bra she had peeled down so it lay like a hank of white cloth under her enormous breasts. The brunette was sticking her tongue out an inch from her friend's pubic hair. She was still wearing her glasses.

After this it was positions.

The photographer knew his business. Though the blonde had the more outrageous body, it was the smaller-breasted brunette who had by far the more expressive face. He always caught her looks for the camera: her naughty glee, fingering her friend, or her blind, naive ecstasy, pulling the blond's ponytail tightly between the lips of her vulva.

The brunette never took off her glasses. Her friend never rolled down her stockings. It was impossible to tell which one was Tammy and which was Sue.

"Forget what it says in *Cosmo*. First lesson: guys like to see women fucking each other."

"Good Lord, these aren't boobs, they're volleyballs."

Candy said, "Does it turn you on, Toni?"

"Isn't it about five thousand to get your boobs done? I guess she wanted her money's worth."

Candy gently reached out and turned my face so I had to look at her. "Toni. Does it turn you on?"

I stared blindly at the photographs. One part of me was greedy to take them in, but I couldn't. Embarrassment blinded me. More than embarrassment. Shame. My eyes saw the pictures but my brain slid away from them. "Leave me alone."

Candy turned the page. A redhead in a nightie lolled on a frilly little-girl's bed with her legs spread. Clown and balloon wallpaper. Stuffed animals all around. Nineteen pretending to be fourteen, I guessed.

"How about her?"

"Candy!"

"Lesson Two: they all like young bodies. A lot of them also like the idea of fucking really young girls."

She flipped forward to the next pictorial. "Lesson three: they like the idea of fucking you in the ass." In this set of pictures a guy in a NASCAR jumpsuit was fucking a woman in mechanic's overalls. They screwed on, in, and around a cherry-red racing car. You could never see actual penetration, but in several pictures they were clearly supposed to be having anal sex, her sitting in his lap with her back to him, spreading the lips of her vulva with her fingers, obviously in part to show that wasn't where his cock was. His hands grabbed tight on her huge breasts.

"I think you don't know what turns you on," Candy said. "You can't tell. You can't even think about it."

"Screw off! Does it turn you on?"

"Yeah. Some of it." She tapped the anal sex picture. "This one. I like her face. He doesn't do it for me. I could skip these," she said, pointing to another couple of pictures. She sat down beside me and paged back through the magazine. She passed the young woman pretending to be a schoolgirl. "That's not what it's like when you're a teenager. I don't like what it's selling." Back to Tammy and Sue. "These two, and that one," she said, pointing to an early picture, the brunette's hand stealing slowly into the blonde's crotch while the blonde licked at her nipple. "I could be turned on by almost any of them, if I decided to be."

"Are you mad at me, Candy?"

"Why should I be?"

"Something in your voice. You just . . . you don't seem like yourself."

Candy said, "You don't know me very well, Toni. You think you do, but you don't."

The two college girls kissed sweetly and fucked on the page in front of me. I looked back at my sister, sitting beside me in her panties and halter top. "Have you . . . ?"

"Had sex with girls? Yeah. More than once. Mostly it's been good, if you're interested. One time, not so good." Candy drank a sip of her tea. "Ever wonder if maybe you were a repressed lesbian?"

"Candy!"

"You're saying that a lot today."

"You're being outrageous!"

"Well, the way your dates have gone, you're thirty and still single, turned down marriage to What's-his-name—"

"Steve."

"Whatever. Maybe you just don't like guys in the sack, but haven't let yourself think about alternatives."

"Candace Jane!"

She laughed at me. "Just an idle thought. You want an

ice cube for your face? You look like you're about to catch
fire."

"Not everybody thinks about sex all the time, you
know."

"Not even me." Candy put her glass of iced tea down
on top of Tammy and Sue. "I decided to lose my virginity
at fourteen. May thirtieth, 1984. School had been out
three days. I put on my pink halter-top and a pair of tight
shorts and I went and sat on the curb by our house until
someone stopped."

"Jesus, Candy. Why?"

"Lots of cars slowed down," Candy said. "Finally this
one guy drove by in a green Duster. His hair was receding
and he had put it in a ponytail in back to compensate. He
was real nervous and kind of skinny. I thought he was
about thirty. He asked if I wanted a ride." Candy looked
at me. "Well, you were always fighting with Momma,
Toni. I didn't have the guts for that. You were always the
straight A student and you called the shots on the baseball
team. I wasn't like that." She picked up her iced tea, leaving a ring of condensation that wrinkled Tammy and Sue's
beautiful young bodies. "Everything had to be out in the
open with you. I wasn't like that. I liked secrets. I liked
sex. I liked it because it was fun. I liked it because it was
dirty and nobody would talk about it. I liked it because I
knew Momma was wrong about it. It was somewhere she
couldn't follow me."

"Jesus, Candy. You got into a strange man's *car*?"

"I wasn't being naive, Toni. I didn't think it would be
glamorous. I wasn't that stupid. I thought I was pretty
worldly about it. He took me back to his apartment,
which was a hole. He was so nervous I finally had to ask
him if he wanted to do it. When he took off his underwear

and I saw his cock, I just couldn't stop giggling." She laughed and I laughed against my will at the merriment in her eyes. "When we did it he kept asking if I was a virgin and I kept telling him I wasn't and it was okay. I was really tight and really dry and it hurt a lot. He took me home right afterwards. I don't know what he was expecting, but he got chafed something fierce." She snickered.

"What if you'd gotten pregnant?"

"Momma had me on the pill. She was wrong about sex but she wasn't stupid."

"God." I looked at my baby sister, her sad-funny smile and her scent of burnt cinnamon.

"Okay, looking back I admit it was pretty stupid."

"Unbelievably stupid."

"But that night I was incredibly happy. I was even happy *because* it hurt. It was supposed to hurt. That made it real. Like getting your ears pierced. You wouldn't feel grown-up if it didn't hurt. It was my passport, you see? It was my ticket to a new world, and you and Momma couldn't get in."

Candy drank again. "I liked boys better than girls in high school. To be around, I mean. Boys were more like you. They said what they thought and they didn't think too much. Lots of times they were creeps and cowards. They weren't complicated. Of course I got everything wrong." She flipped casually past Tammy and Sue. "That first guy's name was Randy, by the way. True story."

I laughed again. "I fucked a couple of more men early on," she continued. "But it was the boys I really wanted, those beautiful dirty high school boys with their fingers greasy from French fries. I wanted . . . oh, I don't know. Their mouths that tasted of stolen cigarettes. Their skinny muscly bodies and the hard-ons they totally had no control over. They *wanted* me and I really liked that. They wanted me. I liked the way they would pretend to touch my tit by accident when we were kissing, the way a boy's dick would buck up in his jeans when I pulled his hand onto my tit and squeezed it there. It was something nobody would talk about. It was something *true*."

She shrugged. "Now, as it turns out, there are problems with being the class slut too. Darryl, the first boy I fucked, we did it in his bedroom a couple of times under a big Metallica poster. I must have said something about us being boyfriend-girlfriend now, and he laughed at me. He told me he had a real girlfriend and I wasn't it. He told me real girlfriends didn't let you fuck them. Would you believe I was shocked? Shocked! The whole point about sex was that it was *true*, dammit. All the rest of what they told us was lies and scenes and shit, but this was supposed to be it, the real thing: that skinny little cock, and me letting him put it in me."

"I feel terrible." I looked at her. "I had no idea. I didn't know any of this."

"I know." She turned the page to Tiffany, the pretend schoolgirl, an innocent with her red-haired pussy showing under the hem of her nightie. *Tonite I turn 19, and the party's between my legs!*

I imagined my sister, fourteen years old in some strange man's apartment, her panties around her ankles, looking past his shoulder, running away from our family on her back. "I'm sorry."

"I think you had exams or something." Candy shrugged. "Seriously, Toni, you had all that *fighting* to do. All that *winning*. I didn't want you to notice. I didn't want you to know."

Softly I said, "Did you think I would be ashamed of you?"

Candy's eyes rolled up and she fell back to lie stretched out on the carpet staring at the ceiling. "Are you *deaf?* I didn't want you in my fucking life, Toni. You were already using up most of the available oxygen. I didn't give a damn what you thought of me back then, to be frank. You had your world and you were welcome to it. I just wanted to have something to myself."

"Oh."

She sat up and patted my hand. "Hey—the truth is hard. I care what you think of me now. A little, anyway. Especially now." She glanced at my belly. "I've gotten pretty used to being your sister. This aunt-to-be thing is freaking me out. No, I mean it. I think about it every day."

"Hunh." I sipped some iced tea. "Do you know if it's going to be a boy, or a girl?"

"Girl."

"I didn't want you to tell me! I just wondered if you knew!"

"Oops. Now you know."

". . . Damn."

I touched my belly, and wondered if my baby could feel my hand there. My daughter. Slowly I said, "I think there are some things . . . there are some things a daughter ought to know, that would be hard to hear, coming from her mom."

"You reckon?" Candy said.

"I do." I looked back down at the magazine and shook my head. "Mr. Copper, eh?"

"In sex? All of them, sooner or later," Candy said. "Gods are big that way. Look at that anthropologist of yours. Rick. It's the Preacher in him that you want to fuck, you know."

"Candy!"

"The Widow . . . She's the one I—" Candy shook her head. "The Widow is a bit hard." She went looking through the stack of magazines and pulled out another one, called *damage*. There was a bound woman on the cover. She was tightly tied to a bench, facing away from the camera so you could see little of her beyond her bottom, exposed through a pair of panties that had been cut to ribbons. A man in a mask stood over her, holding a long pair of scissors.

Candy flipped the magazine open to a picture of a woman tied to a tree with clothesline. The line was cinched tight at her ankles, her waist, her breasts, and around her throat. Her breasts were normal-sized and droopy. It made the scene much creepier and more real. There was a red rubber ball in her mouth as a gag, and she had wooden clothespins clamped to each of her nipples. She looked scared.

My heart slowed, thumping very hard.

"Lesson four: a lot of men like the idea of hurting women. This picture is kind of exciting," Candy said quietly. "It's also really wrong. You have to be . . . It isn't Sugar that can enjoy this. Sugar doesn't like raping or being raped. Hurting or being hurt."

"Jesus Christ, Candy."

"You can learn to be turned on by this stuff. You can learn to love being . . . violated, if you know how to open up to it. But you have to be very careful. If you don't do it right, it feels bad. It feels horrible if you aren't turned on, and if you do get turned on, that can be horrible too, if you don't handle it just right. And in real life if you do this stuff with a jerk or a psycho, you are getting into some very serious shit.''

I couldn't say anything. I couldn't even open my mouth.

She paged through the magazine and stopped at an ad. This time it wasn't a photograph, just a line drawing of a woman bound and gagged and stuck full of pins. Pins in her belly and genitals and all over her breasts. Her eyes were wide. Underneath the picture it said, ''Sexy girls Bound! Gagged! Cut!'' It was an ad for a line of comic books. There was an address to send money.

''How can you look at this, Candy?''

''How can you afford not to?''

She closed the magazine. ''Of course that's extreme. I've only ever met one guy who wanted to do that stuff to me for real. Looking at the pictures would probably get a lot of guys hard, but they would never do it to a real woman. But you've got to acknowledge it, okay? You have to face the world and *look* at it and see the truth. The torture stuff, it's not a big part of the truth, but it's there.'' She closed the copy of *damage* and paged through another *Hustler*, quickly this time. ''Ten years ago nobody showed pictures of women's assholes. Now they're everywhere. Lots of pictorials of anal sex. It's the hot taboo in the air today. All men want to try it, but they won't say that out loud. Show them that you want it, they think you're hotter than an oil-field fire.''

''This sounds like Sugar to me.''

''The sexiest thing a woman can do is to want sex,'' Candy said.

''What about those other pictures? The violence.''

''That's . . . that's a little different. That's not about fucking, that's about jerking off. That's men not really wanting to think about their partner. Jerking off is about forbidden things. Screwing your boss, your secretary, your eighth grade teacher, your babysitter. Go a little to the fringe and you can include your sister. Five years ago anal sex was *it*. Now maybe anal sex is becoming routine, so the magazines have to find a new taboo." She stopped and tapped a photo with one fingernail.

In a moment of shock I recognized it as essentially the same scene as the one in *damage*, only without the overtones of real violence. In the *Hustler* picture, two naked babes were on a beach. One of them had "broken the rules" and was being punished. She was tied to a post with a few loose loops of twine, arms above her head. Everything about the picture, from the stagey poses to the enormous breasts, had a jokey, let's-pretend feeling—but once again there were clothespins clamped to the victim's nipples. "I don't know exactly how far this is going to go," Candy said thoughtfully. "Not too far, I hope. I mean this, this is just playing. This much can even be fun. But you look at the stuff underground or on the Internet, a lot of it is very rough. Really rough. Some of it is people playing with dominance and submission and getting a kick from it, but a lot of it is by men who truly hate women. Just hate us. Just hate the fact they can't fuck us at will. We're not people to them."

"So what do you do?"

Candy shrugged. "Lots of people want to steal your car, too. I don't know. Watch your back."

I finished my iced tea. "Candy?"

"Yeah?"

"I'm sorry about, about what you told me. I always wanted to look after you. Always. And I'm sorry that—"

"Hey! Here I am, mailing out wedding invitations.

Gonna be an aunt soon. Tía Candy. No tragedy. You keep acting as if sex were just dirty, nothing else. I like it. And it's not the only thing in my life, okay?"

"Okay."

She looked at me. "Jesus. I'm gonna start feeling like I didn't turn out good or something."

I wanted to laugh at that but I couldn't quite manage it. "I think you turned out fine. Really. And you've been really good to me since this happened," I said, pointing to my belly.

"Hey, Ms. Magnum cum laude. Someone has to look after *you* sometimes too, you know." Candy scooped up her magazines and shoved them back in a drawer. Over her shoulder she said, "By the way, if it makes you feel any better, we're both going to make it through the hurricane okay."

"Hurricane! You dreamed one?"

"Mm. Last night. At first I couldn't figure out what was going on, there was all this noise. We were in the garden at the house and it was a *mess*: all the flowers gone, the bananas hanging from the tree with their peels split open. Mud everywhere. Big cracked branch hanging in the middle of the garden. Then I realized the racket was chain saws. Zillions of 'em, all around us, like the morning after Alicia blew into town."

I leaned back in my chair. Hurricane Alicia had been an early lesson in privateering and free enterprise gone wild; in the aftermath of the storm, ten-pound bags of ice had been going for ten or even twenty bucks as people tried desperately to save the contents of their freezers from going bad in the protracted power outages. Parts of the city had taken two full weeks to get power back.

Things spoil fast in a Houston summer. "There has to be some way to make a profit out of this."

"What?"

"Momma did it. She made money off the future. We've never really tried."

Candy looked at me. "Momma paid for it, too."

"Well, the Riders are in my head anyway, and I'm not getting a thing from it. Paying off Momma's debts again."

"Toni, don't. You just . . . it's no good messing with that stuff. The future doesn't work that easily."

"I need the money."

She looked at me even longer.

"Oh," I said. "Oh Lord."

"What?"

"Mary Jo. A *hurricane*, Candy. It's going to bring her house down. Her roof will never take it. The water will be three feet deep on her living room floor."

"Oh my God," Candy said. "Then I guess you better make some money in a hurry."

Candy said that in her dream I had been grossly fat—thanks, sis—meaning the hurricane must be coming late in my pregnancy, August or September. Assuming it might take a week of work to get Mary Jo's roof in shape, that meant I had better have the money to pay for it before the end of July. Just over two months.

As a last resort I could use the American Express gold card I got while making good money at Friesen Investments, but I swore I would rather wash cars or flip burgers than go tens of thousands of dollars in debt. Momma would do that kind of thing: run up a gargantuan bill and then count on some miracle to let her pay it off. Of course Momma could make her own miracles. But there isn't anything in this life you get for free, not even miracles. Every debt she ran up, the Riders made her pay in full.

I couldn't live like that. First, I didn't have the talent. The Riders mounted me at their pleasure, as far as I could tell, without giving anything in return. Probably Momma left them creditors too, when she slipped out of her life, and I had been left behind to foot the bill.

And thanks to Bill Friesen Jr. and his need to prove his manhood, I no longer had the comfortable job I had trained for years to earn.

The phone was ringing when I got back from Candy's place. "Toni Beauchamp speaking."

"Toni?"

"Bill?" I said. "Bill Friesen Jr.?"

"Uh—"

"I was just thinking about you," I said. "Not good thoughts."

"Oh. Um, look, Toni, I guess you're still angry at me, but I need your help."

"Then you are in one sorry predicament."

"Please. I'm willing to pay."

"You know I have my own consulting firm now." As of exactly this second, in fact.

"Toni. I'm begging. Things have gone . . . Things aren't very good for me." He sounded desperate. I could imagine his blinking round face, the bemused expression he wore whenever things started to go wrong, as if he could evade any responsibility by slipping into a doze while events careened around him.

I really did not wish to see him. "Always glad to help an old friend of the family. My rates are, ah"—pick something insane and impossible—"four hundred dollars an hour."

"Fine. Is now a good time?"

I dropped the phone. "Damn, wait just . . ." I got it back onto my shoulder. "Did you hear me, Bill? I charge four hundred dollars an hour."

"Yes, fine, look, it's just past one now, can you do a late lunch meeting today?"

I kept forgetting what life was like for the really rich. I kicked myself for not charging a thousand. "Actually, I've just finished with a client here." Lord, Toni, you just lied again. You're getting more like Momma every day. "Lunch might not be a bad idea."

"Oh, great." The relief in his voice surprised me. "Where do you want to go?"

Since Bill would be buying, I tried to think of an obscenely expensive restaurant, but ended up asking to go to Pappadeux instead. It was moderate by Bill's standards—fifteen to twenty dollars for the entrees—but I worshipped their food. The Pappas brothers were Greek immigrants who came to Houston in the thirties and opened a restaurant. As time went by, they grew more and more successful, opening Pappasitos Tex-Mex Cantinas, Pappamia Italian food joints, Pappas Brothers Steak House (with a selection of fine cigars and a smoking room to enjoy them in), and Pappadeux cajun seafood restaurants. The one kind of food the Pappas family does not serve, anywhere, is Greek.

Pappadeux is always loud and full of junior executives and upwardly mobile twenty-somethings and an unfailingly pleasant "waitstaff." It has a lot of cheerleader yuppie ambiance I usually don't like, but I forgive it for the sake of the food, which is unfailingly superb. Even their iced tea is superior.

By the time Bill and I arrived, there was a fifteen minute wait for a table in nonsmoking, so we sat on stools at the full service bar and studied the menus. Bill ordered a frozen strawberry daiquiri. I meant to be good and take only a glass of water. There was no point breaking my pregnancy diet, caffeine was a one-way ticket to a low birthweight baby. I was not my mother's daughter in this. I had some strength of character.

"Glass of iced tea," I said. "And could you put a wedge of lime in that?"

How much caffeine could there be in one little glass of iced tea? Anyway, I promised myself I would make up for my weakness by feeling guilty and miserable the whole time I drank it.

Without booze—I certainly wasn't risking fetal alcohol syndrome—there was no way I could run up a truly horrendous tab for Bill, but at least I could order the day's special: grilled mahi-mahi in a sherry cream sauce with shrimp, scallops, and roasted pecans; served with fresh green beans and dirty rice. (Dirty rice, if you have not had it, is sort of like the shrimp fried rice you might get at a good Chinese restaurant, only instead of soy sauce, the dish is flavored with a particularly tasty sprinkle of mud. It is hard to explain why this is appetizing. Trust me.)

Bill ordered the same. His frozen daiquiri came. He poked at it with his straw and then looked up at me. "You were right. First we took a couple of hits on some currency speculations. Nothing major, but enough to hurt. We saw an opportunity in a biomedical company, way undervalued. We went for it. Two days later the FDA repealed their chief product."

"What was it?"

"Something for hair loss. Didn't work. At first the FDA passed it because it didn't do any harm, you know. It wasn't toxic. Then it turned out the company was making false claims about the success rates of their treatment. This stuff was nothing. Nothing! Like insect repellent without the stinky stuff in it."

"You invested in hair tonic, Bill?"

"The growth was just too good, Toni, really. Dollar growth, that is. Not hair. Obviously." He ran his hand over his own hair. It was starting to recede, making his face look even rounder. He sucked up a little more daiquiri. "But it's the oil deal that has me strapped. Go ahead and say 'I told you so' if you want."

"I told you so." One of the bartenders dropped a salver in front of us with a miniature baguette wrapped in white linen. I cut off a slice and slathered it in whipped butter. Fat is good for babies. Truly. You can look it up. "You're paying good money for my advice, Bill. Let's hear the details."

They weren't pretty. About a year before, Jim Edmonds, a friend of Bill Sr.'s, had come to him trying to sell his company. He had invested heavily in a parcel of land in the Hill Country not too far from Fredericksburg. The geologicals indicated good potential for large oil reservoirs. The oil was deep in Ordovician-age rock, about 10,000 feet down. Edmonds drilled four test wells; two of them hit, one stripper well at about ten barrels a day, but one good one at three hundred and twenty. No gushers, but decent production. He was making very good money off a series of wells he had drilled in Cuba for a song, so he decided to expand both the Hill Country and Cuban fields into major plays. He had stepped up drilling on both sites, starting ten wells in the Hill Country play, when the President slapped an embargo on Cuba. Not only could he not get his already-bought new equipment *into* Cuba, he couldn't get the oil from his existing wells *out* of it. His loans came due and he found himself suddenly stretched out like a drumhead, effectively broke, even though he had hundreds of millions of dollars worth of functioning equipment sitting on perfectly good oil fields.

So he came to Bill Sr., who said he was no longer of an age to be interested. He was content to put his money in T-bills, dabble in the market, watch his mutual funds grow and play a lot of golf. Bill Jr. was more ambitious. "I wanted to *do* something for once. Dad was funny about it, not saying much . . . I thought maybe he was testing me. Seeing if I had the guts to make a move on my own."

"So you bought the Hill Country play. The week Momma died, as I remember."

"That's right."

"How much?"

Bill looked down at the bar. "A hundred million."

"What! We were only valued at sixty-five million, and that's with obligations of our own!" I noticed Friesen had become "our" company again in my speech. So much for Antoinette Beauchamp, lone wolf consultant.

"Work it out, Toni. He had started ten more wells. If seven of them hit, even at only a hundred barrels a day, we would make the money back plenty fast enough."

"If," I said. Bill looked away. "Okay. Tell me about the financing."

"The hundred million for the company I borrowed at the bank."

"Sixty-five of that secured? Eight percent interest?" I dug my calculator out of my purse.

"Seventy secured, eight percent, and simple interest, not compound."

"Good deal. You did that part right, anyhow."

"The banker was a friend of Dad's."

"Ah. Go on."

The other thirty million dollars of the bank loan had been unsecured at eleven percent, but against the company, meaning that, should things go sour, Friesen Investments would be the only party liable; Bill Jr. could walk away untouched.

"So much for buying the company. How about completing the new wells?"

Bill didn't answer at once. Our entrees arrived in a cloud of scented steam. I tried a mouthful of the mahi-mahi and closed my eyes in bliss. After three months of noodle soup, hamburger, and red beans and rice, the taste of restaurant food was overwhelming.

Bill still hadn't answered. I opened my eyes and looked at him. Then I stared. Then I squinted. "Oh. Oh, Bill. You put out a junk bond issue, didn't you?"

"We were nearly in the clear, Toni. All I needed was another thirty-five million to finish the wells."

"What did you offer?"

"Thirteen percent."

I asked a passing bartender for an extra napkin and started making notes on it. "Okay. But where did you get the money to back the bonds?"

"Borrowed it from a private investor. Five million at seventeen percent. The bond offering went well. Sold fifty million worth."

"Seventeen percent! What were you using as collateral?" I wrote the figure on my napkin. "Oh. At that percentage, you must have put it against yourself."

Bill nodded unhappily.

"Uh-oh. Okay, what are your repayment schedules?"

The news was ugly. I got busy with my calculator between bites and tried to organize my scribbles on the other side of the napkin.

<u>Friesen Inc. owes</u>
70 M to Bank @ 8% (30 year term) = $515,451.72 per month
30 M to Bank @ 11% (30 year term) = <u>$287,049.49</u> per month

$$\text{\bf 802,501.21 per month to Bank}$$

Plus
50 M, bonds @ 13% = **3.25M** every 6 months to bondholders
<u>Bill Jr. owes</u>
5 M, self @ 17% over 5 years = **$125,106** per month

"Bill, how much oil are you pumping?"

"Seven hundred and forty barrels a day."

I worked my calculator. I checked the result twice. "Wow. I meant to laugh in your face, after you fired me and all. But this . . . You're going to lose your dad's company." I looked up. "Now I see why spending four hundred dollars on me is no big deal. What about the hundred and twenty-five thousand a month against yourself, how are you covering that?"

"When my father was my age, he owned eight producing wells. Starting from nothing."

"Gave yourself a hell of a raise out of company funds, I guess." I ate some more of my entree. Now I was sorry I had ordered the most expensive thing on the menu. Bill sat hunched on the stool beside me, big and fleshy, defeat in the soft droop of his shoulders. "Oh Bill. Cash is cold, you know? You can't make decisions to impress your dad."

"I didn't want to impress the old bastard."

I ate.

"You know, after we bought stock in that hair tonic

company, I picked up a bottle of the stuff." Bill rubbed his big knuckles on the forehead his receding hairline had left bare. "Didn't work worth a damn. The whole fiasco has my distinctive signature on it, doesn't it?" I bit my lip. Bill shook his head, sheepish and amused, and for the first time in months I remembered why he had been okay to work for, most of the time. "Toni, I was a fool. My dad was Bill Friesen. And I'm just . . . Junior. So all right, I get the message." He caught my eye and held it. "I know what you're going to say, you're going to say that even Bill Friesen wasn't Bill Friesen—he was Elena Beauchamp, in any way that mattered. He was just another salesman, like your dad. Only with a richer class of client. Maybe you're right. I was wrong, I apologize. I'm eating my crow."

"Are you offering me a job, Bill?"

"No. I can't afford to. I just laid off Kennedy yesterday. There are only three of us in the office now. But I will give you a job, your old job back, as soon as the company gets on its feet again." He put down his fork. "Take off the curse, Toni. I'm begging you."

"Bill! Bill, there is no curse. There was never a curse. That was Momma's kind of thing. I can't do that."

"I remember you putting a curse on my company," he said quietly, blushing. "I remember every word, Toni, and it all came true. The currency thing. The wells running dry."

"Wasn't there something about carpet stains, too?"

"Oh, yeah. I forgot to check."

"Bill! Get a grip. I solemnly swear there was no curse." But inside, I was remembering the feel of the Preacher in my head, his smell of old books in the Spindletop as I pronounced my malediction. "Even if Momma's ghost put one on, I wouldn't have the faintest idea how to take it off."

"This is sorry news," Bill said.

I needed a moment by myself to think over the situation. Was it possible I had actually managed to ruin Friesen Investments? I felt a guilty thrill of power at the thought. There would be a certain irony if I had destroyed the only thing my mother ever built. "Excuse me," I said, slipping off my stool. "I'll be right back."

I needed a moment to think. Also, to be truthful, I needed to pee. One thing I was quickly learning about the second half of pregnancy is that you pee a lot. With a kind of grim glee my books told me that as the baby got larger it would press ever more inexorably on my bladder, until I could hold about a dropperful of urine at a time.

Bill was frowning as I came back to my place. "You didn't order a margarita."

"Is that against the law?"

"You always used to order a margarita when we came here."

"Didn't feel like it."

"You're pregnant, aren't you? I just noticed when you got up. I wasn't paying attention earlier. I wondered if you were just, ah . . . ."

"Getting fat."

"But then I remembered about the margarita."

This was unusually observant of Bill. I was surprised. "I'm almost six months," I said, before he could ask. "Due September twentieth. A girl."

"Wow. It's hard to imagine you being a mom. Wow." Bill blanched. "Were you . . . did you know, at the Spindletop?"

"Yes."

"Oh, Lord. Toni, I had no idea. You should have told me! I never would have laid you off if I had known."

"I did not wish to be beholden to you, Bill Friesen."

"For God's sake, Toni, it's not a matter of charity, it's simple human kindness." He shook his head, moodily forking up another mouthful of his mahi-mahi. He had tucked away a good bit of it while I was in the restroom. Bill's heart might be torn to pieces by the threat of losing his father's company; his stomach was more reliable. "Your problem is you always look for the worst side of everything. If I gave ten bucks to a beggar on the street, you'd say I was trying to impress you, or buying off my conscience, or doing it as a back-hand way to brag."

"True enough."

A green bean waggled between his big lips as he shook his head. "That's where you're wrong. Maybe all of those slimy things would be true, but wanting to help another guy out would also be true. Probably the truest part. It's not as simple as you being able to see through pretty illusions, Toni. It's that you think only ugly things are true."

"It's worked for me so far, bucko."

"Has it?" Bill clasped his daiquiri in one big paw. "Is that what you will teach your daughter? Remember to wear your scarf or you'll catch pneumonia and die. Look both ways so you can put off the day you are hit and killed by a drunk driver. Don't talk to strangers; they're just waiting to—"

"Stop it. Leave my kid out of it."

Bill finished off his fish and took a slurp of his daiquiri. "Your mother scared the hell out of me."

"Me too."

"That's what I'm saying. You're frightened, Toni. You're frightened all the time. Maybe I am trying to impress my dad, but at least I'm not running away from my mother's ghost."

I told Bill to pay off his personal debt as fast as he could so only the company was liable. Then I told him to finish drilling the Hill Country wells, drill more if he had to, drill until he hit a gusher or the bank foreclosed. "Somehow I thought you'd have some more conservative advice," he said, half-smiling. "T-bills. Stock options. Restructuring."

"Conservative advice won't save you," I said. "You're in too deep for that."

"Is that really your advice?"

"It really is. And to show you how much I think of it, I'm giving it to you absolutely free. Forget the four hundred dollars."

He laughed. "Can I at least pay for lunch?"

"Mr. Friesen," I said, "you can even leave the tip."

If there was one thing I hated, it was debt. This had never made me popular back at Friesen Investments. The same Bill Jr. who was willing to embarrass himself and order a Peachy Keen was always willing to mortgage tomorrow when he wanted something today. To be fair, that's the way the eighties taught us all to play the game: pick your spot, make your strike with borrowed money, take your profit and move on. As long as everything keeps increasing in value, it's a good tactic. A bull market favors the bold.

Unfortunately, I had used up most of my short-term savings getting pregnant and settling up Momma's final account with the IRS. I even had to cash out one of my mutual funds. What savings I had left were tied up in my IRA, money I couldn't get at until I was sixty-two and a half! What had I been thinking? My daughter would be grown with children of her own by that time. What was I going to do about her doctor, dentist, college?

Let alone a father. That was not so easy. Even Candy, for all her looks and charm, even for Candy it turned out love was not easy. I thought again of her magazines, of Candy a teenager waiting for men on the corner and me too wrapped up in myself to notice. She was the first baby I had meant to take care of, pretty Candy. I prayed I would do a better job with the little girl in my womb.

I had never had Candy's looks. Knowing what I knew now, I'm not sure I would have wanted the price they had exacted from her. Maybe all our gifts are Riders, in a way. Maybe all our treasures exact a certain price.

For me, it would take more than a negligee to bring a man in and keep him. If I hadn't known that before, my embarrassing rendezvous with Greg had pretty much proved it. Like Mary Jo said, if a woman wants to find true love, she better have some cash of her own. There's a reason the girls in all those fairy tales are princesses. Only the independently wealthy can wait around for Prince Charming.

I had to have a source of income.

Going home from my meeting with Bill I told myself I had run out of time waiting for Prince Anybody to rescue me. It was time to rescue myself. Once home I took my calculator out of my purse and opened the notebook where I had been playing my pretend stock market port-folios and futures trades. Up in my room, I turned the TV onto CNBC and started making systematic notes on the commodities prices that scrolled along the bottom of the screen every ten minutes. I was looking for a way that a woman with my training could make money from home without a big initial investment. Stocks you usually have to pay full price for; but with futures, your money is hugely leveraged. If I really really dared to try it, speculating in futures was the best option I had.

Just as the heart of the stock market is in New York, the commodities exchange that matters is in Chicago. Commodities futures originally sprang up as a way to protect farmers and their buyers from wild fluctuations in the market. By using futures, a seller can come to the market and say, "I want to sell wheat that will be delivered in July or October. What can I get?" He sells the wheat before he has grown it. Both the farmer and the buyer can budget accordingly. The farmer knows that even if there's a glut that year, his price won't go down; the buyer knows that a drought or flood can't drive the price up.

Speculators buy and sell contracts for commodities. For instance: here it was the fifteenth of May. Suppose I bought a contract for five thousand bushels of July wheat at $1/bushel. If, tomorrow, the price offered for July wheat was $1.10/bushel, I could sell that contract. I would have made ten cents for every bushel of wheat, for a profit of $500.00.

That was the idea, anyway.

Now, just a tiny bit more explanation. You may have heard of being "long" or "short" in something. When you're *long* in a commodity, it means that you have bought a contract and expect its value to rise. When its value has gone as high as you think it will go (or as high as your nerves can stand), you sell it, and take your profit. When you are *short*, on the other hand, you sell a contract for a given commodity *before you've even bought it*, with a promise to buy one at a later date. Obviously, you go short when you think something is overvalued and you expect its price to drop. To use the example above, if I sold my five thousand bushels of wheat at $1/bushel, then waited three days and filled the contract by buying the wheat after the price had dropped to $0.90, then once again I would have made my ten-cent profit per bushel equalling $500.00.

Of course, in the real world, prices hop like a frog on a hot tin roof. Markets that look like they will go up forever dip when you least expect it, while other ones peak, drop just enough to scare you out, and then rocket up again. Even expert speculators lose money seven trades out of ten.

Still, it's very hard to make a lot of money fast in a mutual fund or other comparatively safe investment. Investing in individual stocks can give you a stratospheric rate of return, if your timing is perfect, but unless you are very lucky, you need more access to inside information than I had. So: commodity futures.

Over the next few days I got very serious about making paper trades. I would watch the ticker scroll by on CNBC, pick something that looked to be on the rise, and then make a pretend purchase. My first paper trade was a contract for Deutsche Mark. I bought in at .6772 at 10:20 in the morning. By eleven the DM was at .6781 and climbing. Finally at 11:40 it began to break and I sold off at .6785. As each contract for Deutsche Mark controls 125,000 DM, I had made an imaginary profit of $162.50. (Had this been a real trade, my net profit would have been less, as I would have had to pay brokers' fees: $20 for a discount house, or as much as $100 for a full service broker).

The next time the ticker rolled by, at 11:50, the price for Deutsche Mark had rebounded to .6790. It continued to climb for the rest of the afternoon, levelling off at .6796 twenty minutes before the two o'clock close in Chicago. If I had stayed on for the full ride, I could have made $300.00.

"But if the price really had been going down for good," Daddy said that night at dinner, "you stood to lose money. When you have a little more cash you can afford to sit tight. Right now, you can't risk it."

"No, I blew it," I said gloomily. "It's like batting: even the best traders only get a hit three times out of ten. The books say that to make a living you have to cut your losses off short, but ride your winners as long as you can."

"Hm," Daddy said. "Slugging percentage."

"That's about the size of it."

I threw myself into trading. I took Schwager's *A Complete Guide to the Futures Markets* out of the the library and studied it like Holy Scripture. When I couldn't absorb one more word about the intricacies of the soybean distribution system, or the role of the Japanese markets in the trading of copper, I reread Edwin Lefevre's classic, tragic, exhilarating *Reminisces of a Stock Operator* and hoped it would give me daring. I kept the TV on with the sound off all the time. I pored over the *Wall Street Journal* until past midnight, and then woke up every couple of hours through the night and stared at it from my pillow. I kept my transaction book by the bed, ready twenty-four hours a day in case an idea should present itself.

I started with a kitty of six thousand dollars of imaginary money. That was Mary Jo's savings plus all I could cash out of my IRA after paying the early withdrawal penalties. I had originally intended to go with only five thousand, but I began to see there was money to be made in coffee, and I wanted to be able to make a trade in it, should the opportunity present itself. It only cost $3,150.00 to buy a contract in coffee, but I found I was also required to keep a margin of a couple of thousand dollars in my account to cover possible losses. (Generally, the more volatile a commodity, the higher the price of the margin for a single contract.)

I agonized constantly over trades, but in fact I only had enough money to be in one or two contracts at a time, so I was only making five or six pretend trades a day. Still, over the next two weeks I traded an amazing range of things: coffee, copper, soybeans, pork bellies, Swiss Francs, Japanese Yen, Deutsche Mark—I had an affinity for Deutsche Mark—unleaded gasoline, and frozen orange juice products (each contract worth 20, 000 lb of frozen orange concentrate, the contents of an entire tanker truck!)

I was a nervous wreck, sleepless and exhausted. I was also incredibly exhilarated. Trading gave me a rush unlike anything I had ever done before. This, I imagined, must be how people felt at the roulette wheel or the racetrack. As an actuary, all I had ever done was assume the worst. An actuary's bottom line is death and taxes. But playing the market is like jumping into the whirlwind of life itself, a tornado that booms and buzzes as prices rise and fall, goods and money change hands, empires wax and wane. Each hour spun around with its load of panic and blood-lust and greed and fear. It was quite a trip.

I dithered for several days, trying to decide whether to go with a full-service broker or a discount house. Full-service brokers give you advice. They treat you well. You can leave them with instructions when you go on vacation, so they will sell or buy for you at given price points. They cover your behind for you. In exchange, they charge around $100 for each round trip; that is, for each time you get into and out of a market.

A discount broker doesn't treat you nice, nor will he cover your butt. A discount broker supplies a voice at the other end of the phone who will relay your buy and sell orders to a runner who will take them down to the pit floor in Chicago where some poor hollering sinner who can't get any other job will scream out your order until he gets the attention of a buyer or seller.

(The life of a Chicago floor trader is not a happy one. They spend all day on their feet screaming; their rates of laryngeal cancer are through the roof. The job is so conducive to hypertension that floor traders are insured at the same rates as skydivers; this I had noticed when studying mortality and claims tables for my actuarial exams. Floor traders also suffer excessively from pencil wounds, if you can believe it, delivered by people running around madly waving their arms.)

With the discount broker, you have to watch the ticker yourself and phone in every buy or sell in real time. If you fall asleep and lose your life savings, that's your lookout. But a discount broker charges $20 for a round trip.

I went with the discount broker. My profit margins required me to supply my own vigilance.

After two weeks of imaginary trades, my six thousand dollars of pretend money had become $9370. I was ready to take the real plunge. I picked my broker and pored over the fat *Global Futures Trading Handbook* he faxed me. I resolved to make my first live trade on Monday morning when the market opened.

Friday afternoon I decided to amuse myself by initiating

a few last imaginary currency trades to hold over the weekend and liquidate Monday morning.

I hadn't realized how nerve-racking it would be to have a trade held across the weekend. Friday night I realized that a G7 meeting going on in Paris could have a huge impact on my speculation. I bought European newspapers to follow the progress of trade talks, hating the Brits for browbeating the German chancellor. The market in Germany opened late Sunday afternoon, Houston time, but a small player like me wouldn't have access until Chicago opened Monday morning.

Sunday night I lost eight hours of sleep and seven thousand dollars thanks to the resolve of the G7 leaders to attack the high value of the U.S. dollar. My imaginary stash was down to $2440. I could only take out one cheap contract at a time, currencies or unleaded gasoline. I was one mistake away from being out of the game.

So I sat in an agony of indecision all day with $2440 imaginary dollars in my notebook and $6000 real ones on account with my broker. I saw an opportunity in wheat that I would have taken in an instant the previous week, when I had been winning. Now, I didn't dare. All day Monday I watched the price of wheat wobble upward. If I had bought in the morning and sold at quitting time, I would have made almost six hundred dollars profit. But throughout the day there were six or seven times I could have lost substantially if I had bailed, and I would have bailed. I knew myself. Tapped out as I was, not daring to lose, I could not dare to win.

I turned off the TV and bought a paper to look through the want ads. Nothing for someone with my qualifications. Nothing for someone with *any* qualifications. If the job required any brain at all, you had to have seven years experience to apply.

I turned the TV back on to see what was happening with the Deutsche Mark.

I made chicken sopa for Dad and ate it myself when I remembered he was on the road again. I hadn't noticed him leaving.

The Astros middle relief blew a game to the Cubs.

That night I couldn't sleep. I went back over all my paper trades. I plugged data points into an Excel spreadsheet to get a better picture of what the markets had done in the two weeks I had been taking notes. I watched the ticker and tried to build an hour-by-hour profile of all the majors: currencies, coffee, cocoa, copper, soy, unleaded, wheat, corn, pork bellies, orange juice . . . Dawn came as I graphed the movement of the S & P stock index. At $14,000 for a contract, the S & P was far out of my reach, but a lot of people traded in it.

Still I could not sleep.

(It's 9:30 at night. Momma has just come back from a meeting with Bill Friesen. These late meetings only happen when Daddy is out of town. Momma looks tired and her makeup is smeared. "Where's your sister? Did you give her dinner? What is she yelling about?"

"I locked her in our room. Why do you have to work so much?" I am nine. "Why do you leave us alone?"

Momma takes her purse off her shoulder. "If there is a God—which I pray there is not—I will go to hell knowing that whatever I did wrong, at least I provided for my children.")

Even Momma—haunted, god-ridden, laughing Momma—had done that much for her children. And I, who was so smart, who did so well in school, who played by all the rules, who wore the clothes she was supposed to wear and said the things she was supposed to say—I could not do so much. I was a woman now and I had a daughter and I could not provide for her.

I wept. And wept more when I found, deep down, that it wasn't my daughter I felt guiltiest about. It was Momma I had failed first. I let her live and I let her die and I never made her life easier, my mother, who suffered so much.

Dawn Tuesday. CNBC's morning show came on. I made a pot of coffee and drank it all before I remembered that pregnant women weren't supposed to use caffeine.

I realized I was starving.

I went down to the kitchen and stared into the fridge and the pantry and then walked to the patio to look out at the garden. Let the kid eat me hollow from inside.

I felt as if I would never sleep again. I could have been a Rider puppet myself, made of sticks and strips of threadbare cloth, buttons and hanks of leather. It was seven in the morning, June 4. Already the thermometer on the patio read 85°. My hair was greasy and I smelled dirty. The sky was cloudless and the heat oppressive. From somewhere in the live-oak tree above me a mockingbird began to sing, beautiful liquid songs. It didn't know about me, that I was broke and pregnant, that after a whole life of being the responsible one I was failing everyone around me, my daughter and my daddy, Mary Jo and Momma most of all. It just sang.

Hard to believe that any creature born into this world could have such a beautiful song. She may be a mimic, she may steal her songs from others, or change them, or forget them, but I still say there is no creature that does more honor to God than a mockingbird. If she is inconstant, it is her nature. If her songs are stolen, well, there is nothing false in the moment of her singing.

Back upstairs I picked up a pregnancy book and read the section on caffeine and wondered how I would feel if I gave birth prematurely to a low birth-weight baby. I imagined my daughter in an incubator, her tiny head sallow, struggling to draw air into lungs still wet with amniotic fluid. Tiny fingers curling and uncurling like flower petals.

I previewed the seventh month of pregnancy and found I should be prepared for heavy white vaginal discharge, constipation, heartburn, indigestion, flatulence, bloating (there it was again), occasional headaches and dizziness, nasal congestion and possibly nosebleeds as my blood volume soared; bleeding gums, leg cramps and backaches, swelling ankles, varicose veins in my legs, hemorrhoids, shortness of breath, difficulty sleeping (they weren't wrong about that), clumsiness, and just possibly leaking breasts.

There was also a chance, they said, that I might be feeling "increased apprehension about the prospect of motherhood."

I cried some more.

Back at my desk I printed out graphs and studied them. The stock market was opening in New York. Pretty people who never made the grades I did appeared on CNBC to chat over coffee and croissants on the morning show. Every one of them was perky and well-groomed, no doubt eager to spend another day celebrating all the little ways the rich were getting richer. Afterwards they would drive off in their wonderfully engineered foreign cars to families of sleek children in the suburbs.

The clock crawled on. It was hot. My hands were shaking badly with caffeine and exhaustion.

I thought about Candy's magazines. They say one girl in four is subjected to some kind of sexual abuse before the age of twenty-one. One in twelve is the victim of rape or attempted rape.

How do you live in a world like that? How do you even look at it?

How do you look at Mary Keith, stepping off that building in Phoenix with her daughter in her arms? How do you look at the ads in Candy's magazines? *Sexy girls cut!* How do you get up in the morning in that world? How could you ever think to bring a child into such a slaughterhouse?

A stink of gasoline and hot dust came through the balcony door, thick enough to make me gag. The smell filled me with terror. I think I might have screamed.

A long, brindled snake slid across the floor toward me. I jumped to my feet—too fast. Blood drained from my head, my vision went black and I staggered, tripping over my chair. I fell heavily to the floor, head swimming, vision gone, the room a blackness spangled with stars. I threw myself to the side, grabbed the edge of my bed and pulled. I screamed again as a nail of ice split through my left foot.

I grabbed at the bed but the covers slipped off, leaving me with an arm full of blankets. Something dry and smooth and terribly cold slid around my foot. It coiled around my ankle; paused; and then inched up my calf. The skin where it passed screamed and then went dead. I could no longer feel my foot. The room stank with the smell of dust and gasoline.

I struggled for breath. My leg went dead from the knee down. The snake's cold head wound around the inside of my thigh. I cried, shaking uncontrollably. My vision came back for a moment and I saw Mr. Copper wrapped around me.

Then frost flowered across my eyes and I was gone.

TEN

I woke up cold and stiff with the sound of a telephone still echoing in my ears. I was holding the receiver. The voice at the other end of the line said, "18628, you bought one June S & P at 649.50, ticket number 126."

I was sitting at my desk, utterly destroyed. My head ached fiercely and the stench of gasoline made me blind and dizzy. "What?" I whispered, but whoever was on the other end of the line had already hung up.

I put the phone down. I had been possessed. That's what had happened. Mr. Copper had mounted me. I felt a quick memory of the skin on my calf going numb. A tree roach the length of my thumb scuttled across the top of my computer monitor. I didn't have the strength to kill him. Tree roaches are so big they don't squish when you step on them, they crunch. Another aspect of Houston I hadn't mentioned to Angela when I was trying to get her to visit.

My eyes were watering and I was hollow with hunger. The computer's clock said it was 1:02 P.M. I had been gone from my body for at least five hours. I remembered the cold press of Mr. Copper's skin against mine. I had never heard Momma talk about meeting a Rider outside her head.

I thought of my daughter, the little voyager in my womb I had come to call the G, and I was seized with panic. What kind of mother was I, to let myself go so long without sleep and food? Too weak to stand, I crawled downstairs to the kitchen. I dragged some milk out of the refrigerator and ate a bowl of raisin bran. Pregnancy books are very keen on raisin bran: extra iron in the raisins, bran to ease your constipation. Probably some cereal company could make a killing off pregnant women if they were to offer New Improved Raisin Bran—Now With Wheat Germ!

Halfway through my second helping the words of the phone call jumped back into my brain. "18628, you bought one June S & P at 649.50, ticket number 126."

That had been my broker calling to confirm an order to buy. I had *bought a contract for the S & P!* Minimum margin: $14,000. A perfectly normal dip in the market could be costing me thousands of dollars while I sat stupidly on the kitchen floor eating breakfast cereal.

I scrambled upstairs to the TV and stared at the CNBC ticker. It was listing mining and lumber stocks, no use to me at all. I nearly screamed. Back over to the desk. Nothing showing on the computer, but my transaction book was lying next to the mouse pad with a pencil in it. I grabbed it off the desk.

Oh my God. There were four transactions noted, all occurring after the time Mr. Copper had mounted me, all listed in a cold, neat script that was not my handwriting. I stared at the notes, trying to understand them, my heart about to burst inside my chest—and then I made a long, strange noise, halfway between a moan and a laugh.

Mr. Copper had been perfect. Of course. He had made money. A lot of money. I forced myself to look at the entries in the transaction book more carefully, pulling the terse numbers into the story of what had happened while I had been banished from my own head.

At 9:20 A.M. Mr. Copper had bought one July coffee at the market, filling it at 129.00/lb. The exit fill at 9:55 was at 133.80. A single contract controlled 37,500 pounds of coffee. The Rider who told Momma once that all cash was cold had made a profit of $1800 in just over thirty-five minutes.

Now, with more money in my account to cover contracts and margins, he could afford to buy two contracts, this time in unleaded gasoline. At 10:25 A.M. he picked up positions at 70.20. One hour and ten minutes later he sold at 72.10. Total profit for that seventy minutes' work: $1596.00

He had made his next move immediately, probably on the same phone call, also marked for 11:35 A.M. This time he shorted July coffee, selling two positions at 131.50. The market promptly burst like a popped jellyfish. When he made his exit fill just over an hour later, the price had dropped to 122.50. Time elapsed: eighty minutes. Total profit, a staggering $6750.

In three transactions Mr. Copper had realized a profit of $10,146.00. Which, added to my starting $6000.00, had given him just enough to cover his margins while picking up the S & P future at an entry fill of 649.50.

I scrambled across the room and died a thousand times

waiting for the market index ticker. When it finally came at 1:40 P.M., the S & P was trading at 651.25. Up one and three quarters.

I thanked God, all the gods, Mr. Copper in particular, and crawled to the phone. I dialled my broker as fast as I could, made a mistake, hung up, dialed again, made another mistake, dialled a third time and let it ring. Someone at the other end picked up. "Account number?"

And I didn't speak.

"Account number?" said a woman's voice impatiently. Still I said nothing. She hung up. Discount brokers don't have time to waste.

Slowly I put the receiver down. Mr. Copper had put me in a position to win, and all I was doing was trying not to lose. That was the actuary in me. But I could never make a living as a speculator by playing it safe. The key to the art was to cut my losers and ride my winners out. Just for once, I had to try and ride my winner out.

Knowing it would be ten minutes before the S & P scrolled by, I forced myself downstairs for another bowl of cereal and a glass of water. By the time the 1:50 ticker ran I was feeling less shaky. Dreadfully tired in my body, but my mind was alert, humming with a keen adrenaline buzz.

The S & P had climbed to just over 652.

I watched it rise that whole afternoon. Finally at 2:20 it started to dip, giving me an excuse to sell. Tension had coiled me up like a mattress spring and I was only too grateful to end my trading for the day. The ticker read 655.25, but by the time my sell order was executed in Chicago, the price had dipped to 655 even. As luck would have it, the S & P immediately rallied, and went on to reach a high of 656.50 at New York closing time. I had bailed too early after all. Even so, I had made a profit of $3000 on the S & P ride.

My day's take exceeded $13,000, leaving me with more than $19,000 on account with the broker. I could take ten thousand out to cover the cost of fixing Mary Jo's roof and still have almost 10K left. A fierce exaltation gripped me, wringing out my poor exhausted body like a rag. I had found a way to make a living. I had found a way to combine my head for numbers with Momma's gift for prophecy. What more perfect job could there be for a woman one-half accountant and one-half fortuneteller? If I was cautious and I paid attention, if I picked the best trades I could find and was willing to make just a hundred or two a day, I could twist a living from my own precious art, my own secret magic.

For the first time, the Riders had done me a favor in exchange for mounting me.

For the first time, we were even.

To believe the Riders and I might be partners felt so good it was almost immoral. Ever since I could remember, they had been cruising like alligators just below the surface of my life, but now I could point to a moment when one of them had done right by me.

Candy, perversely, chose this of all times to lose her cheer and get suspicious. "Mr. Copper was just playing, Toni. That's what he does," she said when I told her about our winnings. "He doesn't mean anything good by it. He just likes to win."

"But sometimes it is personal, Candy. We're tied together, the Riders and us. They have to look out for us, or when would they get a chance to walk the world? Look at what happened with Angela when she was a baby.

Momma was about to hurt her, or go crazy, or God knows what. So the Widow stepped in and removed her from the situation."

"Now you think the Widow is a kindly grandmother?"

"Well, all right, not that exactly. But she has the best interests of the family in mind."

"What *she* thinks are the best interests. She's like La Hag Gonzales, Toni. They want what they want. Just because your interests and Mr. Copper's were the same for one afternoon, don't think that suddenly the Riders care about you."

"I didn't think Momma could do it to you."

"Do what?"

"I hoped you would escape. I hoped you could believe that something beautiful was true. That not everything real was ugly."

Candy said, "I don't want you to get hurt."

She was not alone in her opinion that the Riders were not to be trusted. Expecting to get a big hug and a coffee-stained smile, I had gone to Mary Jo in triumph with the news that Mr. Copper had come through with the money to fix her roof. I had been disappointed. Immediately she began to fret at the thought of workmen cracking her little home open and letting the light into its dim corners. The morning the crew arrived from Sears, Mary Jo refused to open the door for them. I had to drive over and unlock her house using the spare key Momma kept on a hook above our kitchen sink.

Mary Jo was huddled in her bedroom with the blinds drawn, refusing to speak. I talked to the Sears guys and then brought Mary Jo to our house, where she spent the next four days, sleeping in Momma's bed while Daddy slept in a cot on the first floor. I felt sad to see her so upset. With Momma gone, the spark seemed to have fled from Mary Jo. I wished, helplessly, that I could be the friend to her that Momma had been, but that could never happen. Elena and Mary Jo had been blood-sisters, cronies, conspirators and accomplices. When Mary Jo's husband left her, Momma had been there, offering to put a curse on him free of charge. When her son, Travis, had left home to wander America, sponging off relatives rather than finding an honest job, Momma had listened to Mary Jo explain how he really wasn't a bad boy at heart. Chain-smoking, she had looked at baby pictures and nodded as Mary Jo tried against all the evidence to imagine a future in which her boy might make good.

At best I was Mary Jo's grateful goddaughter. I am ashamed to admit I was a little bit glad when the work was done and she could return home.

When Momma died, Mary Jo lost her last link to life outside her little house. She had some money coming in from her pension, some from Social Security, and some from a part-time job stuffing envelopes. Taken together, it was enough to buy her loaves of Wonder Bread and pay for her cable TV. If Momma had kept her promises and put Mary Jo down for some meaningful dollars in her will, things might have been different. She was bitter about that, but not surprised. Mary Jo had known my mother too long to be surprised when her promises broke like soap bubbles in the sun.

On the twelfth of July, Mary Jo called to complain about one of her dizzy spells just as I was heading out the door to pick Angela up at the airport. "What it is, is that new roof," Mary Jo finished. "I think there's some radon or asbestos or something in those new shingles, got my head in a whirl."

"Mary Jo, I have to go now. Angela is visiting from Canada. I have to pick her up at the airport and I'm fixing to be late. Maybe you should call a doctor about this dizzy spell of yours."

"What? Oh. Oh, sure then." Another long pause. "Your momma's dead, isn't she?"

"Yes, ma'am. She is."

"Yeah."

Another long pause. "Mary Jo, I have to go. Promise you'll call the doctor, all right? This isn't like you. I'll call when I get back to see how you're doing."

"It's just a dizzy spell, dear. You don't have to call . . . Tell you what, you get Travis to give me a call," she said with a sudden burst of bitterness. "You get that boy to give me a call and I'll tell him how I feel."

"Call Dr. Richmond, Mary Jo. You like her," I said, glancing at the clock on the kitchen stove. I was ten mintues behind schedule.

"You know, I still think he would amount to something if he got himself a good wife. If he knew what was good for him, he'd come back home and marry you, Toni Beauchamp. You're a good girl, Toni, but you could use a bit of a spark. One thing about Travis, he's lazy but he's got a spark. Just like his daddy."

"I'll call you later," I said, and I hung up the phone before I could hear her say anything else.

(Momma is lying on her chaise three months before her death. "They should rename this the Grandmother State," she says. "We're always hip-deep in hunchbacked little old ladies who never complain. That's horseshit," she says to me. "Don't be fooled. Getting old is hell. I just wish my brain had given out first. I don't think I'd mind dying so much if I were senile. God damn, but there's a lot of things I would be glad to forget.")

I promised myself I would call Mary Jo when I got back from the airport and prayed her dizzy spell was a temporary thing, brought on by the sweltering July heat. I had been in her house many a summer afternoon, and without air conditioning it was a furnace.

At least my mother had been spared the humiliation of losing her mind. At least she had gone to her grave with her wits intact.

As I grabbed my purse and dug around for my car keys I found my hands were shaking and I was on the verge of tears. The sound of Mary Jo's voice, and the memory of my mother, shaking and bald in the chaise longue on the patio . . . Lord, I wished I could have made life easier for my mother. For all my resentments, I could see now how hard it must have been for her. How hard. Gods whispering inside her head and a little girl lost in the cold cold north. And me, who should have been some comfort to her. But instead I was the hatefulest child. And no way now to make it up to her.

I arrived just in time to catch Angela at the gate. We had exchanged pictures, but I would have recognized her without the photograph, so much did she look like the mother I remembered from my childhood. It took my breath away. Angela spotted me and her smile broadened as our eyes met. She strode past the other passengers, purse bumping at her hip, and stuck out her hand when she got to me.

"My Lord, do you ever look like Momma," I said. She was leggy, like Momma had been, but instead of Momma's long skirts, she wore jeans and not much makeup. She was lean and looked fit. I sure wouldn't look as good when my daughter was seventeen.

Angela blinked. "Hello to you too." She had Momma's low voice, but without the bourbon and cigarrete huskiness to it, and instead of Momma's lazy drawl, Angela talked in an accent that made her sound like a TV anchor on the national news.

"Forgive me. It's just so . . . The set of your shoulders, the way you walk, it's exactly like Momma. It's amazing."

"Hunh. You know I've never even seen a picture of her?"

"I'll show you some, if you like." I felt myself beginning to flush. "Look, can I carry something for you? Is this all you've got?" I asked, looking at her purse and attaché case.

"Nope. Two suitcases to claim. I haven't learned how to travel light. I just ditched Darth Vader; if I let go of any more stuff, I'd float into the air like a balloon."

"Welcome to Houston," I said, picking up the attaché.

Once I got over the shock of how much Angela looked like Momma, I liked her just as much in person as I had on the phone. She was funny and energetic. "Hey, look at that!" "What?" "The Walk sign. In Canada, our little stick men stand straight up and down, very proper. But here, look at that little guy leaning! Go Go GO!"

Or, "So whose idea was it, anyway, to base *health care* on the *profit motive?*"

"Insurance companies," I said. An actuary knows the answer to that one.

Or, as we were nearing the house, "What *is* it with you guys and street signs? Five blocks back the streets were spelled out in tile on the curb. Three blocks ago the names were, like, etched in these little concrete pylons. Now they're regular metal signposts, only they're being strangled by vines. It's all higgledy-piggledy."

"Um, never noticed that. I guess it goes with being the only city in North America with no zoning laws."

"No *zoning* laws? *No* zoning laws?"

"None. Our next door neighbor has a convenience store in his garage. A few years ago someone moved into a mansion in River Oaks and opened a strip club on his second floor."

"What about the neighbors? Didn't their property values drop?"

"About three hundred thousand overnight. Yep."

Angela cackled. "Life, liberty, and the pursuit of young butt." I parked in front of our house and then levered myself out of the front seat. Sigh. There was no doubt that I was pregnant now. I could no longer bear the feeling of anything across my tummy, not in the sweltering damp July heat, so the last of my maternity shorts with their elasticized panels had gone into the closet for good. It was knee-length granola dresses from here on in. Yuck.

I put her suitcases up in my room and fixed a pitcher of decaf iced tea and a mango for us to eat on the patio. I prepared the mango the way Momma taught me, cutting the two halves away from the stone, then scoring a grid into the flesh with a dull knife and popping the skin inside-out so the flesh stood out in raised rectangles. Angela had settled into one wrought-iron chair and I maneuvered myself into the other with the wary awkwardness of a hippo on a trampoline. The day was wretchedly hot, the sun a glaring spangle glinting through the live-oak limbs, but we were in the deeper shadow under the broad leaves of the big banana tree. A mockingbird sang to us, hidden, and the gulf breeze lazed through the ferns and monkey grass.

Angela rolled up the sleeves of her white blouse. Damp stains showed at her armpits and the sweat had beaded up on her forehead. "It's hot! Whew!"

I drank some tea. I had put wedges of lime in the glasses, and the fresh green smell cut through the lazy heat a little. Angela followed suit and drained half her glass at a swallow. She looked at me, and smiled. "Kind of like dating, isn't it?"

"What?"

"This. Talking. You and me. Hard to know where to start."

"So, Angela, what's your sign?"

" 'Stop!'" she said. "Or was it 'Beware of Dog'? Monica—that's my daughter—Monica would love this place. She thinks Calgary is boring. She thinks we're boring. So did her dad, come to think of it."

"Ouch." I thought of Mary Jo, afraid to leave Chester and then ditched by him anyway, and wondered if the same thing had happened to Angela.

"At least Darth Vader is helping to pay for Monica's college. We were very particular about that. Neither one of us wanted me taking his money for myself."

"Did you know that in the year after a divorce, the average American man's standard of living goes up by forty-three percent?"

"And the ex-wife?"

"Down seventy-three percent," I said. "Some people remember TV theme songs. I remember statistics."

She tried the mango. "Hey! This is great. Kind of like a peach wearing sexy perfume. Just remember that stats aren't everything. You know the old line about lies, damned lies, and statistics."

"Mark Twain," I said. "You'd be amazed how many times you hear that joke when you're an actuary. Usually from people trying to buck the odds." I thought of Bill Jr. frantically drilling for oil in the Hill Country. "It's true odds aren't everything. But they're still the way to bet, you know. Not many casinos go broke."

"I suppose not." After another drink of tea she said, "Did Elena's death cost a lot? Because if it did, if you're in debt—"

"No, no problem." I didn't mention the IRS. Candy would call me foolish, but I wasn't going to start out with my half-sister by begging for money.

We finished the mango, and the heat drove us inside to the cool tile floors and the ceiling fan. Angela asked what I had been working on, so I lumbered upstairs and showed her my transactions book and the CNBC ticker and tried to answer her questions as best I could.

"Fantastic!" she said after fifteen minutes. "I want to make a trade."

"I'm very new at this, Angela. I would rather not—"

"I've got the money, okay? We'll just let something run for ten minutes: one scroll on the ticker and I'll cash out, win or lose. Okay?"

Reluctantly I nodded. In the three and a half weeks since Mr. Copper made thirteen thousand dollars for me, I was up four hundred bucks. Better to be up than down, no doubt, but $100 a week was not going to send my daughter through medical school. The G squirmed in my womb and gave me a little kick in the bladder for emphasis.

Angela flipped through the brokerage handbook. Her

sweaty hands left fingerprints on the pages. "Twenty thousand pounds of frozen orange products," she said. "Buy some. In this heat, the idea of owning twenty thousand pounds of frozen orange juice sounds divine."

I laughed. "You want to go short or long?"

"Um . . . long. It's too hot for the price to drop."

I grinned and phoned in the order. A moment later the brokerage called back with the exact entry fill price and Angela watched me note the trade down in my book. "Now what?" she said.

"We wait for it to come by on the ticker and see how you did."

Angela stared at the screen. The CNBC types were talking about Mexican opposition to NAFTA. Down below they were listing NASDAQ stocks. "Doesn't this waiting kill you? Is this what the big traders do, sit and watch TV?"

"No, they have second-by-second price updates coming in by satellite to computer setups. I can't really afford to take that much of a plunge."

"What would it cost?"

"Maybe five thousand for the computers, and another five hundred a month or so for the service. Two thousand dollars for the software. That would get me an Omega Tradestation."

"You want one?"

I laughed. "Like Candy wanted a Corvette when she was seventeen. Prices can change so fast that ten minutes is an eternity. If I had a full-service broker, oddly enough, I wouldn't need the setup so much, because then at least I wouldn't have to recall my stops every day."

"Stops?"

"When you leave instructions with the broker to sell as

soon as your contracts hit a certain price. Stops are how you keep yourself from taking a really big loss."

"I see." Angela looked at the TV. "Okay, I can't just sit here. Let's go where it's cooler and get some more to drink."

"More iced tea?" I said, when we got down to the kitchen. "Or maybe some orange juice?"

"OJ. Definitely OJ. Hey—there's a message on your answering machine."

"I must not have noticed it earlier." I punched the replay button. The machine hummed and whined for a moment. Then came a crackle of static. Then a terrible voice, strained with desperate effort, like the voice of someone with MS or a stroke. "TO-NNNUH! Tone, z'mar! Mrj-uh. Uhl!" The voice gasped, hoarse and ragged. Momma's breathing had sounded like that, in the last hour before she died.

"Mary Jo," I whispered.

A bang and another rush of static. The phone had fallen. Mary Jo must have dropped the receiver. I could see it hanging there in the dim pantryway between her kitchen and her back door, bumping against her ancient washing machine. A long scrabble, squeaking linoleum, the receiver banging against the washer. Mary Jo called out my name in that strangled voice, grunting, strangely faint most of the time, but shot through with sudden loudness, as if she were getting her mouth near the receiver only for instants before it swung away. "She's lying on the floor," I said. "She's lying where she dropped the phone."

The machine beeped, cutting off Mary Jo's message.

"Jesus," Angela said.

My fingers were shaking as I dialed Mary Jo's number. The line rang busy. "Oh shit. Shit. I've got to go."

Five minutes later I was fumbling for the lock at her side door. I opened it and a wave of hot darkness rushed from the house, smelling of mold. I ran inside into the kitchen. The drapes were all drawn tight and I couldn't see a damn thing. "Mary Jo? Mary—shit!" I said, tripping over a chair. It had been left in the middle of the kitchen floor. I fell down hard, hurting my right knee. It was hot, dark and burning hot inside Mary Jo's house.

"You okay?" Angela said behind me, voice tense.

"No. Hold the door open." Enough daylight came in for me to find the light switch by the front door.   Mary Jo was sitting on the kitchen floor with her back against the refrigerator. She was staring at the cabinets in front of her and her head did not turn as I ran in. I scrambled across the kitchen floor. "Mary Jo!" Her eyes were wide open, alert and terrified. I could tell at once that she recognized me. She was barely breathing: shallow, curiously slow breaths that caught in her throat. I held her hands. "Mary Jo, what's wrong? What's wrong?"

"Call an ambulance," Angela said. She stepped over me and Mary Jo, hung up the phone and then dialed 911.

I gave the ambulance directions and handed the receiver back. "Okay, honey," I said to Mary Jo, "the ambulance is on its way." I took her hands. They were completely unresponsive. "Can you move your fingers?" Nothing. A moment later, Mary Jo's feet twitched on the linoleum. "Good. Good. Now, can you move your hands, Mary Jo?"

Nothing.

"Stroke?" Angela said.

"I don't know. Mary Jo, I'm here, it's Toni. Listen, the ambulance is on its way. I'm going to take care of you, okay? I'm going to make sure everything is okay. Got that?" I tried to smile into her terrified eyes.

She stopped breathing.

"*Shit!* Mary Jo, don't quit on me here. Come on, breathe, sweetie. Breathe. Breathe." She did not breathe. Her feet kicked and rattled against the cabinets. "Breathe!" I shouted. I put both hands on her chest and shoved hard. Air pushed out of her in a soft, painful grunt, but when I pulled back, her chest stayed still. I had forced the last air out of her, and no new air was going in. "Angela!"

"I don't know, I don't know!"

"What should I do? Oh God—" I tipped Mary Jo sideways and laid her on the floor on her back. Putting one hand behind her head, I covered her mouth with mine and blew, soft and steady, as if I were trying to fan an embering campfire. I heard a faint sound and felt a little current of air on my cheek.

"Her nose. Pinch her nose shut," Angela said.

I tried again, pinching her nose shut. It was very awkward, bending over my own pregnant tummy. All I could remember about mouth-to-mouth was from ads I had seen as a kid for the St. John's Ambulance course; they had a man blowing into a dummy beside a swimming pool. Mary Jo's mouth tasted like cigarettes and mold and she smelled like an old person. Her skin was very soft and furred with fine hair. I blew into her mouth again, and again, and again, and again. "She's not breathing!"

"Keep going, Toni. The ambulance will be here soon. Do you need help?"

I shook my head, breathed into Mary Jo again, tried to remember the old St. John's Ambulance ads. Shit—the guy used to do mouth-to-mouth three times and then listen to the dummy's chest. I put my ear on Mary Jo's chest. Something bad was happening. Her heart wasn't beating right, it was in spasms, like a rag being wrung out. Her legs kicked and twitched, but her face when I went back to give her more air was slack.

Breathe. Breathe. Breathe.

I put my head on her chest. No heartbeat.

"Where the fuck is that ambulance!" I put my hands together on Mary Jo's chest and pumped hard.

"Oh God, has her heart stopped?"

Pump. Pump. Pump. I put my head on her chest. No heartbeat. Pump. Pump. No heartbeat. I blew some more air into her mouth, and again. My back was on fire from bending over her and my shoulders hurt. Pump. Pump. Pump.

"Toni."

"I don't know what to do." Breathe. Breathe.

Angela put one hand on my shoulder.

Pump. Pump. Pump. "I don't know what to do." I was crying. I had meant to take a CPR course for the baby's sake, there was a special infant CPR course they offered out of Methodist Hospital and I had meant to sign up but I hadn't gotten around to it. This could be my baby on the floor and I wouldn't know what to do. My face was wet with tears. Pump. Pump. Breathe. Breathe. Breathe.

An eternity later I gave up. My arms were too tired. I couldn't breathe. I was dizzy from lack of air and I couldn't see for crying. I wouldn't let Angela help. I realized the moldy smell wasn't from Mary Jo's skin, it was the Widow. It was the mold in the house and the smell of the Widow, who watched from behind my eyes as Mary

Jo died. Her smell of mold and scorched cloth and silver polish that made my head spin when I ran out of air.

Mary Jo stared up at the ceiling. Her pupils were huge. I tried to stop Angela from touching her. Angela pushed me away, gently, and bent down to feel for a pulse. She shook her head. I was crying.

The ambulance came. Paramedics ran into the house and examined Mary Jo. Then they closed her eyes and stopped hurrying. They asked some questions about her. I told them how we had found her, what I had done. One of them was black. He said I had done the best I could. The white guy stood up and looked around the kitchen. The other asked if Mary Jo had seemed confused earlier in the day. I told him about the phone call, how she had said she was dizzy and had almost forgotten that my mother had died.

"Here it is," the white guy said. He was holding a Tupperware dish. "Green beans. Found it on the kitchen table."

"What?" Angela said.

The black paramedic said that Mary Jo had probably died of botulism. She had left the beans in the Tupperware too long. He said it happened to old people a lot. Mary Jo wasn't old. She was only sixty-two. She died of botulism. He said there was nothing I could have done to save her, and he held my hands.

Every day after Mary Jo died I could feel the Widow looking out from behind my eyes.

You get what you pay for, I guess; the Widow in my head was the price for failing Mary Jo. I could have saved her if I had gone to her house after she called me, dizzy and almost forgetting that Momma was dead. I let her down. I let her die. And doing that, I let Momma down too.

This time I knew better than to leave the funeral arrangements to someone else. I called lawyers, mortuaries, funeral homes, insurance agents. I even tried my best to track down Travis. I found a letter from him in Mary Jo's house, postmarked Boulder, Colorado in 1991. I called Directory Assistance, but they had no listing for a Travis Turner at that address. The operator said there were thirteen T. Turners in Boulder. I called them all. None was Mary Jo's son.

It seemed incredible to me that a parent could die and the child not even know it.

Angela did what she could to help. I suggested she move to a hotel where they would have air conditioning. To my surprise Daddy stepped in and asked her to stay with us. She agreed. She was a terrible cook.

We buried Mary Jo in the Memorial Cemetery on a morning in July when the sun pounded down like a hammer on our black suits and gabardines.

After Mary Jo's funeral the combination of my pregnancy and the terrible heat seemed to leave me with no energy left for anything. I never had the long talks with Angela I had meant to.

The Widow watched her, though. She couldn't get enough of Angela. When I was so tired I was nearly asleep in my chair at the end of dinner, the old witch still paced back and forth behind my eyes, staring greedily at Angela, the lost girl, drinking in her walk and her laugh and her flat Canadian accent, her hips that were Momma's hips and the few grey strands in her hair.

Carrying the Widow like this was almost worse than the actual possessions. When a Rider climbed into my head, I felt a few instants of horror, a few hours were erased from my life, and then things returned to normal. Now the Widow didn't need me to go away to ride in my head. The scorched cloth and silver polish smell of her was always faintly in the house, like the smell of Momma's hairspray.

When she looked through my eyes, she turned everything to skeletons. I would look across the table at Daddy and see only his smallness and the loneliness of his endless trips to Beaumont and Longview and Shreveport and Jackson. I saw how old he had become: how round his shoulders were, how thin his hair. Even baseball seemed to have lost its interest for him; he fell asleep in the middle of games, he read the capsule summaries in the paper and didn't bother with the box scores.

When the Widow looked at my body, she saw the cradle of cancers to come.

One thing I noticed, though, was that she bothered me less when Candy was around. I had never been so grateful for my sister's cheer and energy. Angela found her amusing, but I thought it was deeper than that. I had come to see that there was great power in Candy's will to be happy. In her own way, she was as ruthless about taking pleasure from her life as I had ever been about making my grades or succeeding at work. It was Candy more than I who had inherited our mother's strength.

Even stranger than Candy's effect on the Widow was Carlos's. The Widow never cowered, it was not in her nature; but when Carlos was around, she hid herself so deeply in my head that I could forget she was still riding there. Candy had told me Carlos could talk to spirits. I was willing to believe this—there was no point in one of Elena Beauchamp's daughters getting skeptical—but frankly I had never really seen the point. Now with the Widow in me I began to feel Carlos's power . . . and, finally, I asked him for help. He agreed.

I was more nervous than I expected, waiting for him the night he was to intercede between me and the Widow. I changed clothes three times, wishing I could wear a business suit but stuck instead in a sleeveless flower-print maternity dress the size of a three-man tent. I lumbered from the kitchen to the front door and back again, wondering what was involved in his Mexican sorcery and if it would hurt. Wondering what the Widow would do. Surely nothing that would injure my baby.

Angela had said she would stay up with me until Carlos came. She dragged herself over to the refrigerator and stood there for a long moment with the freezer door open, pretending to get ice for a glass of tea. The day had been muggy, nearly 100 degrees until late in the afternoon. Just before midnight I wandered over to the patio and read the thermometer. Mockingbirds still called and sang among the branches of the live oak outside, invisible in the darkness. "Eighty-five degrees," I said. By day the Houston summer is unbearable, but a July night in Texas is surely one of God's gifts to the world, a mysterious velvety blackness, softer than a whispered promise, so rich and luxuriant you can almost feel it brush against your skin like the flesh of unseen flowers.

The birds fell silent. A moment later I felt a faint vibration in the soles of my feet as the floor tiles began to tremble. "The Muertomobile," I said. "He's coming."

The grandfather clock in Daddy's room was striking twelve when Carlos knocked at the front door. Instead of jeans and an undershirt, he was wearing a black tuxedo with a shawl-cut collar and black velvet lapels framing a strip of ruffled white shirt. Each cuff was pinned with garnet studs. In the light that streamed from our door I could see the reflection of my swelling stomach in his shiny black patent leather shoes.

Somewhere in the lace of branches looming overhead a single mockingbird began to sing again, singing and singing as if calling me into the darkness. The sultry air was rich with smells: asphalt still soft with heat, oleanders, clay, exhaust fumes, cilantro still on my hands from making that night's dinner, and cumin and chilis, and sage and jasmine from our garden, and still the mockingbird made the dark air sweet with song.

"I'm kind of nervous," I said, trying to laugh.

Carlos looked at me with the Preacher's eyes and did not smile. "*Sígueme*," he said. I did not know the meaning of those words, my Spanish was a decade old, but I felt the power in his voice, and when he turned I followed him.

The Muertomobile was a hulk of shadow by the curb, rimed and crusted with photographs and watches and silver dollars, candles and bits of bone. Brass and gilt and glass and silver winked in the light from our house and then went out as Angela closed the door behind me. I didn't like the sudden darkness. The new moon had not yet been born, and the thick canopy of interlacing live oaks that lined our street throttled lamplight and starshine.

Carlos handed me in the passenger side; fat and awkward, I eased into the blood-red upholstery. Crushed velvet slid and whispered. Carlos swung the heavy door to; it shut with a clank like a bank vault closing. Inside me, the G kicked once and fell still. Carlos got behind the wheel and crossed himself and said, "*Podemos entrar, debemos entrar, entraremos las tinieblas. En nombre del padre y el hijo y la sagrada virgen, estamos agarrados en el puño de la mano más poderosa y llevados a la oscuridad.*" In the name of the Father, the Son, and the Sacred Virgin, with the strength of the Most Powerful Hand, we are going into the darkness. The words so heavy with power I felt the skin crawl on my arms and back, the little hairs prickling at the base of my neck.

Carlos turned the key and the engine of the Muertomobile throbbed in a deep bass note: turbines revolving under heavy rivers; machines turning far underground. He pulled out from the curb. He left his headlights off.

"Carlos? There's no seat belt." No answer. "It's not lost in the upholstery either. You took it out, didn't you?" I thought of the G, riding helpless and vulnerable in my womb. "This isn't safe. I want to go back."

Carlos did not slow down or turn back. *"Háblame de los duendes."*

"What? What?"

"Los duendes. Habla de ellos."

"I haven't taken Spanish since high school." We passed flickering between the street lamps, watching their brightness intensify, the live-oak branches laced above the road gaining definition, the pavement coming into focus, the glare shining on the windshield, blinding and then gone, and our own shadow creeping ahead of us as the light faded behind. Carlos had left the windows rolled down and I found I could still hear the mockingbird, now nearer, now farther away, as if she were keeping pace with us, flitting from tree to tree in the darkness along the road, singing and singing.

"Quién es la primera?"

"The first? Of *los duendes*? Um. The Widow, I guess. Yes, the Widow." My heart was beating fast and painfully hard. I realized I was holding the door handle so hard my fingers were starting to ache. "I shouldn't be here, Carlos. This is crazy. What sort of mother would go driving around in the dark with no seat belt?" A mother with Riders climbing into her head, that's who would be out in this damn sorcerer's car at midnight. Momma had done things like this all the time, I thought bitterly. Why should I be surprised to find myself doing it too? Oh Christ.

"Habla de ella."

Talk of her, speak of her, something like that. "She watches the family. She hoards. She is a miser. She owns us without loving us."

"*Te ha cogido? La has llevado?*"

Had I carried her? "*Sí.* Yes. These days I feel her behind my eyes all the time."

Carlos swung the car down a new road. The street marker was clotted with vines, the street name choked and hidden. I did not know where we were. Houses stood by the road with their mouths closed, their eyes dark.

"*Anciana!*" Carlos called. Old woman!

There was a sharp thump from the back of the hearse. I screamed.

Carlos ignored me. "*Habla del segundo.*" Speak of the second.

I told Carlos of the Preacher, with his smell of old books and his hard silence. I told about the laughter he had taken away and his iron principles and his tablecloth made of real girls' hair. I told Carlos about Sugar, the sweetness in her breath and her smell of peaches and sex. I told him of Pierrot's cruel marvels, his razor smile, his hidden sadness, that lonely clown. I told him about Mr. Copper, who knew neither love nor pity; who played to win but paid his debts. And after I had finished telling of each Rider, Carlos would call out its name, and a sharp bump would come from the back of the Muertomobile, and the hearse would ride a little lower, and creep more slowly along the deserted roads.

Still the mockingbird sang, now farther, now nearer. Shotgun shacks and mansions rolled by, tenements and little white churches. I recognized none of them. Slowly, slowly I was filled with the certainty that we were not in Houston anymore, but in another city, a dream city like the one Rick Manzetti had wandered into on his trip to New Orleans. Perhaps a real town threw off five or six unreal ones, like shadows thrown from one object lit from several sides. Or perhaps there was only one city, and you could get to it from any town in America if you were lucky or drunk or damned enough, if you took just the right turn at just the wrong time. A city where gods might lounge in the doorways or sit whispering on their porches late into the night. And somewhere out there, beyond the mockingbird's song, a little lost girl was walking, walking, walking through those midnight streets.

"Y la última duende?"

"The Mockingbird," I said. "I . . . I don't know what to say about her."

"No tiene olor? Ni historia? Ni deseo?" She has no smell, no stories, no desire?

"Nothing. Momma never told any stories about her. She was only singing. Only the song. She mounted Momma more than any of the others, but I can't remember a single story about her. And she is the only one I haven't felt near me since Momma died. Sugar has mounted me, and Mr. Copper and the Widow. Pierrot— I've felt Pierrot," I said, remembering his nasty laughter as I spoke with Rick Manzetti. "Some days I see the Preacher everywhere. But not the Mockingbird. Never her."

Carlos nodded. *"La sinsonte!"* he called, but no bump came from the back of the hearse. *"Está perdida,"* he said. *"Tienes que buscarla."*

She is lost. You must find her.

The black velvet curtain between us and the back of the hearse twitched and I jumped in my seat, praying it would not open.

"Ahora. Háblame de tu madre."

"My mother? Why do we have to talk about her?"

Carlos did not answer. In the long silence that followed I thought I heard Pierrot snigger. The G moved, turning in my womb like a child in a restless sleep. I should think of a name for her soon. I was at thirty-one weeks already. Babies had been born this premature and lived. "My mother knew a lot about mascara but used too much foundation," I said. "She went through a can of hairspray in six weeks and her second favorite fingernail polish was Purple Plum. Is this what you want?"

"Háblame más," said Carlos the sorcerer, so I rambled on, my fingers clenched around the door handle, my other hand on the dashboard to protect my womb in case we crashed. Sweat running in my eyes. My heart pounding and pounding.

"Mosquitoes didn't like her much, which is probably why she kept the doors open all the time. They'd like to have eaten me alive. She hung garlic and tansy to keep them off; said her mother taught her that. She didn't talk about her people very often. I do not believe they were educated folk. Momma didn't have a hillbilly accent, but every now and then she would come up with these back-woods expressions: 'He was the runningest ol' dog you ever did see,' or I'd ask if dinner were ready and she'd say, 'Purt nigh, but not plumb.' I guess you would call her a liberal; she was in favor of integration and she wanted to vote for a woman president. She used butter, never margarine. She always wanted to go to Paris, but never did."

I glanced over at Carlos to see what he was getting out of all this, and gasped. He was driving with his eyes closed. For a long moment I stared at him with my heart hammering in my chest. I must have tensed up fiercely, because the G gave a kick like a mad colt.

The car started to drift off the road. *"Habla,"* Carlos murmured. His voice was low and hazy. I had seen people in trances before—Momma had friends who would go into trances as soon as look at you—and I knew he was far gone.

"She, she, she loved biscuits but she hated making them herself," I squeaked. The car steadied in its lane and we picked up speed. "She always said biscuits in a can were one of God's special acts of grace. She could drink just about anything. With liquor she didn't care if she was drinking single malt Scotch or cheap mixed rye, but she was fond of a good bourbon. When I was little she was the only mom who let me do just what I liked with my hair, grow it out or cut it short or wear it in curls. She told me once her mother made her wear the same little swing for eight years and she swore she would never do that to her child. Uh . . ."

My mind went blank. The Muertomobile began to drift toward the right curb. I groped around for something to say about Momma, some little detail, anything, but for some reason all I could think about was that I could no longer hear the mockingbird.

A girl stepped into the road in front of us. "Christ!" I yelled. I lunged for the wheel just as Carlos slammed on the brakes. I felt a shock as we hit something and then I jerked forward hard, slamming my shoulder on the dashboard so hard it made my arm go numb. The Riders Carlos had summoned into the back of the hearse shot forward and smacked into the wall behind me, then dropped painfully down as the hearse jerked to a stop. The black velvet curtain had pulled off four of its rings. I could hear snarls and mutters coming from behind it.

Adrenaline went whizzing through my bloodstream like ice water, so intense I froze for an instant in pure shock. "Swing and a miss," I breathed. The G jumped and twisted like a pike in my womb. I blessed her, blind with relief to feel her thrashing strongly inside me. Sensation returned to my right arm, and my shoulder started to ache as if someone had taken a home run cut at it with a baseball bat.

Carlos got out, hurried to the front of the hearse and crouched down in the roadway, talking to someone I couldn't see. Groaning, I eased myself out the passenger side of the Muertomobile.

I didn't recognize the neighborhood we were in; I couldn't even be sure if we were in Houston or in the Little Lost Girl's city, or at some intersection between the two. Three blocks away, traffic streamed down a well-lit road: Richmond, maybe, or Westheimer? Most of this block seemed to be houses, big ones sectioned into apartments to judge by the cars scattered outside. Ahead of us, at the end of the block, music pulsed dully from a tiny club or bar.

The girl we had hit sat in the roadway examining her hands. "Wow. Blood," she said. "You're definitely going to have to give me your name and number in case I need to sue the shit out of you." She was a white girl with dirty-blond hair. "Fuck, there's gravel stuck in my skin." She wore a black skirt and leggings with china flats on her feet, and an oversize black T-shirt with the words *Fear* slashed on it in white. She had an East Texas white-trash accent. A bad kid from Baytown or Beaumont or Port Arthur.

"We should take you to a hospital," Carlos said in English.

"Do I know you? No, I'm not getting into some stranger's bizarro car in the middle of the night, thank you very much. You think I never watched a Movie of the Week?"

"Are you hurt? Besides your hands," I said.

"I don't know. I been hit harder with worse things, probably." She held her hands up to the streetlight and squinted at them. "That stung."

"Please. Let me take you to the hospital."

"Uh, no offense, friend," the girl said, glancing back at the Muertomobile, "but you drive like a complete fucking loon. Even if I didn't think you were going to, like, torture me on videotape or something, I'm not getting into a car with a skull glued to the hood. With a guy who drives without his fucking headlights on in the middle of the night."

"Okay, let's call your parents," I said.

"No."

"Do they know you're out this—"

"No," she said again, very fast. "Look. I don't want any trouble with you guys, okay? I'll be fine. I was just going to meet some friends in the bar. I'll go in, wash my hands, and then seek repairs as necessary."

She couldn't have been more than sixteen. "You don't want to phone your parents."

"It's really none of your business, okay?"

"They don't know you're here, do they?" I said slowly. "They don't know you're out. In fact, I bet they don't know you're in Houston." No answer. Bull's-eye. I thought of Candy sneaking out to get screwed by men twice her age while I studied for my freshman exams.

"Look, get Speedy Gonzales here to write down his name and number and I'll call him if I start to hemorrhage," the girl said. " 'Hundred twenty cc of glycocholine—STAT!' " She laughed. "Could either of you characters spare a cigarette? I gave my last one to my mom."

I turned to Carlos. "Let's call her a cab and take her to the hospital."

"I don't have any insurance," the girl said. She stood up and rubbed her bloody hands on the side of her skirt. She was a little taller than me, but thin, thin, with shadows under her eyes.

"Where are you staying?" I said.

"I told you, I've got friends. A lot of friends. Waiting for me," she said, backing up a step.

"We're not trying to hassle you."

She looked at the Muertomobile. "Yeah, well, sorry." She wiped her hands on her skirt again.

In the darkness I heard the mockingbird begin to sing, and looking at this girl, I thought of Momma running away to New Orleans as a teenager. She never talked about her folks much, never talked about her life between the ages of twelve and twenty. I wondered what the girl in front of me was running from. A stepfather who beat her or a drunken mother, or maybe just her own mistakes? Maybe she was running from nothing worse than Baytown itself, or Beaumont or Port Arthur: those little Texas refinery towns that beat all the hope out of you. Maybe she didn't know what she wanted, except that it was not to grow up to work at the drycleaner's or Dad's plant. Maybe she checked out of school because she couldn't do math and didn't have anyone around to make her good at it. I thought of Candy again in her pink halter top, and me behind my books, hiding, and I thought of the daughter in my womb and prayed that she would always be running toward the light in front of her, and never from the darkness behind. Maybe this girl was a bitch or a brat. But looking at her, so young, I thought I could forgive her anything if only I could take her home and feed her and keep her safe until morning.

"Can I go now?" the girl said. "I'm going. Don't worry about the name and number. On second thought, I really don't want to know."

"No, let me give you my number," I said. "Let's go over to the club where I can get a pen, I'll write down my name, and you call me if you need any help." I was crying. "If you need anything," I said.

She turned her back, embarrassed. "Yeah. Whatever," she said.

The next day Rick Manzetti dropped by to tape another one of Momma's stories, but instead I ended up telling him about my late-night ride with Carlos. "So then what happened?" he asked.

"I took her to the club and wrote my name and number on a napkin."

"That's it?"

"I bought her a pack of cigarettes."

He looked disapproving, but I didn't care. "Momma smoked," I said.

"I beg your pardon?"

"Momma. She smoked." I was drinking cold milk at the kitchen table. Rick was drinking a Dos Equis with a wedge of lime. "Do you see? Carlos found Momma for me." Rick made another note on his little yellow pad of paper. He had great hands. "But not the Momma I knew, the one who was so much bigger than me. He showed me that other Elena Beauchamp, the girl from Longview or Tyler or Port Aransas who got out of some small-town Texas hellhole and made her way in the big city.''

"The Little Lost Girl," Rick said.

"Maybe." I looked at him. "Maybe you're right. Maybe Angela wasn't the Little Lost Girl. Maybe Momma was talking about herself all the time, but I never understood it. I guess we're all Little Lost Girls. One way or another.''

"There's a lot of people lost," Rick said. "So did Carlos's exorcism work?"

I nodded. "By the time we got back from the club there were no Riders in the Muertomobile, and the Widow was gone from behind my eyes." I watched him take a drink of beer. "Rick, can I ask you a question?"

"Shoot.''

"Would you marry me? Not now, of course. But I mean, if we got to know one another better, and got along and all that. Could you see yourself married to me?"

"Mm. I . . . No. I don't think so.''

"Figures." I drank some more milk, wishing I could have his beer instead. "Why not?" He glanced at my distended tummy. "You want to marry a virgin?"

"I don't want to be a father to another man's child." He scratched his beard. "I don't think that's admirable of me, but that's how I honestly feel, deep down.''

"Good thing to be honest about," I said. "Did you know that the rate of child abuse is twelve times higher for stepparents than natural ones? I guess blood really is thicker than water." I patted my tummy. "I've been thinking about that.''

"I'm sorry.''

"You could tell me that you'd marry me if it weren't for the baby. Just to keep my spirits up."

He smiled. "Okay."

"You're not just humoring me, now, are you?"

"Of course not."

I laughed and finished my milk. "I think I've told you all the Little Lost Girl stories I can remember. I'll call you if any more come to me."

Angela's voice came down the stairwell. "Knock knock?"

"Come on down," I said. "You aren't interrupting anything. More's the pity." Rick grinned into his beard and put his tablet of yellow scratch paper into his leather briefcase.

Angela poked her head around the corner of the stairwell. "I just thought of something," she said. "What about that orange juice?"

She was quite right. With Mary Jo's death and the funeral and the Widow in my head, I had forgotten all about the Frozen Orange Products contract we had purchased. I called my broker in a panic and made him sell immediately, terrified I had missed a deadline and that at any moment I would see a container truck filled with twenty thousand pounds of frozen orange juice concentrate backing up to our yard.

As it turned out, we had two days to spare before we would have been forced to take delivery and pay for the balance of the contract. Apparently even my pitiless discount broker had tried to call, but I had unplugged my answering machine and thrown out the tape with Mary Jo's horrible message, and they had been unable to reach me.

"Well?" Angela asked as I hung up the phone in my bedroom.

I swivelled around in the office chair in front of the computer. "I'm afraid we—" Dramatic pause. "Made six hundred and twelve dollars!"

"Made? Did you say—!" Angela whooped. "Six hundred bucks for forgetting to make a phone call!"

I was grinning like an idiot. "It always happens this way. Everyone makes money on their first trade. And everyone loses money on the second. It's a rule."

"Quick, let's go make a little one right away and get the losing over with," Angela said. She had her hair up in a bandanna. A few strands of white showed amidst the brown. It was somehow hugely reassuring that a woman with white in her hair and a seventeen-year-old daughter could still whoop with such conviction. She grabbed the notebook I had been using as a transaction log, flipping past the page written in Mr. Copper's cold clean hand. To my surprise I saw a couple of pages with notes in her messy scribble. "I've been following the Deutsche Mark this week and I think we can still get on the train."

"You've been following the Deutsche Mark? When?"

"Frankly, Toni, you haven't been a lot of fun the last couple of weeks," Angela said. She hefted the copy of Schwager's *Complete Guide to the Futures Markets* I had finally broken down and bought after comitting myself to life as a speculator. "I've been sitting in front of the fan reading this stuff for the last ten days while you've been moping."

"Lord. I'm so sorry. I haven't been much of a host."

"It's too bad, because you're a way better cook."

Which was true. I had slowly gathered that a Canadian's idea of spicy food pretty much topped out at dill pickles. I resolved to get back in the kitchen that night. Maybe stuff some poblano peppers for chili rellenos. Then a thought struck me. "Um, when are you supposed to be going back to Calgary?"

"Two days ago."

"What!"

Angela shrugged. "I thought you could still use a hand around here, so I exchanged my ticket."

"I didn't know you could do that."

"I bought a full-fare ticket, in case I got here and, um . . ."

"In case you wanted to get the heck out of Dodge after meeting us." I leaned back in the office chair, pushing hard against the pillows I had piled there to give some relief to my back, which was aching all the time now. "Good planning."

Angela picked her current glass of iced tea off the computer desk and held it against her forehead. "To be honest, Toni, I didn't know how you guys would react to me. I mean, I'm the one who got Elena's money." She smiled wearily, and I saw the crow's-feet around her eyes, the lines beginning to deepen on her forehead and around her mouth that she did not bother to cover with foundation, as Momma would have. "And I thought I might be too angry to stay here. I always hated you, growing up. Not *you* you. Whoever my mother had left me for. Because she loved you more than me."

"She lived with us, at any rate."

"It's the same thing," Angela said.

She sat on the edge of my bed, watching the CNBC ticker. The black iron fan whirred, tugging at her sweaty shirt. "Toni, what does 'directly' mean? You've been using that word a lot the last two weeks. As in, 'I'll get to that directly.' "

"Um . . . 'not now.' "

"I had finally begun to figure that out."

I squirmed in my chair, pressing my fists into my back. It was stinking hot and sweaty, even with the fan on. I couldn't remember the last time I had been able to have even a sheet on me at night. My face was always flushed and my body felt as if I had just stepped out of a long hot bath twenty-four hours a day. "It goes with 'fixin' to,' which means, 'The thought had crossed my mind.' As in, 'I'm fixin' to cut the lawn.' "

Angela laughed. She picked up the transaction book and read over her notes, then looked at me. "How about going into business together?"

"Business?"

"Trading futures."

I stared stupidly at her, then wiped at my perspiring face, managing mostly to get a little more sweat into my eyes, where it stung. "Are you *kidding?* " I said, blinking. "You've made one trade, Angela. You made some money. I made money on my first trade too. It's not a good way to make a living. Ninety-five percent of all independent traders—"

"—go broke within the first year. I know. I've been reading your books, remember?" Angela shrugged, that same lanky, raw-boned nonchalance Momma always had about the future. "If it doesn't work out, it's not as if my life is over. Do you think I don't know what it's like to fail?—Or maybe it's you who's never failed before," Angela said. She poked at me with the transaction book. "That's it, isn't it? You're scared because you've never taken that first big hit, have you? Never been divorced, gone bankrupt, been stuck in hospital with tubes up your nose." She leaned forward and patted my hand. "Honey, don't be scared. It's a rare crash in this life you can't walk away from."

"Did I ever tell you I worked as an actuary?"

Angela laughed. "You see everything as if the very worst was going to happen. Well, guess what? It usually doesn't. If it did, insurance companies would all go broke. Which they don't, in case you hadn't noticed."

"Yeah, yeah, okay." I could not keep myself from smiling. "I hear you."

"Even when the worst does happen, you survive. Hell, I survived a car crash that broke both my legs and the time Monica fell out a window when she was two and a breast lump and a bunch of divorces—you think I'm going to ruin my life over a few commodity trades?"

"Enough!" I said. "How many husbands have you had, anyway?"

"Two of my own," Angela said, considering, "and countless others." She looked at me and burst out laughing. "Toni, you look like you're choking on a pickle. Are you shocked? At the age of thirty-one?"

Yes! I wanted to say. Yes, you can't be cavalier about screwing other women's husbands! And yet . . . and yet I really liked Angela. I really did. And I didn't know the story behind her affairs. So all I said, after a long, stammering pause, was, "You really do remind me of Momma."

"Uh-oh," Angela said. "I love it when you say that; I love the idea that I have some part of her after all. But I also know *you* well enough to know it's not supposed to be a compliment."

"But it is. Sort of. You have her style. Momma was a

pirate. She was a privateer. You would have liked her. I wish you'd been with us."

"I think I would have stood up to her a little better," Angela said.

"I'm sure you're right. But she was so big, Angela. She devoured the room. But you could have laughed her off." *You're the hatefulest child there ever was, Antoinette.* "I wish you'd been here. I think I would have liked not being the oldest child," I said. And then, "I did the best I could."

Angela said, "I know."

Then she gave my hand a brisk squeeze. "Here's my offer. Between Elena's bequest and the money my wonderful lawyer screwed out of Darth Vader, I'm pretty flush right now. Have you ever heard me talk about the job I have in Calgary?"

"Um, no."

"There's a reason for that. Frankly, I'm itching to call my boss and tell him my vacation is being permanently extended. Since I was supposed to be at work yesterday, he may have fired me already, mind you." She shrugged. "I have enough cash to put us in four or five contracts at a time, which I think we're going to need to do, if we want to see a constant income stream. On top of that, I would buy one of those Omega Tradestations you were talking about." She waved dismissively at the TV. "Waiting every ten minutes for a quote is insane; the market changes too fast. Also, I think we should work with a full-service broker, at least on big trades."

"You really have been reading up!"

"We'd go in as partners. I want to be able to bug you into taking a risk every now and then, but we make no trades except by consensus."

"Sounds fair," I said. My heart was finally beginning to

catch up with the sense of what Angela was saying. To have help arrive unlooked for; to see a chance that I would be able to make a living at home: suddenly all the panic I had been suppressing seemed to clamp around my chest like iron bands. "I don't wish to be beholden to you," I said. "To you or anybody."

"I'm not giving you anything, moron. I said we would be partners. I happen to think you're very smart. You know a lot about the markets, and about business, and about finance. I failed algebra in tenth grade. If you don't think your skills are valuable, that's your opinion. But you might at least be smart enough to shut up about it." Angela laughed. "I cringe to imagine what you would be like at a job interview."

"I never had to do one. I was hired out of school by a friend of Momma's."

"Figures. You know, I think I was dead right. Your big problem, Toni, is that you've never really failed *big*, so you can't imagine picking yourself up off the ground afterwards." She took a swig of iced tea and grinned. "Stick with me, kid, and I will personally guarantee you will fall flat on your face."

"Now that's good to know." I rubbed the sweat around my face a little more. I felt as if my body had been modelled out of margarine and was beginning to run in the heat.

"I do have one nonnegotiable condition." She put her tea down on the table.

"Yes?" I said, waiting for my beautiful future to smash like a glass on the tile floor.

Angela pulled at her sweat-sodden blouse. "We *must* put an air-conditioner in at least one room of this pile.

I've got heat rash up to my boobs. This city is so sticky it makes my earwax turn liquid.''

"Spare me the details. Air conditioning in the bedroom.''

"Then it's a deal. Podner.'' She stuck out her hand and I shook it, giddy with relief and anticipation. "Are we going to topple the corporate world, then?''

"Fixin to,'' I said. "Fixin' to *directly*.''

And then, a moment later, I said, "Angela, you'd know if you were a repressed lesbian, wouldn't you?''

"I'm not.''

I flushed. "I didn't mean *you* you, I meant, you know, anybody.''

"Why do I think you've been talking to Candy?'' Angela popped an ice-cube into her mouth and gnawed on it, considering. "It seems like the sort of thing you would know.''

"Good. That's what I thought.''

She ate the rest of her ice-cube. "Of course, maybe that's what 'repressed' means. That you wouldn't know. If you knew, it wouldn't be repressed, would it?''

"You think so?''

"I have no idea.''

"Oh,'' I said.

"Can we talk about something else now, Toni?''

"I reckon,'' I said.

TWELVE

After my night ride in the Muertomobile it seemed as if the Riders and I had become more comfortable with one another. Sometimes, after long hours of tracking futures on the brand new Omega Tradestation with Angela, I might smell Mr. Copper's scent of dust and gasoline, but only faintly, like a memory, or a possibility of something to come.

The great Joe DiMaggio once said that Houston has three seasons: summer, July, and August. Angela didn't even know who Joe DiMaggio was, but she agreed with the assessment. She spent the better part of August draped around the a.c. unit she'd installed on the third floor. Now that she had experienced the brain-boiling heat and humidity of the endless Houston summer, she said, many things about our family suddenly made sense to her.

We made close to eleven hundred dollars trading futures in August. Not a living, not for two women, but it was an encouraging start, particularly as commodities futures were not the only things on my mind. Mary Jo had named me the executor of her will, which meant I had to sell her house, new roof and all, and disperse her belongings. The water-stained copy of *Little Black Sambo* she had willed to me. I cried when I got it, and put it in the Widow's cubby, I can't say why.

Then there was Candy's wedding to prepare for, which meant dealing with Carlos and La Hag Gonzales, and of course with every day I got hotter and fatter and more pregnant. I wheezed and panted and grunted my way through the first three weeks in September with my head full of Deutsche Mark and canapes, wondering if I would ever find a husband, or even wear a belt again.

The day before Candy's wedding my underpants fell down.

Underwear is designed to fit the normal human shape. But when you are pregnant you are not just fat, you are fat in a funny way. Your abdomen has, say, eight pounds of baby packed like tuna in ten pounds of seawater. Add one fetal cafeteria, also known as the placenta, and then stuff the whole mass into your womb. Now remind yourself that you are not fat. There is no extra flesh below the abdomen; at least there wasn't on me. As a result, my belly had a steep undercurve. This proved too slippery a slope for my poor overstressed underwear to grasp. Despairing, their elastic weakened by my enormous girth, they gave up the struggle and plummeted to earth around my swollen ankles.

I was standing in the checkout line at Whole Earth Foods at the time.

It is extremely embarrassing to have your panties fall around your ankles in the middle of a busy grocery store.

Even a hippie grocery store. With a sigh I shuffled forward and put my basket on the checkout counter and bent down. Bending down is a major operation when one is nine months pregnant, involving a lot of squatting, wheezing, and grunting. More squatting and puffing followed as I stepped out of my panties, left foot, then right, picked them up—no easy task—and stuffed them in my purse.

Straightening, I found myself the object of the fascinated gaze of a middle-aged man with a greying ponytail ahead of me in the line. "What's the matter?" I said with icy dignity. "Never seen a pregnant woman's underwear fall down before?"

Let me tell you about the ninth month of pregnancy. First, it is unbearably hot, especially in Houston in September. I lived like a bat, coming out only after sundown, spending the days wrapped around the new air conditioning unit. I couldn't imagine why we'd never put one in before. It was a miracle. It was divine.

When you are nine months pregnant, your bum hurts all the time, balanced by a dull remorseless ache in the small of your back, an ache that never leaves, and wakes you up eight to ten times every night.

Although you are in severe danger of Bloating throughout pregnancy, you have only touched the swollen edge of Bloat until you come to the ninth month. Mid-pregnancy bloating is to the ninth month as a balloon is to the Goodyear Blimp. Everything bloats. Your breasts. Your bum. Your ankles. Your wrists. Your head bloats, making it ache all the time. Your fingers bloat, making you clumsy. It seems incredible that you could bloat, given how much the indigestion and heartburn suppress your desire to eat, but on the other hand, the ferocious constipation does its part in the swelling process. The constipation was the reason I had waddled out to Whole Earth Foods in the light of day to lay in whole-grain bread, lettuce, celery, bran, wheat germ, and more wheat germ. The writers of pregnancy books love wheat germ. They want you to bake, stir, sprinkle, and substitute it. I'm sure if you got them in private they would admit to rolling and smoking it too.

In the ninth month of pregnancy your tummy feels itchy all the time and your belly button turns inside out.

At six and seven months the G had been quite the acrobat, twisting and tumbling gracefully through the cavern of my womb. It was like having a gopher-sized synchronized swimmer performing in my body cavity, six shows daily with a matinee on weekends. In the eighth month, though, quarters had begun to get crowded. The G responded with admirable feistiness, hammering on all available walls, floors, and ceilings to inform me that she didn't appreciate this loss of living space. In the ninth month, mercifully, there was no longer room for her to wind up for a big haymaker anymore. For a couple of weeks she squirmed and struggled.

Finally, five days before she was due, the G pointed herself head-down and dove to the very bottom of her little grotto, coming to rest like the good baby she was with her tiny head jammed against my cervix. The cervix, I learned, is a little dilating door that wheels open like the one at the beginning of James Bond movies.

When the baby performs this maneuver, turning upside down and plastering herself head-first to your cervix, you call your doctor in a state of great excitement to say that the baby has "dropped." Dropping is a mixed bag. It means that the many varieties of false labor may officially commence: Braxton-Hicks contractions, prodromal contractions—a whole gallery of different squeezing, clenching, flexing movements that range from the simply odd to the very uncomfortable, and all share the quality of advancing your labor not at all, so that you rush to your amused obstetrician only to be told you can expect days, weeks, or even years of this before Real Labor begins. Pain, it turns out, is not in and of itself significant. It's just a bonus.

Another drawback of The Drop is that my poor bladder, which had been squashed down to something with the capacity of a couple of tablespoons, was abruptly crushed to the size of an M & M. I had already been waking up eight times a night with back pain and indigestion. Now I had to get up an extra four times to pee. I was fat, badly centered, and very clumsy, so it was no small task to roll myself groaning out of bed and trudge down three flights of stairs to the bathroom. One night early in September I slipped badly and fell down six stairs to the second-floor landing. When Daddy called sleepily to see if I was okay, I told him everything was fine, but actually my knees were banged and bruised and my heart was going a hundred miles an hour as I imagined what might have happened to the baby if I had fallen down a full flight of stairs. The pregnancy books say that falls rarely do any damage to the fetus, but I had seen *Gone With The Wind*, you bet.

The next night I took a big saucepan upstairs and used it as a chamber pot. I was too embarrassed to tell anyone, but Angela was sleeping in Candy's old bed, and quiet as I tried to be, dragging my pot out from beneath my bed and creeping out to use it on the balcony with the French doors closed behind me, I'm sure she had her guesses. Besides, one time I heard her snicker.

On the plus side, when the baby Drops you get to breathe again. Thanks to the baby, I hadn't drawn a really deep lungful of air in six weeks. When the G dropped, this brooding pressure moved suddenly lower in my body and I gasped, sucking in a great, liberating lungful of 96-degree supersaturated smog. It was glorious.

By the day before Candy's wedding the charms of breathing Houston air had begun to wane. I'd been having Braxton-Hicks contractions all morning. These are strange little clenching movements that wander around your uterus like sheet lighting playing around a cloud bank. One had just finished when my panties fell down.

When I got home, still seething, Daddy helped me carry in the groceries from Whole Foods. "Think we should trade Bell?" I said, referring to Houston's right fielder. I'd had the car radio on, listening to the Astros lose their eighth straight game. Three weeks ago they had had a two and a half game lead in their division, but now they were 4–14 in September, one game away from mathematical elimination.

"Just don't bat him cleanup. He makes some plays in the outfield and he's got a hundred RBIs. Everyone would be talking about what a great year he had if he'd been batting sixth."

"I guess," I said, waddling into the kitchen. "If I hear him ground into one more double play with men in scoring position, though . . ." I puffed and heaved a bag of vegetables up onto the counter.

Angela and Candy were working on the wedding dress, Candy standing on a chair in the middle of the floor, Angela doing up her buttons at the back. "Don't fidget," Angela said. La Hag Gonzales had altered Momma's wedding gown to fit Candy. She looked stunning. Braless,

Candy's breasts stayed high and firm. She rose from that white dress like a calla lily, her throat and shoulders silky smooth, her lovely face framed by her rich black hair. Damn her anyway.

I looked for a casserole dish and a mixing bowl to start making a lasagna. Homemade food for the rehearsal dinner, of course, but there was no point serving Mexican to La Hag. Fidgeting, Candy turned her head to me and tried a smile. "Well, the day before the big day, eh?"

"Probably not. The average first kid comes four to seven days after the due date."

"Oh. I didn't mean the baby."

"I know," I said.

"Stand straight!" Angela said. Candy looked away from me.

Daddy came into the kitchen with the last bag of groceries and stood listening to the radio on the refrigerator. The Florida Marlins were batting in the seventh against one of the hapless middle relievers who had cost Houston their chance at the pennant. The lead-off man had walked. The Marlins played hit-and-run successfully, the man on first breaking to steal and the hitter punching a single to right field through the gap when the second baseman went to cover the bag. Men on first and third, nobody out. I dumped a tub of ricotta cheese into the mixing bowl and then stopped as another Braxton-Hicks crackled across the front of my uterus.

"I'm worried about having the service over in Baytown," Candy said. "If Iris comes close to us there's going to be all kinds of flooding down there." Hurricane Iris had been wandering our way for nearly a week. Hurricane-watching is a popular sport in Houston, although we only get hit every ten or fifteen years. Still, Iris looked very promising. Most hurricanes beat the tar out of a few Caribbean vacation resorts and then plow into Florida, or hit further up the East Coast in the Carolinas. Every now and then, though, a tropical storm like Iris will slide west of the Caribbean and pick up speed over the Gulf of Mexico.

"I've never seen a hurricane," Angela said. "Would it be really dangerous?"

"Not here," Candy said. "We're too far inland."

"It depends on what you mean by dangerous," I said. "If you don't think downed power lines or falling tree-limbs or flying glass or spinoff tornadoes or power outages are dangerous, why then, no, it shouldn't be dangerous at all. You won't drown, though a couple of kids will get eaten by flash floods in the bayous."

"Guess who worked in insurance?" Candy said.

"One thing about living on the Canadian prairies, we never have any kind of natural disasters. Unless you count winter." Angela did up the last button and handed Candy down from the chair. "Ta da!"

Candy curtsied. She was breathtaking. "Do you think Momma would have liked it?" she said softly.

"How the hell should I know?" My whole body felt heavy and hot. I was sweating like a pig and my breasts were starting to leak colostrum and I hadn't gotten around to getting any breast pads yet. My back ached fiercely and my grotesque stomach bumped against the kitchen counter. When I went to plug in the mixer I had to lean until my back strained just to reach the electrical outlet in the wall. "Who knows what Momma would have said? Called you an angel? Asked where you got off wearing white on your wedding day? Told you not to sleep with a wetback? Given you a kiss and left lipstick on your lace? I don't know."

"Don't talk about your mother that way," Daddy said.

"No, on second thought I know exactly what she would have said. She would have told you how beautiful you were. And then she would have told *me* how beautiful you were."

"Don't even bother, Daddy," Candy said. "Toni's determined to be hateful. Who knows why. Let's see: she doesn't drink like Momma. She doesn't cry like Momma. She doesn't make scenes like Momma." I could just catch the faintest trace of Candy's burnt-cinnamon smell from her fine black hair as she shook her head. "Maybe that's why she's so bitter, do you think? Because that's one thing Momma could do, Toni. She could love people. And people loved her. But you! How many people do you think love you?"

"Shut up."

"I'm sorry if it bothers you that it's me wearing this dress, not you. But you don't need a gown to marry a turkey baster, do you?"

My heart seemed to slow, and the blood pushed painfully through the fat skin of my face.

Angela grabbed Candy by the arm and pushed her toward the stairs. "Get out of here before you two say something worse."

Candy and I did not speak for the rest of the day, not through the long afternoon of cooking and not during the rehearsal dinner. Candy sat with Carlos's family and laughed and drank too much red wine and would not look at me. When the party moved into the garden she went with it, entertaining our guests, while I stayed in the kitchen washing dishes. Daddy went upstairs early and lay down in his room. I could hear his TV on. Probably watching the Rangers game on Channel 51. He had been quiet and withdrawn all day.

Angela's reflection approached me in the window over the kitchen sink. "Can I do the washing for a while?"

"I'm all right."

"Don't bullshit me, kiddo. I've been pregnant, remember?" Angela leaned in and stripped the gloves off my hands. "You dry."

"Okay." I pulled a chair over from the kitchen table and watched her work. As soon as I sat down I realized I wouldn't be getting up in a hurry.

Angela splashed into work. "Back hurt?"

"Yes."

"Hips?"

"Yes."

"Headache?"

"Big time."

"Taken any Tylenol?"

"I'm not allowed. The doctor said not to take anything without her permission."

Angela looked at me. "Has this doctor ever been pregnant?"

"Not that she's mentioned."

"Take some Tylenol. They're in my purse."

She scrubbed out the lasagna pan while I took the painkillers, thinking of the guy who had put strychnine in random bottles of Tylenol when I was in junior high school. Thinking of the bondage pictures in Candy's magazines. Thinking of Mary Keith, who stepped off a building in Phoenix with her daughter in her arms.

"Scared?" Angela said.

"Yeah," I said. "Really scared."

Angela took a towel off the rack and started drying plates.

"Did you ever worry that you were going to be a terrible mother?" I asked.

"Me? No way. I knew I would be a great mother." Angela laughed out loud. "What a stupid little shit I was. But no, actually, I never worried about that. I always felt like all I had to do to be a better mother than my mom was to stick around, you know? To be there for more than four months. I was pretty sure I was up to that." She put up a stack of plates.

"What if the hurricane hits and the power goes out while I'm in the delivery room?"

"Hospitals have backup generators, Toni."

"What if the backup malfunctions?"

"And if you're in labor at night and if they have no flashlights at the hospital and nobody can find a candle and they have to do an emergency C-section?"

"Just for instance."

Angela scooped up a handful of silverware and began scrubbing fork tines. "Then your odds of coming through it with a healthy baby are still probably a hundred times better than they were for your great-grandmother."

"I suppose." A breeze had come up and I could hear the live-oak branches creaking. Drifts and swirls of conversation eddied into the house from the garden, where Carlos's numerous relations laughed and talked amongst themselves. "Even if Iris doesn't get us head-on, she's going to come close. Candy dreamed it. Someone has to go out tonight to get masking tape and bottled water. And ice, we'll need ice to keep the food from going bad if the power goes out."

"Where can I find a rag? My scrubbie thing is all slimed up."

"Under the sink," I said. "Because Houston is so flat, the roads fill with water very fast. I've seen Westheimer impassable in ordinary storms. My little car could never make it to the hospital."

"Then you call an ambulance," Angela said.

"Sometimes ambulances are late." As Mary Jo found out the hard way. "You know what my pregnancy books advise to get labor underway?" I said. "Sex. Lots of good sex." Angela probably thought of a bunch of funny things to say, but suppressed them all, for which I was grateful. I hated sounding so sorry for myself. "Candy was supposed to be my labor coach."

"Ah. I see."

"She didn't make it to all the classes, of course. But she made it to some. I guess she and Carlos will be on their honeymoon instead. They're going to San Cristóbal. That's in Mexico. It's in the mountains, not so hot as here. Momma always said it was beautiful. She was going to take us someday."

"Candy isn't going to leave early just because you had a fight," Angela said. "She'll still be there for you, Toni."

"I don't want her there. I don't want her in that room with me."

Angela laughed. "Toni, I hate to break it to you, but when you're in labor you won't be thinking about this little scrap. They could put a branding iron on your butt and you wouldn't notice. But you will want a hand to hold. I strongly suggest that you and Candy kiss and make up."

"That doesn't come very easily to me."

"Then let me help. You have two lines, Toni. 'Candy!

You look so beautiful!' is one. This is tricky because you *have* to say it, and you have to mean it, but it's going to be a tough sell after what you said this morning."

"She doesn't need me to tell her she looks fabulous in that dress. A blind man could tell her that."

"She needs to hear it nonetheless. And more particularly, she needs to hear it from you."

"Why me? Why not you?"

"I'm not her big sister," Angela said. "Whether you like it or not, Toni, on this day you are all the mother Candy has. It's your job. You worked *hard* for her all those years. Are you going to blow it now?"

I grunted. "What's my second line?"

" 'Everything is going to work out between you and Carlos, I just know it.' "

"Why should she believe me? I can't see the future. Fifty-two percent of all marriages fail. Why should she beat the odds?"

"Say it, Toni."

"How convincing could it be, coming from a woman Nobody Could Love?"

"More convincing than it sounds from a woman divorced two times," Angela said drily. She turned back to the sink and reached for a handful of silver. In a pompous British voice she said, "That woman, sir, is not only divorced in herself, she is the cause of divorce in others."

"Shakespeare?" I guessed.

"Winston Churchill," she said. "More or less."

The phone rang at five the following morning. I hadn't gotten to sleep until almost one, and even then my night had been restless and filled with bad dreams. I swung myself out of bed and ran to the phone, amazed at my own speed. "Candy?"

"Iris is coming right for us," my sister said. "She's due to make landfall at Galveston in two hours. I've been watching the Weather Channel all night. We can't do this in Baytown. I'm going to start calling people. We're going to move the ceremony to our house."

"Here!"

"Ten o'clock, Toni. It has to be ready for ten o'clock, the priest is booked for the rest of the day. I'll call him, you call—no, never mind, I'll do the calling. You just get the place cleaned up, get some food, whatever."

"Wouldn't it make more sense to—"

"I'm not getting married in a church, Toni! I just can't. Not with this happening. This is a sign. I never had *one damn dream* about my wedding day!" Candy cried. "I hope that makes you happy," she said, and she slammed down the receiver.

"What's up?" Angela asked through a mouth full of pillow.

"She never dreamed about her wedding."

"What?"

"Candy. She sees the future in dreams. But she only sees happy times."

"So?"

"So she never saw her wedding."

Poor Candy. Knowing her as I did, I imagined her going to sleep for the last eight months, hoping every night that this time she would see a vision of herself, radiant at the altar. And it never happened. No happy wedding vision for the girl who grew up listening to our parents fight, the girl who slipped off at fourteen to get laid because it was the one thing she could call true and only hers . . . If I was worried about the kind of mother I would make, I realized for the first time just how scared Candace Jane must be about the kind of wife she was going to be.

"Better get up," I said to Angela, who moaned and hid her head under her sheet. "We have a lot of work to do."

I woke Daddy and went downstairs and fixed us all a big mess of chorizo and eggs. It was cool downstairs, cooler than it had been in months. The clouds on the storm front had arrived; the sky outside was pitch-black, the moon and stars blotted out. When I opened the French doors to the garden, the night wind blew inside. It smelled of flowers and the sea, it tugged at Pierrot's diamond pants as he sat in the chifforobe, and flapped the tails of the Preacher's black coat. In the kitchen, strings of dried peppers and garlic swung and rustled.

A quick breakfast and then we set to work getting the house ready for a wedding and a hurricane. Angela had gone out for storm supplies the night before, rolling into a twenty-four hour Kroger's. They had been out of nearly everything; she came back with a roll of parcel-wrapping tape and six liters of tonic water. They had been sold out of ice, but shrewdly Angela had brought back a ten-pound bag of charcoal briquettes, on the theory that if the power did go out, we could cook what we couldn't freeze.

I took the parcel tape and taped X's across all the south-facing windows so that if they broke they wouldn't shatter and spray glass inside. I kept both TVs on the Weather Channel and listened while I worked. Iris was moving north-northwest at twelve to fifteen miles an hour. She had been upgraded to a Class 3 hurricane, with sustained wind speeds of 125 mph gusting to 145. The folks at the Weather Channel were having a wonderful time; for them this was as good as a war and a presidential election rolled into one. Regular and infrared satellite photographs tracked the storm's progress while the commentators talked knowledgeably about how hurricanes spawned killer tornadoes when they hit land.

Just past six o'clock in the morning it began to rain.

I looked at Angela as the first drops began spitting against the French doors. "Here we go," I said, scrabbling in the kitchen drawers for flashlight batteries. Although I had been exhausted to the point of uselessness for much of the last two weeks, today I found myself, on five broken hours of sleep, bursting with energy.

"God, you're like a buzz saw," Angela said, yawning.

"Panic."

"I can't panic properly until I've had some coffee," she said.

"That's because you've never been through a hurricane." I tested the big Energizer flashlamp, catching her square in the eyes with the beam.

"Brat!"

"Great. Still working. Close the patio doors, would you?" Ordinarily I loved to hear the sound of the rain drumming down in the garden, but the wind had stiffened enough that the tile floors were beginning to darken. A flash of movement caught my eye as a little green lizard scuttered inside to get out of the storm.

Daddy carried his breakfast plate over to the sink. "I'll get the Coleman lamps out of the garden shed."

"Yuck. Nobody wants to be married by kerosene light. We'll go with candles."

"For later. Just in case."

He took his windbreaker and headed out. When he came back five minutes later he was drenched, and the battering rain was much louder. "You're making puddles on the floor!" I shouted, springing for a mop and starting to hum an old Pogues tune. I mopped the way pirates rowed after a few cups of grog. I was the Mop Queen.

After mopping I made Angela help me heave the table against the wall so it could pretend to be a sideboard. I set out our best china cups and saucers and silverware and dessert plates. I filled Momma's antique sugar bowl but decided that we didn't have enough linen napkins to go around. "Time to bake," I said. "Cookies or brownies or Rice Krispie squares?"

"Brownies first," Angela said decisively. "They're classy and they take the longest. Mine never turn out, though. I'll start on the Rice Krispie squares. They're tacky but everyone likes eating them. To judge by last night, I'll bet Mrs. Gonzales has been baking for a week. Leave the fancy stuff to her. Throw in cookies at the end if you have time, they're easy and fast."

"Spoken like a Professional Mom," I said. "I'm in awe."

I was melting butter and cocoa together at eight o'clock when Candy arrived. The instant the door opened we were deafened by the storm roaring outside. The clamor had crept up so gradually and we had been in such a hurry, I hadn't really paid attention to it. Now it was awesome. I could hear high-power lines singing in the wind. Rain chattered like gunfire against the kitchen window.

"Bitch won't bring the *cake!*" Candy yelled. She staggered inside, wild-eyed and wind-blasted. Outside the world was a howling madhouse. The sun should have been up for an hour, but the shrieking darkness was so thick with rain that not only was it still pitch-black, I couldn't even see a glimmer from the streetlight across the road.

"What?"

"She won't bring the cake! I paid her good money for

a cake, no Royal icing, a good lemon icing 'cause I swore I wouldn't be one of those brides who stands up in front of everyone at the reception and can't cut through the fucking atomic bombproof icing and now the bitch won't *bring it* because of a little fucking rain!''

"Candy? How did you get here?" Daddy said.

Candy stood bristling before us like a wet wolverine. "Walked," she said. "Swam." She pulled off her cowboy boots with a huge sucking sound, her fingers slimed with mud. A cup of water drained from each sock. She was wearing a windbreaker and jeans and looked like she had crawled across a motocross track during a race in a monsoon. Great swaths of mud and live-oak leaves and bits of paper and pine tree needles were stuck to her clothes. In one hand she clenched a king-size JC Penny plastic shopping bag. "I was on the phone arguing with the cake lady when I heard this crashing noise. I thought the roof of the house was tearing off, swear to God. Then the line went dead so I had to come here to use your phone. I put the wedding dress in a dry-cleaning bag and then put the dry-cleaning bag in a Sears bag and put the Sears bag in here," she said, rattling the JC Penny bag menacingly. "When I went outside I found that crashing noise had been the live oak outside my apartment falling over. Guess what broke its fall?"

"Your car," I whispered. "Oh my God. Is there much damage?"

"For Christ's sake, Toni. It's a Civic! A live oak on that is like dropping a cinderblock on a ladybug." Candy was shaking with rage. Or maybe it was delayed fear. "I was three minutes from getting in that car, you know. It looks like a pop can that got squashed under an anvil. I would have been squirted out the windshield like so much tooth-paste."

"My," Angela said. "Isn't this exciting?"

"I need to use the phone," Candy said, stomping past me in her wet socks.

"What for?"

"Gonna get my fucking *cake.*"

"Candy, the cake lady is not coming. She shouldn't come. *You* shouldn't have come. There's a killer storm outside. Nobody is coming," I said.

"I paid good money for that cake," Candy said. She didn't move for the phone. Tears were starting in her eyes.

"You shall have your cake," Angela said. "Toni, don't be ridiculous. Of course people will come. Not everybody, perhaps. But plenty of people will. Carlos will, and that's all that matters."

"But—"

"No, we don't really have time for *buts,*" Angela said smoothly, taking Candy by the arm. "Come upstairs and let me get to work on you. I think we'll use the hair dryer first, before the power goes out."

The room lit with unbearable brightness. Thunder exploded all around us. An instant later the transformer behind our house blew up. Green lightning arced from it like fireworks gone mad. The lights gasped and went out, along with all the electric appliances. At first all I could hear was the ringing the thunder had left in my ears. Then the transformer, spitting and sizzling. Then the moaning winds and the rain battering against the windows. One of our tile shingles tore off the roof and came smashing down onto the patio. A moment later, with a great wrenching, creaking noise, a ten-foot plank pulled out of the back fence and went cartwheeling through the garden.

"Or," said Angela, "we could towel-dry and style with hairspray."

After that there wasn't much to do but listen to the back fence pull apart, one plank at a time.

By eight-thirty the sky had turned a greasy, unnatural copper color. The wind was ferocious, but more fitful, and the rain began to ease up. Five minutes before nine o'clock the clouds split as if being ripped along a seam. The wind died to nothing and a blue window opened in the heavens like a cervix dilating.

"The eye of the storm," I said to Angela, who had popped downstairs for a moment while Candy used the toilet.

"How long will it last?"

"I don't know," I said. "By the way, I'm having contractions."

Angela stopped. "How far apart?"

"Seven minutes, twelve minutes, eight minutes, and thirteen minutes so far. Not regular. It probably isn't real labor. But it isn't Braxton-Hicks."

"Do you feel it in your front or your back?"

"A bit of both. Real labor is supposed to be just in your back, I know. It probably isn't real labor."

Angela held my hand, looking at me. "Probably not. You scared anyway?"

"No," I said. "Well, yes. But I'm okay. I just want to get it over with. Want a brownie?"

The toilet flushed. Angela squeezed my hand. "Later. I have all I can handle upstairs."

Candy stomped out of the bathroom in her bare feet and wedding gown, the buttons undone all down her back. "With any luck the damn priest will drown," she said,

and stomped upstairs. Angela rolled her eyes and followed.

After a moment's thought I waddled over to the chifforobe. Momma's gods gazed out at me, the Preacher
stern, Sugar lazy, Pierrot grinning his cruel smile. "Now,
you listen to me," I said quietly, picking up the Widow
by her test-tube body and staring at her black button eyes.
"This was your idea, remember? This is supposed to be
the happiest day of my little sister's life. And I swear on
Momma's grave that if you ruin it for her, I'm going to
take you down to the Greyhound bus station and bury
you six feet deep in the Lost and Found box, do you hear
me?" I shook the Widow until the dried spiders in her
glass body bounced and jiggled.

I heard what sounded like the ghost of a malicious
laugh. "That goes for the rest of you too. You know what
I'm going to do with you if this doesn't go well?" I said,
glaring at Pierrot. "You're going to be a Christmas present
for a family I know with *two-year-old twins*."

The faint laughter choked off.

I closed the chifforobe doors and got busy setting out
candles.

Just after nine, to my complete surprise, our guests began
to arrive.

Greg was first, sweeping inside with a great stomp and
flourish, resplendent in a London Fog raincoat and bran-
dishing an enormous green umbrella. "I'm early! Can you
imagine it? But I thought I'd better come while the skies
were clear." Whisking through the front door, he spun
around on one heel, accidentally spattering me with rain-
drops from his twirling umbrella, and wound up leaning
against the wall next to the table-cum-sideboard. "Rice

Krispie squares! Yum. But I'll wait until the reception proper, shall I?''

I wiped the water from my face. "Hey, Greg, glad you could make it.'' And suddenly I was. If I were to double over with agonizing contractions in the next thirty seconds, Greg would be instantly available for a spot of Galahading. He wasn't husband material, not for me—nor was I wife fiber for him, apparently—but in the short term, I couldn't ask for a better friend.

"Say, have you met Charisse?'' he asked, as a young black woman walked up behind him. "Charisse, this is Toni Beauchamp, the sister of the bride.''

"Pleased to meet you,'' she said, looking amused as Greg struggled to fold up his umbrella. "Greg told me dates were invited. I hope it's true.'' She held out her hand and I took it.

"The more the merrier. Frankly, we weren't expecting a big turnout.''

"I'm only two blocks away.'' Charisse was wearing a classy skirt, long red nails, gold hoop earrings, short-cropped hair. I figured her for a jazz singer and then wondered if that was racist. Then I tried imagining her as a junior loan executive and decided she could have been that too. I liked her. "Come in, please. Find your favorite place along the wall. So has Greg told you any stories about my mother?''

"No, I don't think so,'' Charisse said. Greg paled.

"Well, he should. Either that, or make him promise to do the alphabet to you,'' I said.

"What?''

"Later,'' Greg said, taking her by the arm. "You should see their garden before the rain comes back.''

La Hag Gonzales was next to arrive, along with all of

Carlos's brothers and sisters, each bearing a platter or basket or tray of wonderful delicacies: at the center, of course, a vast simmering chicken mole, smelling of peppers and bitter chocolate gravy. Second in importance, the *viscochos*, small round cinnamon wedding cookies. And then, loading the table until it groaned, salsa and tortilla chips and pan de dulce, tacitos, shrimps and scallops speared on toothpicks and then wrapped with bacon and basted with lime butter, tamales, fried cheese, fried tomatoes, fried battered jalapeños, and menudo, that delicious combination of hominy and tripe that is so intoxicating in the hands of a master. Nor had La Hag forgotten drinks: two of her brothers wheeled in a massive keg of Dos Equis, and she herself bore six bottles of Jose Cuervo's best tequila.

"Oh, Señora Gonzales! This is so wonderful! *Es excelente! Gracias*, thank you, thank you!"

La Hag shook her head. "I am much embarrassed. We could not get the cake from Señora Gomez. The world will know how she has shamed me." Her look did not bode well for poor Mrs. Gomez, who was doubtless in a dither at having to choose between Hurricane Iris and an enraged Conchita Gonzales. "Also, I am sad to say the mariachi players will be unable to attend. Something about a house falling down."

"I hope nobody was hurt!"

"Nobody," said Carlos's mother, with an unsatisfied air. Clearly she considered failing to perform merely because one's house had washed away tantamount to malingering.

I snuck a glance at the chifforobe and breathed a small thanks to the gods in there. Surely sparing Candy the mariachi band had to count as a small miracle in the Riders' favor. "Carlos is not with you?"

"I sent him to fetch the priest."

"From Baytown? That's . . . that's going to be quite a drive on a day like this."

Señora Gonzales smiled. "Child, do not worry. He is my son. He will come."

The next guest to arrive was the most surprising of all: it was Penny Friesen, Bill Sr.'s wife. "Mrs. Friesen," I said, shocked. I kicked myself for not telling Candy about Momma's affair with Bill Sr. She must have invited the Friesens without my knowing it.

"Hello, Toni." A look passed between us, and I knew my stammering had given me away. Oh yes, Penny Friesen knew about Momma and her husband, and she knew I did too.

She held out an enormous vase of flowers. "I cut them last night. I always do, when a hurricane is coming. If I don't, the storm beats them flat. No use wasting the beautiful things, is it?"

Looking past her shoulder, I saw her Volvo station wagon loaded with a mass of blossoms from her beautiful house and grounds. "Oh, thank you."

"I can't stay for the ceremony," Penny said. "I don't want to be caught outdoors when the eye passes, you know."

I nodded. "And Mr. Friesen?"

"Mr. Friesen . . ." Penny looked at me. She smiled, almost apologetically. "Bill won't be coming today."

"I'm sorry," I said, to the woman my mother had betrayed. I winced through another hard contraction. Penny looked at me sharply. I shook my head. "I don't think I'm in labor. Not yet."

She shook my hand, and then gave me a hug. "I always

liked you girls." She stepped back. "I envied your mother her daughters. Not that I haven't enjoyed my son. But daughters are different, I think."

I touched my tummy. "I think so too."

"Give my best to Candace, will you? Goodbye."

"Goodbye," I said.

The phone rang as I headed back to the kitchen. Angela signed that she would finish arranging the flowers, so I picked up the receiver. "Hello?"

"Toni? We broke down!" It was Carlos.

"We can wait. We aren't going anywhere."

"You don't understand," he yelled. "My *car* broke down. My car never breaks down. Does the Batmobile break down? Does Zorro's horse go lame? No. This is not, this is not a spark plug going out. It is not natural."

"Carlos, you are overreacting—"

"This is a *sign*, Antoinette!"

"Carlos—"

"I am in my car, with a priest, going to a wedding in a hurricane, the car breaks down. Am I *blind*? No. Something is very wrong. I am being told something."

"Carlos, listen to me. Listen to me, Carlos. You're right. You are right, your car didn't break down by accident. It was *los duendes*. They have been playing a few tricks, but I talked to them just now and we all understand one another."

Silence.

"Carlos? Are you listening?"

"You talked to *los duendes*?"

"*Sí*. Yes. Everything will be fine with them. Your mother is here, with all the family and the food and the beer, Carlos. We all look forward to seeing you."

"*Los duendes*. Okay. But what about your mother? She

never liked me. What about her? I think she's the one who broke my car."

"She would be very happy for Candy. I promise you."

Another long silence. "You speak for her, eh?"

I saw Candy's head peeking down the stairs, scanning the room. "Yes. On this I speak for Momma. She gives her blessing, Carlos. I swear it. Now come as quick as you can. You have a beautiful bride here waiting for you."

"I got nothing against Candy. Candy I like. La Beauchamp and *los duendes*, these are other matters."

"I swear I will intercede with them. You should see Candy, Carlos. She's a vision. You better get here before your best man steals her away, is what I think."

"I got nothing against Candy," Carlos said.

I gasped as another contraction hit me. What had that been, four minutes? Five? Please God, don't send me into labor now.

"Okay," Carlos said. "Okay. We're coming. We will be there. *Vámanos, Padre*. Okay, Toni, we will come."

And they did, ten minutes after the eye of the hurricane had passed over us. The storm wall was howling through the neighborhood, tearing the flat leaves from the banana trees and hammering the last of the crepe myrtle blossoms to the ground. Carlos and the priest staggered in, windlashed and blinking the water from their eyes. Carlos had tricked his car into starting again. He had found a short in the electrical system and fixed it with a hank of wire that held almost till he reached us. The last two blocks they came on foot, Carlos and the padre leaning sixty degrees into the wind.

It was a mad, merry celebration, and everyone was drunk on the storm before the first shot of tequila was poured.

My contractions fizzled out, gone completely by the time the ceremony was over, but the strange energy that had filled me since Candy's phone call kept me up and alert all afternoon. I even waltzed, lumbering a few steps when we turned Daddy's battery-powered transistor radio on to KQQK SuperTejano and cleared the center of the ground floor for dancing. Angela had a rare time. She hit it off with La Hag, incredibly enough; the last time I saw them together they were giggling in a corner, Señora Gonzales having challenged Angela to match her in some Mexican drinking game from a girlish past apparently far racier than I had imagined.

Bill Jr. arrived as the hurricane began to weaken, just after the reception had begun. He strode in clutching a bottle of champagne and swung me off my feet—no mean accomplishment, as I had added forty-six pounds to my pre-pregnancy frame. "Twenty-seven hundred and sixty barrels a day!" he shouted in my ear.

"What?"

"We hit a gusher! Twenty-seven hundred and sixty barrels a day! We drilled the wells like you said, and the very last one was a monster!" Which was the kind of glorious day it was—

—for everyone except Carlos and Candy. He was nervous and wet and out of sorts, glancing constantly at me and at the chifforobe, barely looking at his bride. For her part, my sister was beautiful, of course, but not what you would call radiant. I never had seen a wedding at which the bride, when asked if she would take this man, said, "Oh, yeah. Whatever," and looked fit to spit.

Candy didn't look much happier when I saw her the next day. I had been to the Home Depot for some supplies, and was hard at work outside the house. The energy that had come to me with her phone call had not abated, but now I felt desperately pressed for time. Two days before, I couldn't wait for the baby to come. Now I knew there was something I had to do first.

"Hey," Candy said, picking her way through the banana leaves and broken live-oak branches that littered the sidewalk.

"Hey."

The sky was blue, blue, and the storm had washed away all the summer's heat and smog, leaving it clear and empty and ready for autumn. Sunlight glimmered on the wet leaves and sidewalk puddles. The road was littered with twigs and pine needles and pecans; from where I stood by the front door I could see three snapped live-oak limbs dangling into our street. Chain saws chattered and whined up and down the block. "I thought you'd be halfway to San Cristóbal by now," I said.

"Christ, Toni, that's just like you. Of course I'm not going before the baby comes."

"Oh."

"Look, I'm still pissed off at you. It wasn't my idea to come by today. Carlos made me."

"Carlos?"

"He says he isn't getting in a car with me until I make things right with you. He says you're thick with Momma and *los duendes*, and I better treat you nice or there's going to be shit for peace in our house."

I laughed.

"It should have been me the Riders wanted." Candy shrugged. "It should have been me Momma gave her curses to. But it wasn't. And for that, I guess I owe you, Toni. I was jealous, but I was glad, too, that you were there to take care of me. Again. As always."

Tears starting coming down my cheeks. Ever since Momma died I could not seem to stop this wretched dribbling.

"So what are you doing?" Candy asked.

"Painting."

"I see that. Why now?" I didn't answer. She looked at the door trim, which I had finished, and the fence, which I was starting. "Yellow around the door, white on the f—" She looked at me. "The Little Lost Girl's house."

"Want to help?"

"Okay," she said. "Yeah."

"Grab a brush. It's probably crazy to paint this fence. I should replace it first. But I woke up this morning *knowing* I had to get this done before the baby came. My own little spell," I said. "Dad's drilling the swing for me. Where do you think we should hang it, inside the fence or outside?"

"Outside," Candy said. "The Little Lost Girl can see it easier."

I nodded and slapped more paint on the fence. "I guess you think I'm crazy."

Candy picked up a brush. "Actually, Toni, this is the first sane thing you've done since Momma died."

I laughed, but I was crying too. "She was the little lost girl all the time," I said.

Candy looked at me. "You never knew that?"

I shook my head and winced as another contraction hit. They'd been coming all morning, slow but steady. Now they were nine minutes apart. I stopped painting for a moment and tried to breathe through the tears and the pain. These weren't like the clenching feeling of the Braxton Hicks. These were like being stabbed in my lower back. "This means business."

"I'll be there," Candy said. "Angie gave me some coaching on what not to say."

"Like?"

"Whatever else I do, I'm not supposed to say, 'Don't worry, honey, the *baby's* doing fine.' "

I laughed. "And the other one?"

" 'I know how you feel.' "

"Good advice," I said.

I picked up my brush, but before I could lay on another stroke Candy put her arms around me. "Hang on, big sister," she said, smelling of cinnamon. "Everything is going to be all right."

. . .

Just before lunch we hung the swing from a limb of the live-oak tree. Shortly after three o'clock I went into the hospital, and nineteen hours later my daughter, Grace Ellen, was born.

I wish so many things for her.

I hope, I pray, I will be able to give her the gifts which have been given so richly to me all my life. Here I bless her with these blessings. I give her Greg's sly wit and taste for miracles. I give her Bill Jr.'s appetite and hope she too can order a Peachy Keen without blushing when she wants one. I hope she can be as smart as Rick Manzetti, as careful and as principled.

From Mary Jo, the great-aunt she will never know, I give her hard truths and the strength to abide loneliness, and a great power for friendship.

From Uncle Carlos I give her careful wisdom and a love of fine cars and the ability to believe a thing without needing to say it. I have to say I hope she gets her brains from her mother and her looks from her aunt, but if she has even one thimbleful of Candy's joy for life, she will be blessed.

From Daddy I give her slow patience and a knowledge of the strike zone. From him I learned the cost of love, and saw that he was willing to pay it.

I give her the Riders, the Preacher in the strength of his convictions, and Sugar in the fullness of her desires. May she have Mr. Copper's power to claim what she wants, and the vigilance of the Widow to watch her and keep her. I bless her with Pierrot's luck, if not his temperament, and hope she can laugh, even in the darkness.

As for me? I will give her everything, even my failures, because a mother can do no less. She can have my brains and my wariness and my bitterness and my love, I can't deny her anything. She will take what she needs from this strange mixed blessing, and God willing, she will find her own uses for it.

I used to think that there was only one true person living in a body, one truth surrounded by a pack of lies. Now I know I was wrong. We are all of us a hundred different selves, mothers and daughters, busy professionals and lazy housekeepers, zealous reformers and incumbents on the take. And each of these women is true in her turn. Each of us is a mockingbird.

In the time since Grace was born no visions have come to me and no Rider has mounted me, except the Mockingbird, who I have called, and who has come to me every day of this new part of my life. Did you ever really think this was my voice alone, telling this story? Me with the degree in math and a deep knowledge of the General Mortality tables? I could never do it.

But Momma could.

It is Elena's voice, I think, that fills these pages. Or say rather, it is Elena's song, and I am the mockingbird who sings it. I don't think I will ever be able to separate my mother from myself. As long as I live, then part of her lives too; and the same will be true for my daughter, and hers, and hers.

We are all singers, in this family, and we are also songs.

ACKNOWLEDGMENTS

I owe a big debt of gratitude to Maureen McHugh, who believed in this book and backed up that belief with much solid advice. Hamd and Joanna Alkhayat patiently talked me through Commodities Trading for Dummies and, better still, made it sound romantic. Everything right about oil-field exploration and financing is owed to Laurel Holmes; the mistakes, of course, are mine. Sage Walker and Sarah Charlesworth gave freely of their medical and actuarial advice, respectively. Dawn Bryan and Karin Fuog head a long list of Other Excellent Readers; I thank you all.

This book is dedicated to the Texan women in my life—a mess of aunts, cousins and friends, and especially my grandmothers Vivian Stewart and Jeanette Thornton. Most of all I thank my mom, who will never fully escape the Lone Star State; my wife, who couldn't avoid it; and my daughters, who have coped with it so very gracefully.